SNOW &
SOOT

CHRISTINA VEILLETTE

ISBN: PB: 979-8-9935855-0-5; eBook 979-8-9935855-1-2

Published by Christina Veillette
First Edition, 2025

This is a work of fiction. Names, characters, places, and events are either products of the author's imagination or used fictitiously. Any resemblance to actual persons, living or dead, or real events is purely coincidental.

For more about the author and other works, visit: www.christinaveillette.com

Illustrations © 2025 Christina Veillette

For those who find warmth in the cold, and courage in the gray.

CHAPTER ONE

Elowen cupped the steaming mug and ignored the stares. No sugar or whipped cream. Bitter black coffee, the way no self-respecting elf would ever touch. The barista muttered something about "gloom in a cup," but Elowen only tugged her hat lower over her red braids and slipped out before anyone could toss sprinkles out of pity.

The corridor hit her like a choir at full scream. Elves twirled in perfect steps, caroling the same lines she'd heard every day for decades. Smiles gleamed too wide, eyes hollow, voices grinding through worn record grooves. The peppermint polish stung her nose, sharp enough to burn her throat. Her pulse raced with the carols. She fumbled for her earplugs, and shoved them in.

Glorious silence washed over her. Her shoulders sagged, though her throat still felt scraped raw by the cheer.

She walked through the dancers like a ghost, coffee steady in hand. Ahead loomed the golden door: List Registry & Tally.

Another day of judgement. Another day of numbers that weren't really people anymore. She slurped the coffee, let the heat steady her hands, and pushed inside.

At cubicle C-144, she woke the crystal sphere with two taps. Rows of cherub faces blinked across the monitor, tagged in flashing green or red. *Naughty. Nice. Naughty. Nice.* A tidy system, so clean it scraped.

The List was the spine of Kringle Central; every elf was raised to believe it sacred law. Red meant correction; green meant reward. Two colors to order the world. Two colors to rule the mortals. Anything outside those lanes was corruption and a threat to harmony.

She sighed and tapped a file: a boy in rags. His memories spooled in miniature: a bakery counter, hunger gnawing at his ribs, empty pockets. The baker's back turned, and a roll was snatched, clutched, hidden. The code flashed automatically: *naughty*.

Her chest ached. *Push it through. Don't think.*

Her fingers hovered, trembling, and then the word unraveled. Light bled through the letters, edges curling like burning parchment before winking out in a spray of runes, burning, gone. Magic clung to her fingers, fizzing like homemade honeycomb.

Her heart seized. *What did I do?*

The void on the screen gaped like an open wound. Desperate to fill it, she drew a new rune. Not red. Not green. Gray, smoky and alive. The crystal sputtered into uneasy stillness.

They said the old makers used gray before the crown forbade it.

Magic wasn't supposed to look like this. Every elf's gift was bound to their assigned task. There were no flourishes, no freedom, and definitely no public displays of magic. Hers had always smoldered instead of sparkled. A flaw she'd quickly learned to hide. But this rune wasn't a mistake. It was a possibility.

A shadow fell across her cubicle. She ripped the earplugs out.

"Metrics, Elowen." Klaussen's smirk hovered above her, suspenders straining, bells trembling with every breath. Her manager's voice was dead; his eyes, worse.

Her throat dried. They would know. Every orb reported nightly to the Master List. The names and fates were stored in the Ledger, a grand monolith rumored to hide in another realm, the beating heart of Kringle's crown. But maybe, this once, she'd saved a child.

"Yes, sir," she said.

His gaze lingered on her washed-out uniform, disapproval curling his lip. "This is not jolly." Then he vanished back into the chorus.

Elowen sagged into her chair. The crystal pulsed gray, crackling like a heartbeat. She glanced at the narrow window and wondered what lay beyond the perfect, suffocating cheer inside the snow-dusted rooftops.

"Caught you."

Larkspur leaned over the divider, curls bouncing, smile sugared and sharp. "You changed the code," she hissed. "That's tampering. Against protocol. And that..." her gaze darted to the flickering gray, "...is corruption."

"It was a mistake—"

"I'll make a note for Klaussen." A wink. Gone.

The crystal flared. A chime shrieked. *Anomaly detected.*

Klaussen reappeared, suspenders snapping. "What in sugar-sprinkled blazes is this?"

"I...I must have mistyped—"

"Mistyped? You can't invent codes. Naughty or Nice; that's the law."

"Maybe the system's wrong. Maybe—"

He slammed a hand down, rattling the desk. "Careful, Elowen. Doubt is contagious. And treasonous." His bells jingled as he leaned close. "Our Chief Cheer Officer will hear about this. They say the old makers used gray and paid a price."

Her blood chilled. *Kringle.*

The summons came before her coffee cooled.

Toy soldiers escorted her through peppermint corridors and frost-gilt stairwells. Whispers followed in her path: *Naughty. Tampering. Gray.*

The throne room glared gold and red. Mountains of gifts stacked like walls, their shimmer already fading when she looked too long.

And there he was.

Kris Kringle.

Tall, broad-shouldered, golden hair gleaming beneath a gilded crown with holly and frost. Not jolly but terrible. His smile was polished ivory, and his eyes twinkled with hunger. The suit shimmered with woven gold thread, heavy as chain-mail.

He glanced up from the report in hand.

"Elowen of C-144," he said, voice smooth as caramel. "Tampering with the List is a serious offense." He smiled wider. "You've served faithfully for decades, a valuable elf in our merry kingdom."

From the shadows shuffled a semicircle of jurors: gingerbread men, nutcrackers, and dolls with glassy eyes. Burnt sugar clung to them as if baked too long. Jurors murmured in unison: *How merciful. How just.* Their voices overlapped like broken music boxes.

Kringle paced around her, silk over steel. "You rewrote the code?"

The boy's face flashed in her mind. "Naughty or Nice...it isn't always that simple."

Gasps rippled. Kringle's bells jingled, sharp as chains.

"But it is," he said. "Sing off-key, and I'll silence your voice before the whole choir falters."

Her knees wavered, but she held. "Maybe your design is wrong."

Frost rimed the air. Gingerbread men clutched their buttons, and nutcrackers clacked their jaws in disapproval.

"Elowen of cubicle C-144," Kringle intoned, "you are hereby stripped of your station and exiled. You will serve as a warning to all who doubt the Order of Cheer."

Applause erupted, hollow and rehearsed.

Toy soldiers dragged Elowen into the square beneath banners that read: *Deliver Cheer. Maintain Order. Uphold the List.*

The Black Door loomed. Twelve feet tall. Veins of light writhed across its surface. Runes pulsed, half-familiar, half-wrong. Doors were stable, rune-safe, built by ancient hands. Rifts were wild. Sleighways, bureaucratic, reserved for Kringle's sleigh travel. Magic mattered. Runes mattered. With the wrong shape or wrong sequence, you might not like where you land.

This was no punishment. It was banishment.

She focused on the door, trying to memorize the order and shape of the inscribed runes, her key to returning home. *If* she could come home.

Kringle stepped onto the balcony, radiant in red and gold. "Beloved elves of Kringle Central," he called. "Today we preserve clarity. One has challenged the List."

The gingerbread jurors nodded, cookie faces stiff.

Kringle's arms spread, regal and terrible. "Without lines bright as stars, what are we?"

The crowd thundered: *Lost! Chaos! Darkness!*

"Elowen of List Registry & Tally. Crimes: unregistered magic, tampering, failure to uphold jolliness, and…gray."

Gasps. Even the jurors shrank back. Gray was not a crime to punish. It was not meant to exist.

"By my decree: exile."

Applause erupted.

The door split open, light flaring into a storm of frost and shadow. Wind tore at her clothes.

"May your fall remind us," Kringle said softly, "that joy requires sacrifice."

Soldiers shoved her forward. She plunged into the gale. Shadows clawed.

Alone. Cast out.

But the gray rune pulsed inside her, steady as a heartbeat. She clung to it. Terror bent her knees, yet defiance forced breath through her teeth.

You didn't erase me. You won't.

Frost swallowed her scream, and the portal took her whole.

CHAPTER TWO

Frost crackled beneath Elowen's slippers as she inhaled the frigid air. Snow slashed in thin sheets across a ruined courtyard before her. Shattered columns jutted from the ground like ribs, carvings long worn to ghosts.

This was no Kringle Central. There were no gilded banners snapping in the wind or carols in the air, only silence broken by the moan of wind through hollow arches. Icicles hung from lintels like teeth. Next to her, half-buried in the snow, lay a toppled statue with curling horns, its face split down the center.

Where in the frost did Kringle send me?

She passed beneath a crumbling arch. Each step deepened the quiet until she could hear her own heartbeat thudding against the cold. Beneath it, fainter still, she felt something older: the pulse of the place itself, patient and watching.

A shape loomed ahead. At first, a ruin. Then it moved.

A hulking figure stalked between the broken columns. Shoulders broad as walls, a cloak of tattered fur dragging through the snow. Shackles bound both wrists, chains heavy as anchors, links thick as her arm.

Elowen froze.

The figure turned. Two eyes burned through the storm, unblinking.

Every story she'd ever heard clawed up her throat. *Run, hide, pray.* But the snow had swallowed her tracks. She was lost with nowhere to go.

The chains clinked as he came closer, each step deliberate. His horns curved back like black antlers dusted with frost. The storm bent around him, snow swirling away as though afraid. She wasn't the tallest of elves, by any measure, but his silhouette was monstrous against the storm.

"Hello?" she managed, voice barely a thread. *Jumping gingersnaps, he's going to eat me.*

The figure paused, tilting his head, as if surprised prey had spoken. His voice rumbled like splitting stone.

"You should not be here."

"Trust me," she said, forcing herself upright. "I didn't exactly choose this."

A sound between a laugh and a growl shuddered from him. "No one ever does."

He stepped closer, shadows coiling. "Where are you from, little elf?"

"Kringle Central." Her breath fogged the air.

The growl that followed was low and bitter. His hand shot out, seizing hers in an iron grip, impossible to break. He dragged her toward the far end of the courtyard, where the rift still smoldered. A faint glow clung to its rim like dying embers.

He thrust a scarred palm to it. Power rippled outward, shaking the stones beneath their feet. The runes flared, then his shackles ignited crimson. The backlash threw him aside as the rift slammed shut.

Elowen stared, pulse hammering. The fissure's edge shimmered faintly gray, the same hue that had clung to her fingers in the Registry. Then the light died.

He snarled, chains rattling. "How did you cross?"

"I...was banished."

He stared, the silence heavy as the storm itself.

Finally, he turned away, cloak sweeping snow aside. He gestured once. On the horizon, through the storm, rose a fortress of black stone; its towers were jagged, its spires like claws against the pale sky.

"Come," he said, voice a tolling bell. "Or the cold will finish what Kringle began."

She stumbled after him, each step heavier. The storm stole her breath, her vision swimming. Just before she fell, she saw the faint red glow of chains bending toward her, then darkness.

❄ ❄ ❄

Squeak. Squeak.

Elowen groaned and swatted at something tugging her slipper, then bolted upright as claws skittered up her leg. A red gumdrop rat vanished through a hole in the stone, a scrap of green fabric clenched in its jaws.

She blinked into the gloom. Frost rimed iron bars across one wall; a corridor stretched beyond, lit by lanterns hung from crooked candy cane brackets. Water dripped somewhere, echoing into black puddles.

A cell.

Childlike drawings of suns and presents faded on the walls, their colors leeched away. A high, barred-window showed only the bruised sky.

She tried the bars but found them cold and unmoving. "Hello?" Her voice cracked. "Is anyone there?" Only her echo answered.

She sank back into the straw. Silence pressed close until her eyes drifted shut.

"Oh dear. What have we here?"

Elowen jerked upright. Something tugged at her badge.

A gingerbread man stood across the cell, stitched together from mismatched cookie pieces, seams piped with blue-glowing icing. One doughy hand held her badge.

"'Cheerful Conduct Coder,'" he read. "Fancy title. What's that then?"

"My job," she said faintly.

"What kind of job?"

"List Maker."

His grin widened, icing stretching. "You make *the* List?"

"In a nutshell."

"Well, jingle my seams! That's proper scandalous."

"It's not as jolly as it sounds."

"Name's Cinnamon," he said, bowing with a crack of icing. "But my friends call me Cinn."

"We're friends already?"

"You're not trying to eat me. That's a start." He giggled and tossed her badge back. Then, without warning, unlocked the cell.

"Come on."

"You're…letting me out?"

Cinn shrugged. "Can't keep a guest rotting in straw, can we? Besides," he added, voice dropping to a conspiratorial whisper, "*he'll* want to see you."

"He?"

"You'll see."

Against her better judgement, she took his stubby, surprisingly warm hand.

They passed frost-coated cells and dripping arches. Cinn chattered as they went, his voice bouncing off stone: stories of gumdrop rats, near-misses with collapsed arches, and how his "Lord" once glued him back together after a blizzard. Elowen barely heard him. Dread built with every step.

They stopped before a vast door of black stone, carved with curling antlers and bound in icy chains that pulsed faintly with light.

"Here we are," Cinn chirped.

"Where is…here?"

"You'll see." He pushed the door open.

❄ ❄ ❄

"She's here!"

Before her stretched a hall, its vaulted beams heavy with icicles, black banners drooping like shrouds, with light slicing through the gloom like frozen lances. The air smelled of iron and pine. This was power carved from ruin, beautiful but merciless.

At the far end, upon a throne of twisted black wood inlaid with veins of ice, sat the dark figure from the ruins.

Horns curled through a mane of dark hair, wild and regal. His eyes glowed faintly red as they fixed on her. The cold itself seemed to wait for his command.

Cinn bounded to the foot of the throne. "See? I told you she woke up fine. Not even frostbitten!"

The figure's gaze flicked to him, then back to her. "You survived the storm."

"I suppose I should thank you for dragging me out of it."

For a heartbeat, the corner of his mouth twitched, as though the admission made him uncomfortable. "Do not mistake survival for mercy," he said. "I do not make a habit of letting strays freeze on my doorstep."

"Then thank you anyway."

Cinn giggled. "Oh, she's bold."

The figure leaned forward, chains clinking softly. "No elf belongs here. Kringle's golden doors will not open for me, and I am bound to this realm. Which means..." his gaze sharpened, "...you are my problem."

"I didn't exactly *choose* this either," she snapped, surprising herself. "Maybe Kringle's *system* is the problem. Lists, rules, binaries."

"Explain."

Her heart pounded in her ears. "I coded for years. Children marked 'naughty' for stealing bread because they were starving. Branded because they weren't perfect. Maybe Kringle likes his world neat, but life isn't neat. It isn't red or green. Sometimes... sometimes it's gray."

He rose from the throne. Shadows rippled like breath around him. "You think you can teach *me* about injustice?" His voice cracked like thunder. "You stand in *my* hall, elf, because Kringle deemed you an imperfection to be discarded."

"Maybe," she said, voice shaking but steady. "But I'm not worthless."

"She's a List Maker," Cinn piped up. "Not a murderer."

The figure let out a bitter laugh and sank back onto his throne. "So. A castoff who believes in gray. How inconvenient."

"Inconvenient?"

"Because it means you'll be staying." His gaze darkened. "And I have no use for idealists."

"I like her," Cinn said brightly. "She talks back."

"Who are you, anyway?"

The hall froze with her words. Even the draft was quiet, as though the ancient castle was offended.

Cinn slapped both doughy hands over his mouth, icing eyes widening.

The figure went still. Then his head tilted, horns catching the dim light, his eyes narrowing with something that looked dangerously close to insult.

"You do not know me?"

"Should I?"

He exhaled a sound half sigh, half growl, shackles shifting at his wrists. "Krampus."

The name struck her like ice water.

Every story she'd heard as a child came rushing back. The monster who crept into attics to drag away the disobedient. The shadow with chains who swallowed the naughty whole. Mothers used his name as a warning: *be good, or Krampus will take you.*

Elowen's legs trembled. She wanted to shrink into the straw again, vanish into the cracks. And yet, her mouth betrayed her.

"Don't you…" she swallowed hard, "…eat children?"

"I most certainly do *not* consume children," Krampus rumbled.

"Where I'm from, that's what everyone says."

"Yes," he said, eyes gleaming like banked coals. "I'm sure that's what Kringle wants them to say."

"So…all those stories…"

"Lies." His jaw tightened. "Kringle needed a monster. So he made one. And gave it my name."

"I always thought the bit about the sack was a pleasant touch," Cinn said, a hum under his breath.

Elowen's heart thudded in her chest. She had expected terror but not this storm of bitterness; the edge of something rawer than cruelty.

She stared at him, brows furrowed. Maybe the stories were wrong.

"Dramatic today, aren't we?" Cinn chuckled from the floor, arms crossed over his icing stitches.

"Enough," Krampus growled, pointing to a side door. "Take her."

Cinn saluted. "You heard the boss. Don't mind him; he broods. It's his thing."

The horned figure sat unmoving in the half-light, shackles glowing faintly red. The name echoed through her mind, old as fear.

Krampus.

As the heavy door groaned shut behind them, she wondered if monsters were born or made.

CHAPTER THREE

The corridor beyond was no less eerie. Torches sputtered in sconces shaped like twisted branches, shadows clawing the walls. Cinn tugged her along cheerfully, utterly at odds with the oppressive air.

"So," Elowen murmured, hugging her arms, "Krampus?"

"The one and only!" Cinn said brightly, hopping over a puddle. "Shackled by Kringle to deal with all the dirty work. Got a naughty mortal? He has to fetch 'em. Need punishment? Call Krampus."

Shackled. Bound. Forced to be the monster. The thought churned in her stomach.

Cinn swung open a heavy door. "Welcome to hospitality duty!"

Inside, the "kitchen" was a sugar-coated nightmare; vaulted ceilings dripped with frost, cauldrons bubbled with blackened caramel, and shelves sagged with jars labeled *Sooted Sugar*, *Licorice Tar*, and *Salt of Tears*. A wooden butler loomed beside a counter, his painted smile frozen.

"Dinner is served," he intoned.

"Correction," Cinn muttered. "Chores are served."

Elowen swept sticky taffy that clung to the floor, scrubbed cauldrons until her hands blistered, and chopped frozen tubers that left her sneezing glitter. By the time she stumbled out, hair frizzed and slippers soaked, the butler thrust a silver tray into her hands.

"You will deliver this to the Lord."

She blinked. "Wait. Me?"

His jaw snapped shut with a click.

"Right," she muttered. "Because nothing says hospitality like feeding your own captor."

The castle's corridors twisted like a labyrinth. Carrying the tray required both hands, leaving her helpless against the cobwebs and whispering drafts. She turned a corner and froze.

The air was different here. Torches burned blue; frost spread in filigree across the stone. A door loomed ahead, carved with runes that writhed if she stared too long.

Her fingers brushed the handle...

"Turn back."

She almost dropped the tray. Krampus stood at the end of the hall, his chains clinking softly, red eyes burning.

"Sugarplum sticks," she gasped. "You could warn someone!"

"I did," he rumbled. "This corridor is forbidden."

She gestured with the tray. "Maybe you could give me a map before sending me on delivery duty? Not all of us navigate through brooding menace and ominous doorways."

One dark brow arched. "You mock me?"

"Here." She shoved the tray against his chest. "Your mystery stew. Enjoy."

He caught it effortlessly. "You forget you are a prisoner."

She squared her shoulders. "I don't forget. But if you expect me to cower every second, you'll be disappointed. I've done enough of that back home in cubicle C-144."

A subtle shift passed over his face. Quickly buried. "Defiance will not save you from what hunts these halls."

"What hunts these—?"

"Go," he said, thrusting the tray back into her arms. "Before the corridor keeps you."

"That's not cryptic at all," she muttered, retreating. She thought she had heard the faintest chuckle before the door shut behind her.

✳ ✳ ✳

That night, Elowen could not sleep. The stone walls wept with drafts; her blanket was too thin to stop the cold. Her thoughts circled Krampus' words: *what hunts these halls.* A soft melody slipped through the window cracks.

A lullaby.

It was faint at first, then swelling, sweet and sharp as spun sugar. The song crawled beneath her skin, stirring something deep and aching. Her breath caught as she crossed to the window.

Through the storm, pale figures drifted across the ice. Hair like ribbons. Smiles too wide.

The Sugared Choir.

The melody thickened, wrapping her mind in syrupy warmth. Her hand rose without permission. She opened the door and stepped into the hall.

"Elowen…" The song whispered her name.

Barefoot, she followed it through torch-lit corridors, down spiral stairs, and out into the storm.

The Choir danced across the snow, white and red ribbons streaming from their limbs. Their teeth gleamed like crystal sugar.

Her pulse slowed. She stepped closer, trembling, her gray magic sparking weakly between her fingers. "Go away," she whispered through chattering teeth. The energy burst outward, cracking the ice.

The song faltered, then turned savage. They lunged.

Claws slashed her arm, hot blood spilling into the snow. She screamed, magic flaring wild and uncontrolled, heat exploding in her chest. The recoil sent her sprawling in the snow, coughing blood.

The Choir shrieked triumphantly…

…and a roar split the storm.

Krampus charged through the blizzard, a shadow made of fury. His chains cracked lightning across the ice, scattering the Choir like startled birds.

"Go!" he thundered, shadows unfurling behind him.

They fled, wailing, into the storm.

Elowen crumpled, blood slicking her sleeve. Pain tore through her ribs. Krampus' shadow fell over her. "Foolish woman!" he snarled. "Do you *wish* to be torn apart?"

"I wasn't..." she coughed, "...going to sit and sing along.

Something shifted on his face; anger, yes, but buried under it, something tighter. Something like fear. His jaw tightened. Without another word, he tore off his cloak and wrapped it around her. The weight nearly crushed her, but it was warm, smelling faintly of smoke and pine.

Then he lifted her, careful enough not to hurt her wound. His shackles burned red, searing his wrists as he carried her through the gale.

Her eyelids fluttered, heavy as stone. She struggled to hold on to the cloak as the wind whipped around her.

Krampus' stride slowed as the storm pressed harder against him. His jaw clenched, arms tightening around her as he fought each step. He glanced down at her face, paling, eyes half-shut.

"Stay awake," he barked, voice breaking through the wind. He clutched her tighter, chains rattling as his massive arms braced her closer against him.

She tried. The world spun. That was when she noticed it: warmth seeping through her frozen body. Comforting at first, until she realized the heat wasn't her own, it came from him. It grew hotter, searing, and Krampus groaned in pain. She saw the smoke curl from his wrists as the glowing shackles blistered his flesh.

Her eyes fluttered shut at the sound of his ragged breathing and the hiss of snow beneath his boots. Somewhere in the blur, her mind caught on a single, jarring thought:

The monster didn't leave her to die.

The monster held her; the shackles burned him as much as the cold burned her, his voice raw with a desperation no story had ever told. No claws dragged her to punishment, or a shadow snatched her away.

Arms. Carrying her. Shielding her.

What kind of monster burned to keep you alive?

CHAPTER FOUR

When Elowen woke, she was warm for the first time in days. Cinn perched at her bedside, crumbs dusting the blanket.

"Oh crumbs, you're alive!" he squeaked. "Don't move, I'll get him!"

Before she could reply, he was gone. Moments later, the wooden butler glided in, setting a bowl of broth beside her.

"The Lord insists you eat," he said.

She was halfway through her first spoonful when the door slammed open. Krampus filled the frame, hair unbound, eyes red as embers. His shirt hung rumpled, sleeves rolled to his elbows, the fabric straining against his broad chest. Tattoos of ice and frost curled down his forearms like living runes. And above the iron shackles, angry burns marred his skin, raw and blistered.

Elowen stared.

The butler stepped smoothly aside, as though long accustomed to this storming entrance. "Lord."

"Leave us, Balthazar," Krampus growled. His crimson eyes burned as he fixed them on Elowen.

Balthazar inclined his wooden head with a dignified click and retreated.

Silence filled the chamber for a heartbeat, only broken by the sound of Krampus' boots pacing across the floor. His gaze locked on her, unrelenting.

"You dare walk into the night," he growled, "into *them*." His chains rattled with fury. "They could have torn you apart."

"I heard them calling," she said softly. "They knew my name."

"You thought curiosity worth the risk of death?" His shadow fell across her. "They are not merely songs on the wind. The Choir are Kringle's dogs. Once they taste your name in their song, they will not stop."

She wanted to shrink back. Instead, she lifted her gaze to him, noticing the burns again, glowing faintly above the shackles. "You're hurt."

His jaw snapped tight. He glanced down at the scorched skin, then grunted. "It is nothing."

"Doesn't look like nothing."

From the corner, Cinn piped, "Yeah, boss, real healthy."

Krampus' glare could have curdled milk. "I should have left you broken."

She caught the way his ears reddened beneath his wild hair before he turned back to her. "Tell me why they banished you."

Her stomach twisted. She looked down at her hands. "I changed the List."

He went still.

Then, in two strides he was at her bedside, looming. His hands slammed down on either side of her pillow, the mattress dipping beneath his weight. The chains clinked, cold links brushing the coverlet.

"You did *what*?" His voice cracked like a whip, echoing through the chamber. His face was inches from hers, breath warm upon her face, his body carrying the scent of smoke, pine, and frost.

Elowen shrank back instinctively, her shoulders pressing against the headboard. Heat flushed her skin despite the icy chill in the room. "I—"

"Speak!" His horns gleamed as his voice thundered, but his nearness was worse than his volume. She felt the warmth radiating from him, and the smell of earth, storm, and something older than time itself, enveloped her completely. His form, his presence, his muscles straining on either side of her called to her in her core.

Her cheeks flushed, and she shifted beneath him, trying to make space, to clear that warm feeling, and that tiny movement undid him. His ears darkened red. His jaw clenched.

The shackles flared. Iron glowed faintly, searing his wrists. He hissed, pulling away abruptly as smoke curled up from the scorched skin.

He straightened, clearing his throat, his expression sliding back into steel. "How?"

"I rewrote one child's code," she said as her fingers knotted in the blanket. "He stole bread because he was starving. I couldn't mark him naughty. So I made a new code."

Krampus' eyes never left her, glowing even as he prowled the chamber like a caged beast. "So," he said, low, dangerous, "you erased his crime?"

"I erased the punishment," she corrected. "I gave him another chance."

Krampus' pacing faltered. His gaze pinned her, something shifting in its depth. "And then they cast you out."

"In front of everyone." Her voice cracked. "They cheered."

His expression hardened, but his voice lowered. "Then we are both prisoners of his order."

❄ ❄ ❄

The chamber felt too small once Krampus stormed off.

Elowen stared at the door long after his heavy footsteps faded, her chest tight as if the walls themselves dared to crush her. The soup on the bedside table chilled, her appetite gone.

He had looked ready to burn her alive when she admitted what she had done. And yet…beneath the fury, beneath the roar, she saw something else flash in his crimson eyes. Not disbelief. Not disgust.

Recognition.

She pulled the blanket tighter around her shoulders. "It's just gray. Why can't anyone else see that?"

A soft scraping sound broke her thoughts.

Cinn peeked around the half-open door, icing eyes wide, grin cracked into a nervous smile. "He didn't throw you in the dungeon again, so...progress?"

Elowen exhaled, half-laugh, half-sob. "If that's what you call progress."

Cinn trotted into the room, hopping onto the end of the bed with a puff of crumbs. "He's...like that. Yells a lot. Broods even more. But if you ask me, yelling is better than silence."

"Is it?" she muttered.

"Oh yes. Silence means he's thinking. And when he's thinking, he remembers." Cinn tilted his head. "And when he remembers, the shackles burn."

"Why do they burn?"

Cinn shook his head, crumbs falling from his jaw. "Sorry. Not my story to tell."

Before she could press further, Balthazar glided in, balancing another tray as if nothing in the world were amiss. His wooden face was unreadable as ever, but his painted eyes lingered on her a fraction too long before he spoke.

"Your pulse is unsteady," he observed. He set the tray down on the table with meticulous care. "You must conserve your strength."

"I'm not fragile."

"You are bleeding beneath your bandages."

Her mouth opened, then shut again. He wasn't wrong. Her arm throbbed with every beat of her heart.

"Eat," Balthazar commanded, and for once she obeyed, spooning a mouthful of broth past her lips.

It was warm, at least. A comfort after the storm.

"Why would Kringle send them?" She asked, lowering the spoon. "The Choir? Isn't banishment enough?"

"Not for him," Balthazar said flatly, with an edge of bitterness to his voice.

Cinn kicked his gingerbread legs, gaze flicking toward the window. "Kringle doesn't like things slipping out of order. You broke the system. He sent the Choir to make sure it doesn't happen again."

Her stomach sank. "So they'll keep coming for me."

Neither answered.

The silence was enough.

※ ※ ※

Later, she wandered into the library, drawn by the whisper of old parchment. Towering shelves rose into the vaulted ceiling, ladders vanishing into shadow. Dust drifted through narrow windows like snow.

She reached toward a cracked spine, then froze. The book hissed. Words slithered from the binding, fragments overlapping like a chorus of accusations: ...*stole the coin...broke the window... lied to her mother...*

Her stomach twisted.

"You're bleeding," Krampus said behind her.

She jumped. The bandage had slipped; blood seeped through the linen. "It's fine—"

He took a step forward, then reeled. The shackles pulsed, and he hissed, recoiling as if struck, before turning and striding away. The doors slammed behind him like thunder.

Elowen sagged against the shelf, trembling. "What in the frost?"

Moments later, Balthazar appeared. "Your duties have been reassigned. You will serve in the archive."

Her brow furrowed. "Reassigned?"

"Manual labor is beneath your current condition." His painted gaze flicked to her bleeding arm.

He led her to the back of the library. At the end waited a door, iron-banded and unmarked, its hinges carved with curling runes.

"The archive is yours," Balthazar said.

Her brows drew together. "Why me?"

"It is a gift." He pushed open the door, and the hinges wailed; a draft of air brushed over her, charged and alive, prickling her skin.

Inside stretched a small, older chamber, tucked into the castle's marrow. A handful of desks crouched beneath narrow windows rimed with frost. On each desk rested a crystal globe, dim and quiet. One pulsed faintly like a heartbeat muffled in snow, but the rest lay cracked and silent.

Her eyes widened with recognition. Orbs for the List. Not the bright candy-striped terminals of Central, but something darker, quieter.

"His Lordship wishes it to be yours now," Balthazar said from the doorway. "Your work as a List Maker may continue. The orb will answer your call."

He turned without another word and shut the door behind him.

Elowen paused. No guards. No manager hovering. Just her and the crystal.

She crept to the flickering orb and brushed frost from the surface. It pulsed alive, showing a boy's face, tear-streaked, crying in an attic. "Naughty" flashed upon the orb in brilliant red.

Her stomach twisted. Again. The List was always the same, no matter the realm.

Her fingers tingled; if she dared, would the alarms shriek as they had in Central? Would Krampus storm in? Would he exile her, too? She traced the gray rune she had drawn before. Smoke curled, guttering, alive. The crystal shuddered, then swallowed the mark whole. Red vanished. The boy's face faded.

Elowen's breath rushed out in a shaky laugh. No alarms. No bells. No guards. Only silence.

She glanced around the dim room, half-expecting to catch Balthazar lurking or Klaussen running. Nothing. Only frost and dust.

Her shoulders loosened. With a deep breath, she tried again, her hands trembling. Another child blinked into view: a girl with ink-stained fingers and stolen paper hidden under her sleeve. Red flared, 'naughty,' but Elowen drew her rune, anyway. The globe drank it, pulsed once, and dimmed.

Freedom sent a wild thrill through her chest, and then a dread settled. This orb would send its runes to the Master List, just like the others. She groaned. Kringle would know she was still working by the gray filtering the red and green.

She reached to steady herself against the crystal and thought of Krampus.

The globe blazed white, drinking her touch, and then, without warning, the vision shifted.

Snow stretched before her under a sky bleeding with northern lights. Bells chimed faintly through the storm, so clear she could feel the vibrations in her teeth.

A woman knelt in the drifts ahead, tall and radiant, garments spun of frost and midnight stars. Constellations glittered in her ebony hair. Her hands reached skyward as her lips moved, her voice breaking in foreign words. Sorrow throbbed through the sound as if it were her own.

The air shimmered. From starlight and snow, two children emerged. One glowed bright, his laughter booming, blond curls bouncing, silver bells jingling from nowhere and everywhere. The other walked from pine shadows and twilight frost, quiet, solemn, small horns upon his head, carrying night in his eyes. Brothers.

The vision surged forward.

Time raced. The brothers grew taller; years passed, their mother's gaze always upon them. Balance, fragile and perfect, formed between them: light and shadow. Harmony she could almost breathe in.

Then voices. Human voices, sharp with fear, so close they made her flinch. A titan in a mountain of fire forged chains of starlight and a gilded crown. "The Forger," they whispered. The chains cracked across the shadowed brother's wrists. He crumpled. The crowd's cheers cut through her like knives, their prayers lifting only the golden son.

The scene sharpened until the golden man's laughter echoed inside her skull, vast marble halls rising at his back, thrones gleaming beneath the gilded crown. She clapped her hands to her ears, but the sound pushed through.

And the shadowed man? Left in frost and silence. Shackles bit into his flesh, the runes searing with gray light. That light, smoke and ash, the same hue that curled from her own palms. A hollow weight dropped through her chest. Stories warped his name. Punisher. Monster. Villain.

"It wasn't fair," she whispered, but her breath vanished into the storm.

The vision split. Chains swelled before her eyes, links pulsing like a heart she could almost hear. A whisper bled through the wind, ragged and heavy, brushing hot against her ear.

"And so they call me monster. Forevermore."

The world lurched into blinding frost and darkness.

A dungeon, shadows pressing tight. A child huddled in the corner, tears freezing on his skin. Chains rattled behind her, metallic and terrible.

Krampus filled the doorway. Towering. Whip glowing red. Cloak alive with shadow. His voice crashed over her like thunder: "Do you know what you've done?"

The child's sob punched the air from her lungs.

The whip cracked against the wall. Sparks rained. The child screamed.

"No!" The cry tore from Elowen's throat. She stumbled forward, desperate to seize his arm, or comfort the child, but her hand met only cold.

Shadows swarmed, gnashing teeth, and flaring eyes. His roar shook the chamber, and it rattled her bones as if meant for her.

She wrenched her hand back, gasping, bile rising hot in her throat.

And the crystal went dark.

She collapsed at her desk, sobbing. The visions clung like frost. How could the same man who carried her from the storm also bear that cruelty?

Tears blurred the edges of the room. She wanted to hate him, to fear him, and yet she couldn't. A part of her, a quiet, stubborn part, wanted to see the man behind the chains, the heart beneath the mask, that little boy from the forest. Empathy clawed at her conscience, dangerous and unbidden, whispering that there was more to the story than punishment and fear.

Her head hung heavy as she left the archive. She drifted through the library, so lost in thought she didn't hear the chains rattling until his shadow dwarfed over her.

"Elowen."

She whirled. Krampus stood beside her, half-shadow, half-light.

"I was—"

"Working," he finished for her. His boots struck the stone floor like hammers.

"I wasn't digging. But it showed me...you—"

"So you saw," he said, his voice low, stepping closer. "The archive shows the truth."

"Then why show me *that*?" she demanded. "So I could see the monster you want me to believe you are?"

Something flickered across his face. Hurt, maybe, buried beneath iron-hard features. Then, it was gone. "You saw what they have *forced* me to be," he said.

"Kringle," she whispered.

"Yes. The chains bind me to his will." His eyes met hers, fierce and tired all at once.

Tears dripped from her eyes. "You could have chosen—"

"No," he snapped. "Choice was stripped from me long ago."

Elowen's stomach churned, torn between horror and pity. Her throat tightened with the weight of understanding she didn't want to bear. How could punishment be forced, yet inflict such pain? How could someone be both a monster and a victim?

"Be careful," he growled. "You toy with truths you don't

understand."

She wanted to back away, but her feet refused to move. His presence filled the library, pressing against her, stealing her air. And yet, something inside her bristled. She wasn't a child to be cowed by shadows.

"Maybe I understand more than you think," she huffed.

Their gazes locked. Anger, pity, and something else unspoken flickered between them. Then, a faint hum coiled through the walls.

The song again.

Elowen stiffened. Her wound throbbed, the scar burning like fresh fire. The melody coiled around her ears, tugging, beckoning. Her pulse fell into rhythm with the beat, slower, slower.

Krampus stiffened. "His dogs have returned."

The song swelled, pressing against the castle wards, seeping through cracks in the stone. Words twined in its melody, promises whispered on sugared tongues.

"Come outside, little elf. Come where it's warm, where it's sweet."

Elowen clutched her temples, gritting her teeth. "They're calling me."

"Don't listen," he commanded.

But the wound ached, pulling her to her feet. Her magic throbbed. The sweetness of the song twined with it, dizzying and intoxicating.

She staggered toward the doorway.

"Elowen!" His roar rattled the shelves. "Stay."

Her hands braced against a shelf, but her feet betrayed her. The song tugged until she slipped into the corridor, and the storm howled louder, colder, sweeter.

Snow stung her face as she stumbled through the courtyard gates. The Choir waited beyond the walls, their dark silhouettes shifting against the pale drifts. Eyes like candy glass fixed on her, mouths opening in wide, too-perfect smiles.

"Sweet child," they cooed. "Sweet little elf. Come with us. Come home."

Elowen's pulse hammered. Her magic sparked gray, hissing across her fingertips. For a moment, terror strangled her. Then she remembered the starving child in the vision, the injustice, the cruelty. Rage replaced fear.

"No."

Light surged from her hand, a jagged ripple through the snow. It tore into one of the Choir, shattering its glamour. Beneath the sugar shine was something grotesque; its flesh stretched too thin, teeth like splintered glass. The creature screamed and fell, its song warping into static before the body dissolved into sleet.

The two shrieked for their fallen sister.

Another darted forward, ribbons lashing like whips. Elowen's magic flared again, wild and instinctive. A wave of gray light erupted around her, searing through the storm. The blast caught a second singer mid-lunge, its chest cracked open in a burst of crystalline shards before it toppled soundlessly into the drifts, its voice dying with the wind.

"Elowen!"

Krampus burst from the gates, chains blazing with frost fire. The remaining Choir hissed and scattered as he waded toward her, monstrous, eyes blazing with fury.

Elowen stumbled, knees buckling. The song clawed at her skull, trying to drag her under. She hurled another blast, but it sputtered, backfiring in a flash that seared her. She cried out, clutching her arm.

Krampus tore through the snow toward her, scattering the Choir like a shadow before fire. He hauled her back.

"Enough," he snarled, wrapping her in his cloak as the storm swelled.

The Choir screamed as she rushed toward them. Her voice tangled with Elowen's, with his, with the storm itself, until the air cracked.

Elowen's hands sparked at the ground, and it rippled with gray runes. Darkness spread like ink across the snow, swallowing light, swallowing sound.

She gasped as the world tilted, tearing open beneath them.

Krampus' grip tightened. His chains clanged and then snapped with a noise like thunder.

They fell.

Through shadow, through silence, through something colder than the storm itself.

Elowen clung to him, the world dissolving into black.

By gingersnaps, what have I done?

CHAPTER FIVE

The fall had no end.

Elowen clutched Krampus' cloak as the world unraveled into frost and ink. No sound but the clatter of his chains, echoing in a bottomless dark. The storm was gone, yet its memory still scraped her raw.

Impact.

Snow exploded. She tumbled sideways, breath ripped from her lungs. For a moment she lay in a heap, listening to her own rasp.

A shadow with glinting horns rose from the drift. Tall. Broad. Krampus.

His chest heaved, muscles taut, chains dragging black frost through the snow. He turned on her, eyes burning with icy fire. "What did you do?"

Elowen flinched but forced herself upright. "I don't know!"

"Don't lie to me." His growl vibrated in her bones. "Rifts don't tear open on their own."

Cold bit deeper than flesh. She wrapped her arms around herself. "I told you. I'm just a List Maker. That's all I've ever done. Nothing like this. Ever."

The wind howled, tugging at his cloak, but his fury burned hotter. "And yet here we are," he rumbled, gesturing to the endless wilderness.

The Choir's song still clung in her skull, syrupy-sweet and suffocating. "I can't explain it," she admitted, barely above the wind. "It's new to me."

"New," he echoed. His gaze sharpened. "This isn't normal elf magic. It's older. Wilder. I didn't know elves could make rifts."

He turned away, eyes scanning the trees. They stood at the edge of a frozen forest. Pines loomed like skeletal towers, branches clawing at the sky. Snow blanketed the ground in heavy drifts, untouched and endless. The air was sharp enough to cut; every breath seared her lungs.

"Where are we?" she asked.

Krampus crouched, running his hands through the snow. He lifted a handful, letting it fall through his fingers. "Far from the castle."

He straightened, towering again. "At least your rift didn't take us out of the realm."

Elowen froze. *My magic did this?*

His eyes glinted with suspicion, and something like curiosity. "The ancients carved doors for safe crossing between realms. But rifts..." His tone darkened. "Rifts are wild. You need the right runes to make one, or you tear reality instead of opening it."

Her stomach sank. The gray sparks at her fingertips prickled in memory. "I didn't mean to—"

"And yet you did." His voice softened, but it carried weight. "Your runes are reckless and lack control."

The words landed heavy. So this *was* her fault. She hugged herself tighter.

Krampus' gaze flicked to her shivering form. For a moment, his expression softened, then the mask slid back into place.

"We move," he said. "Now."

He strode into the trees, chains whispering over snow.

Elowen scrambled after him, nearly tripping in the drifts. Her slippers were soaked, her toes numb, and her breath burned, but she clenched her jaw and pressed on.

For a while, silence reigned between them. There was only wind and crunching snow.

Finally, she said, "The end of the year is coming."

"Yes."

She kicked at a drift. "Back home, we have a grand celebration. All the names tallied, all the gifts wrapped, a thousand candles to divide Nice from Naughty. We have a large feast and everything."

He didn't turn. "Here it's chains. Old vows renewed. None escape them." He rattled his wrists; frost skittered into the air.

Elowen rubbed her arms, teeth chattering. "What happens if you fail?"

"No one fails," he said simply. "Not when the system devours all who resist it."

A shiver crawled up her spine.

They pressed deeper into the forest. Branches clawed her arms, her legs burned, her lungs screamed. She tripped and caught herself.

Krampus slowed his pace, though his scowl deepened. "You're weak," he muttered.

"I'm not weak. I'm *freezing*," she snapped. "And tired. And I didn't exactly choose to crash into...wherever this is." She waved her arms around, gesturing wildly to the trees towering above them.

His mouth twitched, almost a smirk, before hardening again. "Keep up, or you'll freeze where you stand."

"I'm trying."

"Try harder."

They trudged on in silence. Her limbs felt heavy as lead, but stubbornness drove her. She would not give him the satisfaction of calling her weak again.

Hours blurred. The forest thinned into a frozen plain bathed in milk-white moonlight. The wind screamed across it, tearing at her.

She stumbled. "Cinnamon sticks!" she cursed, sinking into a drift.

Krampus sighed, turning back. For a moment, she expected another scolding. Instead, he extended a hand.

His palm was broad, shackles glowing faintly. "Up."

She hesitated, then slipped her freezing fingers into his. His strength hauled her up effortlessly. Heat bloomed in her chest, a strange warmth that wasn't from the storm.

He released her quickly, grunting as the shackles sparked, and turned away.

They walked on. The storm deepened until he was only a shadow ahead. She drew close, nearly walking into his back. He didn't protest. His arm braced around her when the gale nearly took her down, steadying her each time.

Minutes. Hours. Time lost meaning. There was only the storm, the struggle, and the strange, furious comfort of his presence.

At last, a jagged ridge loomed, a dark cleft cutting into the rock.

Krampus quickened his stride, dragging her with him. They stumbled inside, wind roaring past the entrance before falling to a whisper.

Elowen collapsed against the stone, chest heaving. She slid down to the frozen ground, curling her arms tight.

Krampus stood at the mouth, scanning the storm with narrowed eyes. "We'll rest here."

"Rest," she panted. "Or do you mean freeze slower?"

His lips twitched. Then he unclasped his cloak and draped it over her shoulders.

The weight was immense, lined with fur still carrying his warmth.

"You'll need it more than I," he muttered, settling opposite her as his shackles hissed.

She pulled the cloak tighter, burying her face against the fur. It smelled of frost and smoke, pine and something darker, something that made her heart flutter.

Silence stretched.

"You hate me for this, don't you?" she muttered.

He didn't look at her; his eyes were fixed on the storm. "I don't have the luxury of hate."

Her throat tightened. She listened to the wind shriek beyond their fragile shelter.

The storm raged like a living thing. Snow hissed at the opening; wind howled through the hollow. Elowen huddled under the cloak, trembling despite the weight of fur and shadow.

Finally, Krampus stirred. The scrape of his chains broke the quiet. "It won't break soon," he grumbled. He pressed one hand against the rock, frowned, then slammed his fist into it. Stone cracked. A narrow passage yawned beyond.

Elowen blinked. "You just...broke a mountain?"

"Loosened it," he grunted, brushing debris aside. "Come on."

She hesitated, clutching the cloak tighter. "Is it safe?"

"Safe?" He snorted. "In my realm, nothing is safe, especially in winter. But it's warmer than this."

He offered his hand again. Shackled, scarred, broad.

Her chest tightened as she took it. The warmth in his grip startled her.

The tunnel forced them close; her shoulder brushed his arm as they moved deeper. They emerged into a small cavern, its walls glittering with veins of frost stone. From the ceiling, icicles dripped, the water hitting the floor with a soft echo.

Krampus struck the ground. A pale blue flame rose, cold but luminous.

"You can summon fire?" she breathed.

"Not fire," he corrected. "Frost light. It keeps the dark away."

She sat beside it, letting the icy glow wash over her. The light steadied her heartbeat.

The frost light flickered between them. Elowen studied the cavern walls, tracing the strange shapes etched into the stone. Ancient symbols. Some angular like blades, others curling like vines.

"What are these?" she asked.

Krampus' gaze followed hers. His jaw worked as though he were weighing whether to answer. At last, he said, "Marks of the first wardens. Old magic, older than even I."

She traced one rune, feeling a faint hum beneath her fingertips. A thrill ran down her spine. "It's still alive."

He nodded. "Stronger than the castle wards. That's why I trust this place."

"And where are they?"

"Who?" he asked with a grunt.

"The first wardens."

"Deep within the realm," he said. "They come only if summoned."

The frost light gleamed across his face, softening the harsh planes. He looked weary, more than she'd seen before. His hair fell wild across his shoulders. His icy forearm tattoos were as intricate as the surrounding runes. Above the marks, his skin was blistered raw where the shackles had freshly burned.

"You're hurt," she said softly.

"It is nothing."

"Nothing?" She leaned forward, his cloak pooling at her knees. "You're scorched."

He turned his wrists as if to hide the burns.

Her magic fluttered in her palms, aching to help. She lifted a hand, then stopped when he flinched. "Why does it happen?"

His gaze dropped to her hand, then back to her face.

"You shouldn't," he warned, low.

"I want to help."

Something flickered in his eyes, quick as lightning. He looked away, his shoulders rigid. "No one can help me."

She flinched inwardly, swallowing the sting of rejection, though her chest still ached to prove him wrong.

Her hand fell back into her lap. The frost light crackled softly.

"I don't believe that," she murmured.

He huffed, but didn't reply.

The storm raged beyond, but in the cavern, the air was steady. Shadows felt smaller, closer, almost intimate.

She let her thoughts drift to small comforts but none of it fully reached her.

Elowen wrapped the cloak tighter around herself and leaned closer to the frost light. She studied him from beneath her lashes; the broad shoulders bent under invisible weight, the way his jaw stayed locked, as if keeping secrets trapped inside.

"When I was a girl," she said finally, "I used to sneak out of the dormitories to the attic and paint snowflakes on the ceiling. Dozens of them. Little flurries in unique patterns. It was the only place I felt free."

Krampus looked up from the flame. "Snowflakes."

She smiled faintly. "I wanted to believe there was something beyond work and lists and singing in step. Like there was... something beyond all that."

A shadow passed over her features, and her voice grew quieter, almost a whisper. "But my magic...it wasn't like everyone else's. Not the pretty kind, not neat. It fizzled wrong, or twisted too fast, and had that gray color. Larkspur...she was always there. She loved rules. So, she'd turn me in every time she caught me. She used to tell me it was dirty, like dishwater. Wrong." She let out a shaky breath, almost laughing to herself.

Krampus's stare lingered on her. "Gray."

"It's always come out that way."

He watched her, eyes tracing the lines of her face. "Gray is not wrong," he said. "It's the color of the ancients. Kris hates it because he can't control it. But it's power, not weakness."

She stared, stunned. She had carried that shame like a scar all her life, and he spoke of it as though it were something precious. Warmth rose in her chest, flickering brighter than the frost light.

His gaze softened, and he mumbled, "I used to watch the skies, too. When the chains were new. Snowflakes were all I could see through the bars."

Her eyebrows arched in surprise as she met his gaze.

He had just thrown her a line in the storm, a flicker of connection.

Her shoulder brushed his arm again, deliberately this time. He tensed, his shackles rattling, faint warmth seeping from the metal.

Her heart lurched at the closeness, a blend of fear, awe, and an unnameable pull toward him.

"You're not the monster they say you are," she said.

The words hung in the cold air, fragile and dangerous.

His lips curved in something between a snarl and a laugh. "Careful, little elf. You may regret those words."

But his soft voice betrayed his glare, and when their gazes met, neither looked away.

She drew a slow, steadying breath, feeling the strange courage and warmth rising like dawn.

CHAPTER SIX

The cavern glowed with the last threads of frost light. Outside, the wind shrieked as though the mountains themselves were tearing apart.

Elowen shivered; her breath curled in pale ribbons. The cold clawed into her bones, a living thing. She wondered how someone so immense could still seem so fragile.

Krampus sat opposite her, his broad shoulders bent, gaze fixed on the dimming light as if willing it to last.

"You didn't sleep," she said, her voice raw with cold. Her throat tightened, half from the ache, half from daring to speak into that silence.

His eyes flicked to her. "I don't sleep."

She frowned, pushing herself upright. "At all?"

"Not in storms." The finality in his tone suggested storms were enemies that required vigilance.

Elowen studied him in the blue light. She noticed the subtle twitch of his jaw, the way his hands flexed against the chains, and felt a strange pull toward him despite every warning she had ever been given. The burns on his forearms had darkened overnight, angry red beneath the silver band of chain. His jaw flexed as if each heartbeat cost him. And yet, she thought, he hadn't moved from his watch, not once.

"Your burns…"

He stilled with the same tightening she'd seen before, the recoil of pride. She hesitated, fear and compassion warring in her chest. Her mind whispered the stories they raised her on: *never touch the monster.* But her hands itched to defy them.

The storm outside gnashed its teeth, a low moan through the stone.

Then, unexpectedly, his voice broke the silence. "The shackles bite when I forget what I am," he said roughly. "When I care. When I...ease." He grimaced at the word, as if it soured in his mouth. "They remind me. To stay a monster."

Elowen's throat closed. "Remind you," she echoed. "Or punish you?"

He didn't answer, but the tremor in his jaw was enough.

Carefully, deliberately, she tore a strip from her hem, the fabric whining as it ripped. She crawled closer, her knees brushing the frost. Her hands trembled, betraying her, partly from cold, partly from audacity. Each movement felt like a defiance of the warnings she had lived under.

Krampus didn't move as she took his scarred arm. Her fingers hovered a breath away, then touched skin hot as iron. He flinched but didn't pull away, only watched, his gaze dark and unblinking. Slowly, she wrapped the scorched flesh, layer after layer, her movements tender and sure. Her hands brushed his skin, reverent, deliberate. She marveled at how someone so terrifying could be so still, so unyielding under her touch.

The air between them shifted and became charged, trembling.

She tied the strip off, then tore another. His other arm followed, and the same ritual proceeded, quiet and careful. Each layer felt like a minor rebellion, a silent acknowledgment that she, a mere elf, could protect him, even a little. The only sounds were her shallow breathing and the low growl of wind.

When she finished, he exhaled, as though he'd been holding his breath the whole time. Then, abruptly, he stood. The chains rattled. "I'll be back."

Before she could speak, he vanished into the storm.

Elowen stared after him, heart twisting. *Foolish kindness.*

Foolish, foolish girl. Alone now, in a cavern with fading frost light. She hugged her knees, aware of the strange ache that had lodged in her chest. Had she scared the monster away?

The cold crept deeper into her bones. She cursed herself, pulled his cloak tighter, and curled against the stone. The frost light dimmed, its glow shrinking to embers as shadows closed in. Her teeth chattered violently. Despair felt like icy claws raking across her chest. She wondered if anyone had ever touched him like that, or if her hands had broken something sacred in him.

Time blurred. The storm wailed. She drifted, half-asleep, half-dreaming of fire that would not burn.

❄ ❄ ❄

The storm engulfed him the moment he stepped outside. Wind howled through the mountain's teeth, tearing at him, ice lashing his skin raw. He welcomed it. The cold did not bite like her hands had.

Her strips of fabric around his forearms burned worse than frostbite. Even though they were nothing but cloth, fragile as any elf's whim, they became an echo of her warmth that he couldn't shake. He told himself it was irritation, that her defiance was an insult to his nature. But beneath that, a different heat pulsed.

Kindness. He should have snarled at it, torn the bandages away, roared at her, reminded her what he was. Instead, he had sat still, letting her bind him like a man, not a beast. Worse...he had wanted it.

His heart jumped as he trudged into the gale. The chains rattled with each stride, their glow warning, searing. *Do not ease. Do not care. Remember.* He clenched his jaw against the sting.

He tore through drifts until he found his old cache buried seasons ago: roots wrapped in oilcloth, a haunch from a hunt preserved by frost, a skin of mountain water frozen solid. He dug them free with clawed hands, the effort grounding him in old ritual. Survival. Duty. Those were things he understood. Not warmth. Not her eyes when she looked at him without fear.

Snow clung to his shoulders as he turned back toward the cavern. The snow fought him every step; the wind shrieked to drive him away. Still, he climbed, muscles straining, chest tight. Each step carried not only food but the weight of what she had done: a defiance as simple as tearing a seam and daring to touch him.

Foolish elf. Foolish woman.

He ducked back through the cavern's mouth, ice crusting his hair, arms full.

And there she was; knees hugged to her chest, cloak drowning her small body, eyes wide the moment she saw him. She gasped and scrambled to her feet. Then, before he could shake the snow from his shoulders, she stripped the cloak from herself and threw it over him instead, clutching the fur tight around him as if *he* were the one in need of saving.

"You shouldn't have gone out there!" she cried, voice breaking with fury and fear. "Look at you. You're half frozen!"

Krampus froze under her hands. She was fire in motion. Defiant, trembling, and alive. He tried to shrug her off. "It is nothing," he muttered, but his voice lacked conviction, even to himself.

Her eyes seared through him, fierce and unrelenting. And the bandages burned hotter still. His lips were blue, and his arms trembled. The chains glowed faintly red.

He wanted to say he had carried worse burdens, that the storms and chains were nothing and he didn't need the cloak as much as her, never mind her touch or trembling voice.

But his lips refused the words. He couldn't do that to her.

The sight of his suffering was too much for her to bear. She tugged the cloak tighter around him. "Stop saying that," she whispered. "You're not made of stone, no matter how much you pretend."

He stiffened. No one had spoken to him like that. Not in centuries. The words struck deeper than the cold. He saw her body tense, braced for denial, a lash of anger, but none came from him. His shoulders sagged, the fight draining out of him until it was as if the storm inside him went slack.

"Do as you will," he said roughly.

And so she did.

❄ ❄ ❄

Elowen exhaled, relief mingling with frustration. She guided him down to sit by the frost light, wrapping the cloak snugly around them both. Her fingers lingered on his shoulders, tracing warmth back into him, memorizing the curve of them, the breadth of his arms, each detail a paradox of fear and awe. His scent filled her lungs.

When she saw the food he'd brought, her stomach clenched with hunger so sharp it hurt. She tore into a root and devoured it.

Krampus watched in silence, his gaze fixed on her with unnerving intensity. Every glance, every pause, every subtle motion of his shoulders felt like a conversation in itself. The frost light painted him in blue fire. "Do you…want some?" she asked.

"I ate outside," he said too quickly.

Something in her gut told her not to ask *what* that meant. She nodded and ate in silence.

Her hands trembled when she set the last down. The cold still seeped through her bones. She wrapped her arms around herself again, but the shivers only worsened.

Krampus frowned. Without a word, he shifted closer. His form loomed and then settled behind her. The cloak stretched wider, draping over them both.

Startled, she blinked up at him, her breath shallow. His nearness was overwhelming, electric, terrifying. Her heart hammered, a frantic rhythm against her ribs, as she felt his warmth seeping through layers of fur and cloth. She could feel the solidity of his broad chest, his pulse through the air between them. She breathed deep, inhaling his scent; it surrounded her, comforted her.

She leaned back, cautiously, her head resting against him. The world outside howled and shattered, but here, she could hear only his heartbeat.

Her lips parted before she could catch them. She lifted her chin and pressed a trembling kiss to his cheek.

Krampus froze. His eyes widened, glowing faint in the dim frost light. "What," he rasped, "was that for?"

"Thank you," she whispered. She smiled, curling closer under the cloak.

He didn't move, didn't speak. His breath came heavy, his body was rigid, but he didn't pull away; instead, he pressed against her.

Elowen closed her eyes, listening to the steady thrum of his heartbeat beneath her ear. A faint part of her screamed caution, but her heart refused. He was terrifying and comforting all at once. The warmth of the cloak spread through her, wrapping her in comfort. When sleep claimed her, she dreamed not of cubicles or codes, not of Kringle's gleaming smile, but of frost fire and shadows, and him.

❋ ❋ ❋

She slept curled against him, small and warm as a spark in an ember pit. Her breath brushed steadily over his ribs, soft as falling snow. The cloak covered them both, but it was her nearness that burned.

The chains knew. They always knew.

Heat flared along his forearms, bright searing bands where iron kissed skin. Every time his muscles eased, every time his body yielded to the comfort of her weight, the shackles hissed and bit harder, punishing him for peace. The scent of scorched flesh threaded through the frosty air, acrid and sharp.

He gritted his teeth, body rigid. He should have pushed her

away, torn free, left her to the cloak alone. Better for her to shiver than for him to soften. Better to keep a distance from the monster. He didn't.

She had touched him, had wrapped him like something worth saving. His skin still remembered her hands, light as snowfall, defiant as fire.

So he stayed. Let her warmth soak into him, let the shackles carve deeper, let the storm rage outside. He bore the fire in silence, jaw clenched, chest rising under her cheek like stone. Let them burn, he thought. Let them rage.

The chains wanted him rigid, merciless. Yet, for the first time in centuries, he chose not to obey.

❄ ❄ ❄

It wasn't until she woke again that she realized the truth.

She awoke warm, too warm. For a heartbeat, she forgot where she was, only that warmth cocooned her, that a heartbeat thudded under her ear. She stirred, cheek pressed to his chest rising beneath her.

Her eyes opened. He sat motionless, arms around her, face turned toward the dying light. His wrists smoked where iron met flesh, the burns deeper than before.

Krampus shifted as she moved, his arms loosening. He didn't meet her eyes as she pushed the cloak back and sat upright, cheeks flushed.

"Why didn't you wake me?" she whispered. "Why didn't you move?"

"The warmth was good for you," he said simply. "I'll be fine."

Her heart ached as she gazed at the burns above her bandages, at the quiet pain he bore so she could sleep in comfort. *Good for me, never for himself.*

She touched the bandages, now dark with char. "You'll never be fine," she breathed. Not while the chains bound him.

He didn't argue. He rose and coaxed more light from the

fissure beneath the frost, blue fire spilling between them.

"Still snowing?" she asked. She rubbed her arms; her muscles were sore from the night.

He gave a grunt. "Worse."

Her stomach growled in answer.

He lifted the bundle of provisions from where it rested near the wall, unwrapping them on a flat stone. He tore a hunk of meat in half and handed it to her. "Eat."

She took a bite. The simple taste brought tears to her eyes.

"You'll need strength," Krampus added, watching her. "Storms test more than bone."

She chewed slowly, then smiled. "Do you always talk in riddles?" she asked. "Or is that part of the monster routine?"

His lips twitched, almost a smile. "And do you always talk too much?"

She huffed. "Maybe." She swallowed her bite. "At Central, everyone sang in step. Every word had to be cheery, every smile painted on. Silence was...dangerous. So I hid. Got rather good at it too. I guess you're the perfect victim of my words."

He studied her. "And they cast you out anyway."

Elowen paused mid-bite. She lowered her gaze. "Yep."

He grunted. "Fools."

Her head snapped up. He looked away quickly, as though the word had slipped out before he could cage it. His shackles glowed.

The word hit her like warmth. She reached across and tweaked the bandage gently. His muscles tensed beneath her fingers, but he didn't pull away.

"You shouldn't," he murmured, though the warning lacked force.

"I know," she sang, "but I want to."

Their eyes locked, her defiance sparking against his restraint, frost light gleaming between them.

He looked away first, clearing his throat. He reached for the meat and handed her another slice, his eyes averted.

She accepted it with a murmured thanks.

They ate in silence, the storm's fury muffled by stone. When the last scraps were gone, Elowen curled back beneath the cloak. Her body ached with cold, but her heart beat too fast for sleep.

"Tell me something," she said, breaking the quiet.

Krampus glanced at her warily. "What?"

"Anything." She tucked her chin against her knees. "Something no-one else knows."

"You ask dangerous things," he murmured.

"Maybe," she said with a small shrug. "But storms make people honest."

He was silent for so long she thought he wouldn't answer. Then finally he said, "I used to braid the beards of my goats. Before..." He gestured vaguely at the chains. "Before all this."

Elowen blinked, startled. Then a laugh slipped out, light and incredulous.

He scowled. "You mock me?"

"Never!" She giggled, covering her mouth. "That's...sweet." She smiled, warm despite the chill. "I didn't expect that."

The shackles hissed, his skin flinching at the burn. He winced, and she reached toward him without thinking.

"I'd like to see that someday. Braids on the goats."

He gave a grunt, turning his face away. But she didn't miss the faintest trace of color in his ears and the twitch of his lips.

She leaned against him once more, letting the cloak cover them both. His body was a steady wall against the blizzard. Her shivers eased, and her head tipped against his shoulder.

"Thank you," she murmured.

"For what now?" he asked, voice weary.

"For staying. For...not letting me freeze."

His throat worked, but no words came. His shackles glowed, burning brighter in the dark.

CHAPTER SEVEN

The storm broke at last.

Silence filled the cavern. It was not the smothered silence of snow-laden winds, but the brittle, echoing hush of a world half-buried. The cavern's mouth gaped open, pale morning light creeping across the frost-lit stone. The air outside shimmered, crisp and thin, like the aftermath of a held note.

Krampus stood at the threshold, his broad frame blocking most of the light. His cloak hung in tatters, heavy with frost, steam rising faintly where the cold met his skin. He didn't speak for a long while. Only his horns moved, scraping low against the stone as he turned his head.

"It's over?" Elowen's voice was a rasp of sleep and disbelief.

"For now." His voice was quieter than usual, almost reverent, as if storms were gods to be endured. Then: "We move."

Every joint in her body protested as she pushed herself upright. Her muscles ached with cold and stillness. The frost fire had guttered out in the night, leaving the air damp, metallic, and heavy. She rubbed her arms, shook her skirts free of frost, and stepped toward the light.

Outside, the brightness struck her like a blow. Snow lay in heavy sheets across the land, sparkling under the winter sun. Trees bowed beneath their burden of ice. The sky blazed a washed-out blue, streaked with silver clouds, like the storm had scoured the world clean.

"Which way?" She squinted through the glare.

Krampus's eyes narrowed as he scanned the horizon. "East. The castle lies beyond the ridge."

"How far?"

He made a low sound, half a growl, half amusement. "Next time you decide to make a portal, make it closer to the castle, and we'll walk less."

Elowen blinked. Was that—? She almost smiled. "Did you just —?"

But he was already moving, long strides cutting through the snow.

❄ ❄ ❄

Snow crunched beneath her slippers, the air bright with cold that stung every breath. Krampus' long stride forced Elowen to half-trot, but she refused to complain or ask for rest. Between them, silence stretched taut and uncertain; fragile, like glass about to splinter.

The world was endless white and gray shadow. Hills rolled beneath blankets of frost. Her magic had cast them farther than she had imagined. Everything looked clean, but wrong.

Her stomach gnawed at itself. She remembered the taste of the roots, the warmth of his cloak, the heartbeat she'd fallen asleep to. It felt like another lifetime. She bit her lip. He wasn't speaking, and she wouldn't break the silence first, especially not for something so small as hunger.

Then the ground trembled.

A faint vibration at first, like a heartbeat beneath the snow. Then stronger. The air itself seemed to quiver.

Krampus froze. His head tilted. "Stay behind me."

The whisper built to a roar. Snow fell in sheets from the trees, and the forest shuddered awake.

Shapes broke from the ridge, first two, then a dozen. They

burst through the treeline in a blur of gray hide and bone.

Elowen's chest seized. "Reindeer?"

"Once," Krampus said, his tone like thunder. His chains rattled, shadows curling up his arms. "Now, hollow."

The creatures' hides hung in tatters, ribs jutting sharp through flesh half-rotted away. Their eyes glowed like dull lanterns, and from their antlers hung chains of ice that clattered as they moved. Steam curled from their nostrils, ghost-cold.

"They don't forgive the living," he warned.

The herd charged.

The ground shook with the force, snow exploding beneath pounding hooves. The chorus of shattered bells and cracking bone was unbearable.

Krampus moved first, grabbing Elowen's wrist and hurling her behind him just as the lead beast crashed forward. The impact sent a shockwave through the snow. He caught its throat with one clawed hand and wrenched. Bone snapped like a brittle candy cane. The creature toppled in a flurry of snow and ash.

But there were more. Too many. Their antlers lowered, jaws snapped, a storm of death in motion.

Elowen's pulse hammered in her ears. She raised her hands, magic sputtering to life in wild gray sparks. The power crackled against her skin, searing hot. She thrust her palms forward.

Light burst, a jagged ripple through the air. The nearest beast shrieked with a shrill, wooden scream and collapsed, skidding across the ice.

Her breath came in ragged gasps. The smell of scorched sugar and smoke filled her lungs. Her magic left trails of gray across the snow, as though it couldn't decide whether to burn or freeze. There were angry welts on her palms, but she didn't back away.

Krampus glanced back at her, his eyes half shadow, half flame. "You'll hurt yourself—"

Another beast lunged. He spun, slashing upward. Claws raked bone. The reindeer crumpled, collapsing into a heap of brittle bones.

He turned again too fast, his arm sweeping wide.

Pain ripped through her shoulder as his claw raked across her flesh.

Elowen screamed. The world tilted. Fiery blood sprayed across the snow.

Time froze.

Krampus halted mid-motion, horror flooding his face. His hand dripped red. "No…" His voice cracked, raw. "No!"

The hollow herd shrieked as one, their voices a ghastly chorus. They pawed the ground, circling closer, drawn by her blood.

Krampus' roar tore the air apart. Shadows burst from him, black tendrils lashing like a storm. The earth buckled, the beasts scattering in terror before his fury.

Elowen staggered, clutching her shoulder. Her hand came away crimson. The snow swam before her eyes. Her knees gave way.

And then, arms around her. Strong, trembling, careful. Chains hissed as he lifted her. His breath was ragged, chest shaking.

"Elowen," he rasped. "Forgive me. Please—"

She wanted to answer, but the world swam out of focus. The light tilted, and the sky folded in on itself. Only the rhythm of his heartbeat remained, a deep, steady drum against her cheek.

The cold faded. His warmth pressed through layers of shadow. She felt his pulse, his breath catching as if every step cost him pain.

He surged to his feet, bounding across the snow. Snow flung up around them as he ran. His strides devoured the ground as beast, man, and storm fused into one desperate force. The horizon blurred into white and shadow, the air thick with his grief.

Elowen's blood trailed in scarlet ribbons over the snow.

Krampus' roar carried over the wasteland, echoing through the cold like something half prayer, half curse. His shackles glowed white-hot, the iron biting deep, smoke curling from his wrists. With each breath, his throat seared.

He ran as if the world itself might break if he stopped.

Her head lolled against his chest, his heartbeat pounding like a war-drum beneath her cheek.

His face loomed above her, twisted with grief, shadow dripping from his horns, eyes blazing like fire against the endless snow.

And in her dimming mind, Elowen clung to the sound of his heartbeat and thought, *He's not the monster they said he was.*

Then the light went out.

CHAPTER EIGHT

The world returned in jarring fragments: stone underfoot, the snap of tattered pennants in a courtyard gust, the thunder of doors slamming open of their own will.

Krampus burst through the keep's entry with Elowen in his arms. Meltwater streaked his hair, and frost steamed off his cloak. Chains clinked like struck bells; the shackles at his wrists glowed the color of freshly forged iron, veins of light crawling up his arms.

"Balthazar!" His roar rolled up the stairwells and down the galleries, rattling glass and bone alike.

The butler appeared on the landing, as though he had stepped out of the stone. Midnight coat immaculate, carved jaw tight. "My lord." His gaze dipped to Elowen, taking in the blood soaking her torn dress, and didn't so much as flinch. "Infirmary. At once."

Cinn skidded out from a side passage, nearly colliding with Krampus' knee. "Oh, gumdrop buttons." His icing expression folded in on itself. "Elowen! Hey. No dying. Not while I've finally got someone to complain to!"

"Move," Krampus snarled. But the snarl wasn't for Cinn; it was for the shackles biting deeper each time he tightened his grip. The scent of iron and ash curled from his wrists.

They entered a vaulted chamber washed in cold light. Shelves brimmed with glass jars and dried herbs; a brazier burned with a pale frost fire that hissed when Krampus passed. Balthazar cleared a bed before Krampus had finished crossing the threshold.

"Set her here," he said, calm as cut marble.

Krampus paused for a breath, then lowered Elowen as if she were made of spun glass. The moment her weight left his arms, the shackles dimmed to a sullen ember, but his breath still rasped as though fire filled his lungs. He backed away a step, jaw tight, every line of him a man barely holding himself together.

Cinn scrambled onto a stool, hands already rummaging through drawers. "Sugar thread, sugar thread...where is the— ah!" He brandished a spool of a translucent filament that shimmered like frost on spider silk. "Stitches that taste like nothing, hold like everything."

"Fizz," Balthazar snapped, and a tiny ice imp tumbled from the rafters in a tinkling avalanche, chirping. "Numb the wound." He gave Elowen a curt bow, voice grave. "My apologies, miss. This will be rather...bracing."

The imp blew. Frost bloomed across Elowen's shoulder, blanching the skin white. Pain flared, electric. She screamed, then sagged, breath tearing. The ache dulled into something far away.

"Hold on," Cinn murmured, his voice unexpectedly gentle. With surprising precision for a cookie stitched together from chaos, he threaded the sugar filament through a needle of spun glass and sewed. Each stitch melted into the skin and reformed, binding flesh to flesh with a faint crystalline gleam. "You're going to be all right," he chanted like a lullaby half-remembered from a sweeter age.

Elowen tried to focus on his words, but they slipped into nonsense about crumbs and courage and staying whole even when broken.

Krampus stood at the bed's foot, unmoving, eyes fixed on the wound he had caused. The gash was clean, diagonal, merciless.

His claws. His doing. The air thickened with shadow that coiled and uncoiled in time with his breath. His hand twitched toward her, and the shackles hissed. He stopped himself like a man pulling his hand from flame.

Balthazar moved smoothly beside Cinn, decanting thin blue liquid into a cup. "For fever." Another vial, smoky purple, he set aside. "And for the pain. In that order."

"Dinner and dessert. Got it," Cinn muttered.

Elowen's eyes fluttered open. The ceiling swam, then faces: Cinn's icing grin, Balthazar's carved calm, the suggestion of horns and grief in the corner of her vision. Her mind refused to name that shadow. A voice coaxed her to take a sip. The blue tonic tasted of snowmelt and wild mint, cooling the fever behind her eyes.

When her gaze finally met Krampus', he looked away so fast it hurt. As though her eyes were knives, and he deserved each cut.

"Krampus," she rasped, and his name tasted of frost and something softer. Her head pulsed with each word. "It's not—"

"No." His voice broke like cracking ice. "It is my fault." The chains gave a warning hiss. He lowered his voice. "Do not spare me, Elowen. Not for this."

"I was trying to help," she croaked, swallowing. "I moved. The herd—"

"I had it under control," he bit out. His gaze snapped toward her with the violence of a winter squall. "I should never have let you fight."

"Then I'd be dead," she whispered.

He flinched. The shackles burned white. His hands clenched until metal squealed. He turned to Balthazar instead. "Do what you must."

Balthazar glanced up. "We are doing it," he said dryly. "What *you* must do is stop pacing holes into the floor." He lifted an eyebrow. "And not ignite my infirmary."

"I am."

"Try harder."

Cinn tied off the last stitch and patted the bandage with a careful ginger hand. "See? Pretty as a present. If you peel them out before they melt, I'll have your head." He paused and amended brightly, "Metaphorically. Balthazar won't let me keep trophies."

"Quite right," Balthazar retorted.

Elowen exhaled a trembling laugh. "Cinn, you're—"

"Brilliant? Heroic? Full of crumbs?"

"Loud," Balthazar supplied.

He offered her the purple vial. "Drink. Let the edges blur." Then, to Krampus, without looking: "My lord, if you remain, you will haunt her dreams. If you go, she will wonder why. Your choice."

A muscle in Krampus' jaw ticked. He took one step back. Another. The shadow thinned around him. Then he turned, resting one hand on the stone doorframe, head bowed. "If she wakes, send for me."

Balthazar's expression didn't change, but something like approval softened the line of his wooden shoulders. "Of course."

Krampus left, chains shivering. The door shut with a sullen hiss of heat.

Elowen stared at the door for a long moment, the edges of the world fuzzing. "He didn't—" Her tongue felt thick. "He didn't sleep. Before. In the storm. And he ran all the way here."

Cinn tucked the blanket more snugly around her. "He doesn't sleep during many storms," he said.

"Is it true why they burn?" She watched as if the answer might seep through the cracks.

Cinn's eyes slid toward Balthazar, who busied himself with vials as if he hadn't heard. "So you know," Cinn said, his voice carrying none of its usual bounce. "Sometimes kindness costs more than cruelty."

❄ ❄ ❄

Light shifted. Afternoon sank to gold. Torches burned low, casting the room in a gentler glow. Her shoulder ached as if a star had lodged there. Voices murmured outside the door, hushed and frayed.

Balthazar sat at the foot of the bed like a carved sentinel, a book open in his lap.

"How long?" she croaked.

"A couple of days," he said. "Enough to knit the edges but not enough to test them. You will not be sparring today."

"I don't spar."

"Your proclivity for injury suggests otherwise."

Despite the pain, she smiled. "And him?"

"Pacing the west gallery to ruin. Charlie tried tea. Fizz attempted to freeze his feet to the floor. Neither plan succeeded. You've really unsettled him. Whatever you were up to out there."

Her chest tilted dangerously, a fiery ache buried under the throb of her shoulder. The image of him pacing, restless for her, threatened to undo her composure. Secretly, she was pleased he was anxious. Let him stew.

"Can I see him?" Even asking made her stomach flip, but the question left her anyway.

"You can," Balthazar said. His expression softened by degrees. "Should you? That is up to you. He will come if you ask." He rose without a sound. "Ring the bell if you need me." He placed a tiny silver bell on the bedside table. Its sound, she imagined, would be the polite chime that asked disaster to come back later.

After he left, quiet settled in again, so pure she could hear the snow sigh in the courtyard. Pain pulled at her. She stared at the ceiling and tried not to remember the way Krampus' face had broken when he realized what he'd done to her. She tried not to remember the way he had held her, like someone drowning holds a rope. Something precious.

She failed in both.

The door creaked. She turned her head too fast and winced. He filled the doorway, a silhouette of horn and breath, eyes dying coals. The skin above the shackles remained bandaged with her dress linen. Her linen. The sight twisted something in her chest, a thread that pulled tight no matter how she fought it. He looked as if a storm had put on the shape of a man, vast and terrible, and yet, she couldn't look away.

"Elowen." Her name on his tongue was hoarse. He did not move closer. "May I—?"

"Yes," she said, and her pulse jumped traitorously. "Unless you intend to stand there and loom. In which case…no."

One corner of his mouth twitched. He stepped inside and shut the door with care, as if noise might shatter something essential. When he reached her bedside, he stopped a full arm's length away and gripped the bed frame to anchor him.

"I…" He hesitated. "Thank you. For fighting."

She blinked. She had not expected that. "I injured you," she said, meaning the burns he'd taken carrying her, meaning every tremor he'd held back to keep her steady.

"I injured *you*," he corrected, soft and terrible. His voice cracked on the words.

Her chest squeezed too tight. She had to look away; staring at him made the guilt in his eyes feel like her own wound.

"We will not play balances with this," he said.

She searched his face. The monstrous shadow that had poured off him in the snow now skulked in the corners, leashed with will alone. He stood raw and contained, and against her better judgment, she found herself drawn to that restraint.

"Then teach me," she said. "So next time—"

"There will not be a next time." His brows slammed together.

"There's always a next time," she said, not bothering to soften her tone. "Kringle sent the Choir. He won't stop."

The muscles in his forearms flexed under the linen. The shackles warmed, resentful.

"You can't protect me *and* fight them," she pressed, gentler. "Not if you're busy shielding me from my stupidity. I changed the List. That makes me a target. That also makes me…useful."

"Useful," he repeated, voice like ground ice. "You are not a ledger. Some bargaining chip to be played with."

"I'm a List Maker," she said. "And something else I don't fully understand." She lifted her uninjured hand and let a moth-wing flicker of magic shimmer over her palm. It smelled of old paper and winter dusk mixed with fresh peppermint. "I'm already a target," she said softly. "Let me be something else too."

He froze. For a heartbeat, she thought he would refuse out of sheer iron habit. Then he closed his eyes and exhaled slowly, like a man opening a hand that has clutched a knife too long. "I will teach you," he said. The shackles flared; his jaw tightened, and he bore it. "But you will obey."

"Within reason."

He opened his eyes. They were winter bright, infuriated, and, frost help her, relieved. "Within *my* reason."

She considered him, considered his guilt and his temper and the way he'd burned rather than let her freeze. "Deal," she said. "On one condition."

He laughed, a short, disbelieving sound. "You bargain with the monster who injured you."

"I bargain with the man who came when I called," she said, surprising herself with the certainty in it. "Condition: you stop deciding what I can bear."

The laugh died. He looked at her as if she were a landscape he had only ever circled and never entered. His gaze burned, not monstrous, but unbearably human. "Elowen," he murmured, and her name on his tongue did something soft and dangerous inside her. "You do not know what you're asking."

"Then show me."

Silence stretched. The frost fire guttered and caught again. Snow whispered at the window.

At last, he bowed his head in something like surrender. "When you can stand without the room turning," he said, "we begin."

"Tomorrow?" she asked, reckless.

His mouth twitched. "You cannot help yourself."

"No," she said. "And neither can you."

"Balthazar will bring you broth," he stated, as if remembering he owned a voice for practicalities. "Cinn will talk until you wish for mercy. Fizz will try to freeze your toes. Threaten him with a kettle. I will…check the wards. I have work to do."

"Krampus," she said as he turned to go.

He froze, every muscle in his body stiffening.

"I forgive you." The truth of it surprised her with its weight and rightness. Like stepping off a ledge; it was both terrifying and inevitable. "You didn't mean to hurt me."

He did not breathe for three breaths. When he did, it sounded like it scraped his ribs raw. The shackles flared white hot and then dimmed. He did not face her. "Meaning is not the measure," he murmured. "But thank you."

The door clicked behind him. Elowen lay back and stared at the ceiling until tears she hadn't given permission to fall slid warm and traitorous into her hair.

Cinn appeared, tray in hand, timing as impeccable as ever. "Soup?"

Elowen blinked, laughing through the ache. "You're impossible."

"I'm perfect," Cinn said, balancing a tray. "Unlike the seven-and-whatever-foot tall, horned disaster currently pretending he isn't in love with you."

Elowen choked. "Cinn!"

"What? I said *pretending*." He set the tray over her lap and leaned close, voice dropping. "Don't tell him I said the l-word. He'll chew a wall."

"Then why say it?"

Cinn grinned, icing dimples deep. "Because you smiled when I did."

Elowen stared down at the broth, steam curling into her face, and couldn't have stopped the smile if she had tried.

❄ ❄ ❄

Night climbed the keep. In the west gallery, Krampus stood before a black window, snow drifting like ash past the wards. The castle hummed underfoot, a creature old and loyal, listening.

His hands braced the stone sill. The shackles lay quiet, smoldering faintly. The wound they had punished was gone for the hour; the new one, a hope he shouldn't keep, flickered. It was the memory of her eyes when she forgave him.

"I'll help you," he whispered.

Behind him, footsteps clicked with measured grace. "My lord," he said. "The wards need reinforcing only along the east parapet. I have set the lesser gargoyles to watch."

"And her?"

"Sleeping. Cinn threatened to perform an opera if she didn't." A pause. "You will break your teeth if you grind them any harder."

Krampus' fingers curled against the sill. "I hurt her."

"Yes."

"I will again if I keep her close." His voice came out low, cracked, too raw. He still felt the phantom of her skin under his claws, the shock in her breath, the way her blood steamed against the snow.

"Possibly." Balthazar's tone didn't soften. "You will certainly doom her if you keep her ignorant."

The words lodged like hooks. Krampus closed his eyes. When she looked at him tonight, she had wanted him near. Wanted his voice, his presence. That should have repelled her. Instead, she had smiled at him. Instead, she had said, *forgive you.*

His chest ached. Attraction was too small a word for what rattled his bones when she leaned toward him instead of away. He had long ago stripped himself of softer hungers. But now, he wanted to sit at her bedside without her flinching, hear her speak his name without fear, to believe, even for a breath, that he might be something more than the beast who scarred her. To *want* at all scared him.

And there was her hand, warm against his ruined forearm.

Teach me, she'd said. *Show me.*

He did not deserve the request. He would answer it anyway.

"Tomorrow," he said.

"Tomorrow," Balthazar agreed. "And my lord?" The butler's voice, for once, tilted toward something like fondness. "Try sleeping."

Krampus huffed a laugh that wasn't one. "In storms?"

"There are always storms. In hope," Balthazar said, and withdrew.

Krampus watched the snow a moment longer, then bowed his head, only a fraction, only to the dark, and let himself imagine, for the space of a single breath, a winter where the shackles did not burn when he cared. A winter where her smile was meant for him.

Then he straightened, and the castle's bells, stitched into the hem of his fate, rang as he turned toward morning. The sound trembled against his chains.

A promise, or a warning. He couldn't tell which.

But it was a morning closer to the end of the year.

CHAPTER NINE

The morning broke gray, the light thin through frost-coated glass. Elowen pulled her cloak close as she entered the hall, nerves rattling harder than the storm outside.

Krampus waited in the torchlight, massive frame carved in shadow. His dark sleeves were rolled, the shackles raw and still wrapped in the linen she'd torn from her dress. Her gaze snagged there.

He noticed. *Of course he saw.*

"You shouldn't stare at wounds," he rumbled. "They stare back."

"I wasn't staring."

"Liar."

Heat crept up her neck. She gestured to the cleared floor. "So this is where I'm supposed to learn?"

"You insisted," he said, striding forward. "I warned it would not be gentle."

"I can handle it."

"Prove it." Chains clinked as he stopped before her, so close she could feel the brush of his shadow. "Show me your magic."

She wiggled her fingers and extended her palm. A flicker lit like a coal in snow. It sputtered, unstable, then died with a faint hiss.

"That is not control," Krampus said flatly. "That is an

accident."

Her chin lifted. "It's worked enough for my job."

"And yet you bleed," he snapped. "You nearly froze. You nearly died. Call that working?"

Her jaw locked. His words cut too close.

He sighed, raking a hand through his dark mane. The shackles flared, punishing the flicker of concern he let slip. He ignored them. "Magic is not a trick. It's not a shortcut. If you can't master yourself, you can't master it."

"I never asked for it," she muttered.

"No one does," he said. "But it asks for you."

The hall fell quiet with only the pop of torch flames filling the air.

"Again."

She tried. The spark flickered, faltered. Her temper spiked, then gray flared like lightning, a crack splitting the stone floor. She stumbled back.

Krampus caught her shoulder, his grip steady despite the shackles biting. "Better," he murmured.

Snow and smoke clung to him, sharp as firewood, filling her senses. His touch was steady, hot as iron, and lingered longer than needed. She shifted beneath it, heart skittering. His ears reddened. At last his hand fell, leaving her skin colder for the loss.

"Your power responds to anger," he said, too brusque. "Learn to summon without it."

"And how?"

He stepped close, voice low. "Like this."

He took her wrist, guiding her palm outward. His chest brushed her shoulder, his growl a vibration at her back. The sound crawled up her spine. She stiffened at the nearness, but didn't pull away.

"Breathe with it. Not against it."

"I am breathing," she mumbled.

"Not like that," he said. "Draw in. Hold. Release."

She obeyed. Gray shimmered, steadier now, like frost tracing glass. Her jaw dropped in astonishment. It held.

"Good," he said, almost reverently. His shackle seared her sleeve. "Do not fear it. Trust it."

Her lips parted to answer, but the air changed.

The door banged open.

Cinn skidded in, arms carrying a bucket of sugar paste. His icing mouth made an O. "Am I interrupting something?"

Elowen jerked back, magic flaring and burning her palm. "It's not—!"

"Get. Out." Krampus' growl shook the floor.

Cinn set the bucket down with exaggerated care. "Sure, sure. I'll leave the two of you to it." He winked, cackled, and then vanished.

Silence.

Elowen looked at her hands. Krampus dragged a hand over his face, muttering in another tongue, his ears red.

"Again?" she asked.

He studied her, something soft flickering in his eyes. "Again."

Elowen shook her fingers. She tried once more. The shimmer lingered, shaky but alive. Krampus circled, his eyes sharp, burning.

"Better. Why do you stumble like a newborn?"

"Because no one ever taught me," she snapped, her cheeks hot. "Kringle forbade it. Magic was for work. I was a registered List Maker. Nothing else."

The gray smudged like ash in her palm as she spoke, and she let it die with a frustrated sigh. "Naughty. Nice. That was it."

Krampus froze.

Her shrug was casual, but it didn't mask the tightness in her chest. "Not much use for magic in Central otherwise. Do your job, smile, and don't…question."

A growl rumbled deep. "You mean he is controlling it."

"I never thought of it that way."

"You should," he said, stepping closer, storm light in his gaze. "To bind what is born in you and shrink it to a tool, that is theft."

She stared up at him, caught between awe and unease at the

force of his words. "It's the way things are," she grumbled.

His gaze bore into hers as if he could see every moment she'd ever bent her will to Kringle's system. Cubicle C-144. He held out his hand, not commanding, but offering.

Her hand fit perfectly within his, giving a sense of belonging. His palm felt rough, scarred. She swallowed. And warm.

"It's a pity," he murmured. "You are made for more than this."

Her heart stuttered. She traced one scar with her fingertip.

He paused, as if her touch pinned him in place more effectively than the shackles on his wrists. The iron hissed, searing, as if it hated her touch. Pain flickered across his face, but he didn't pull away.

She looked up. His expression was caught between a storm and surrender.

Elowen's breath came shallow as she felt the heat between them. Words stuck in her throat, and her brain raced to force them out. Every nerve screamed that he might close the distance, that if she leaned forward an inch, just an inch...

He closed his fingers gently over hers, just for a heartbeat, before retreating, shadows clinging to his shoulders. His jaw locked, but his eyes betrayed a flicker of something raw, something unsaid.

"That is enough for today," he said, clipped but unsteady.

She nodded, the ghost of his warmth lingering on her skin, her lips tingling with a kiss that hadn't happened.

At the door, Cinn peeked back in, whispering. "Progress."

Krampus snarled. Elowen groaned, cheeks burning with something more than embarrassment.

Krampus stayed behind, staring at the faint scorch her touch had left on his wrist. The shackles pulsed, digging deeper, as though punishing him for a crime he hadn't yet dared commit. With a growl, he tore Elowen's bandages and flung them aside, vanishing into shadow before the pain betrayed him further.

❋ ❋ ❋

The hall emptied of her, but her scent lingered on him, frost and parchment, faint peppermint. It clung like a second skin.

Krampus braced both hands against the stone wall until his claws bit mortar. His breath came ragged, too human. Too close.

He had almost kissed her. In a heartbeat, her eyes had lifted, her lips parted, and the space between them had narrowed to nothing. If she had leaned forward, if he had bent down...

The shackles hissed now, angry red searing. They knew. They punished. His arms trembled, not from weakness but from the knowledge of how much he had wanted it.

Fool, he snarled at himself, though the sound scraped hollow. Foolish to imagine warmth where only fire burned. Foolish to let a touch unravel centuries of iron.

He turned on his heel and strode into the gallery. The castle sensed his unrest; torches guttered, shadows quivered along the walls. Balthazar emerged from a side passage, head tilted in silent question.

"If she asks," Krampus said, voice gravel and restraint, "tell her I am occupied with preparations for the end of the year."

The butler's eyes flicked, too perceptive by half. "And you are not?"

"I said, tell her." Krampus bared his teeth.

Balthazar bowed with courtly calm. "As you wish."

Krampus left before the silence could turn into counsel. He did not go to the lists or his tools, not at first. Instead, he stalked down the spiral into the lowest vaults, where frost coated the walls in jagged runes of his own making. He laid a hand on the stone and fed the wards with his magic until the chains at his wrists smoked.

Preparations? Yes, that much was true. But not the kind Elowen could be allowed to see. He reinforced every barrier, carved new sigils into the ice itself, tested the strength of the iron bells that would toll when the year turned. The work steadied him, but it did not silence the echo of her laugh, the softness in her defiance.

When he paused, breath steaming, the castle hummed low in its bones. The wards flared obediently, but his thoughts were far from duty.

He had almost kissed her. He wanted to again. The desire gnawed sharper than hunger, sharper than the storm clawing at the mountains outside.

And so he buried himself in preparations, rituals, fortifications, anything that kept him away from her touch and her safe within the castle walls. Because if he gave in, even once, the shackles would burn him hollow. And worse...he feared he might not care.

CHAPTER TEN

Elowen padded down the silent corridor, cloak wrapped tight against the lingering chill that seeped from stone and frost alike. By now she would have heard the goats bleating from the stables with Charlie caring for them, or Cinn clattering about humming off-key. But today, the only sound was her own slippers brushing across cold flagstones.

She hadn't seen Krampus since the previous day's lesson. The moment his hand had closed around hers, warm despite the burns, steadying despite the shadows, still threaded in her head like sugar. He had vanished after, leaving her with questions gnawing at her ribs.

She hadn't dared to go searching. But part of her had hoped he would find her.

Instead, she found Balthazar.

The butler's gaunt figure materialized from nowhere, tall and starched in his severe coat, his painted eyes set in permanent disapproval.

"You will not find him," Balthazar said, his voice as flat and final as a slammed book.

Elowen startled. "What?"

"The lord," the butler clarified, as though it were obvious. "He is making preparations for the end of the year."

"Oh." She tried to make the word sound casual, but the little sting bled through. "Of course."

Balthazar studied her, gaze sharp as a quill. "You believe he avoids you."

"I didn't say that."

"You did not need to."

"So what am I supposed to do then? Sit around while he... prepares?"

"The kennels nearly froze you. The scullery nearly scalded you. And the less said about the stables, the better." His voice carried the patient contempt of someone delivering bad news for the hundredth time. "You are ill-suited for chores in your state. The archive will at least keep you occupied without endangering the livestock."

Her cheeks burned hotter. "I wasn't that bad."

"The goats disagree."

"That's hardly fair."

"Fair?" His brows arched with dry incredulity. "My dear, nothing here is fair. But the archive will do you no harm. Unless you choose otherwise."

With that, he gestured toward the northern wing and melted into the shadows.

Elowen stood fuming. She didn't want to be dismissed into a dusty room like a child shooed off to her studies. She wanted to matter. She wanted answers. And if Krampus wouldn't give her any, then she would find them herself.

❅ ❅ ❅

The northern wing stretched long and hushed, windows glazed with frost. She sneezed. Dust lay thick across the floor where even Balthazar's footprints had faded. The air smelled faintly of cedar and candle wax, long extinguished.

Elowen pushed open a warped door. Hinges shrieked, then gave way to a chamber of shadows.

An art gallery.

Paintings crowded the walls, dim beneath layers of dust. She edged closer, breath fogging the air. Figures emerged: elves laughing under auroras, children racing across snowfields, toys conjured midair in spirals of light. The brushstrokes shimmered, catching the glow of the dim light.

Her chest ached. Elves were unbound, wild magic spilling into flame, frost, and song. But here it was memory made permanent, colors fighting to outlast ruin.

She traced the mural with her fingertip. Claw marks had torn through faces, jagged scars gouging the paint. Joy vandalized into warning.

At the end of the gallery, a portrait towered above her: a tall woman crowned in stars, gaze tender, luminous. The same mother she had seen before. Krampus' mother. Frost veined the canvas, threatening to erase her.

Elowen's throat tightened. The castle had once been alive with gardens and light. With her. With all of them.

A cracked mirror beside the painting shimmered. For a heartbeat, it reflected not Elowen's face but the woman's, smiling as though she had been waiting for her. Elowen reached out, only for ice to web across the surface, sealing the vision away.

Her heart ached with grief that wasn't entirely her own. What else was stolen, not only from Krampus, but from everyone sealed to this place? And the elves, Kringle had bound them all.

The corridors shifted underfoot, unfamiliar and treacherous. Twice she thought she heard steps echoing behind her, but only shadows greeted her. At last, the fear of being caught or swallowed by the castle pushed her toward the archive, where the air at least smelled of ink and frost, not dust and regret.

❄ ❄ ❄

Far away in Kringle Central, the List Registry & Tally department thrummed with enforced cheer.

Row upon row of glassy orbs flickered in cubicles, glowing

red or green as elves pressed their palms against them. Every hum of magic lit another name, another judgment.

Carols piped from unseen speakers, every note in perfect pitch, every beat relentless. Clerks' smiles twitched wider to match the rhythm.

From his raised platform, Klaussen puffed out his chest. His green vest was pressed crisp, his collar bristling with peppermint starch, suspenders taut. His candy cane pointer rapped the railing like a conductor's baton. Eyes swept the rows for anyone who slipped off-beat.

"Faster," he trilled, voice slicing through the department. "Quotas don't fill themselves."

Orbs flared and dimmed, clerks shifting in nervous synchrony.

At her station, Larkspur flicked her wrist. Her orb obediently flipped from red to green, and she masked her smirk behind a brittle grin.

Across the row, a nervous junior clerk coaxed his own orb with sparks, but it was too flashy, too desperate. His coffee steamed beside him, warmed by the same magic.

Larkspur hissed. With a snap of her fingers, frost laced over his orb; with another snap, it froze his drink solid. "No unregistered magic use," she muttered. "You want your own name marked naughty?"

The poor elf paled and bowed his head, mouthing apologies. His orb flickered meekly back to green.

"Good girl," Klaussen drawled from above, eyes glinting like glass beads. "Correcting inefficiency keeps us all in His Jolliness' good graces."

The elves chorused a hollow "Yes, sir," their voices merging with the carol in eerie perfection.

Larkspur glanced up at the portrait of Kringle looming over the balcony, his painted crown shimmering with light. For a heartbeat her expression faltered, calculating, hungry, before she bent back to her work with renewed fervor.

Klaussen preened, smoothing his vest. He didn't dirty his hands with grunt work anymore. Better to leave that to mere clerks. He oversaw, he corrected, and he *managed*. And if Kringle looked this way, he intended to be the one seen directing the song.

Red. Green. Red. Green. Names flickered and vanished, added to the great scroll of the Master List. The carol swelled.

It looked like joy.

It sounded like cheer.

But every elf felt the weight of the rhythm grinding them down, one note at a time.

CHAPTER ELEVEN

The corridor wound deeper than Elowen expected, a spine of stone lined with doors that looked too ancient to open. Frost crusted the walls in delicate veins, catching the torchlight in a pale shimmer.

Her resolve that day was simple: find Krampus, demand another lesson, and prove she could master her magic. She kept telling herself that with each step.

But the silence here pressed close, haunted, until her footsteps echoed like trespass. Her pulse climbed higher with every turn.

She should have turned back.

Instead, her curiosity tugged her toward a door set with iron filigree. The carvings curled sharp, like antlers and brambles, and when her fingers brushed the metal, it groaned open as though expecting her.

The room stretched long and dim, lit by lanterns high on iron brackets. Racks lined the walls, each bristling with rods of wood and bone.

Switches. Dozens of them.

Each carved differently, each humming faintly with its own vibration. Some glowed with warm amber light, others pulsed in shadows, and others sparked faintly like frozen stars.

Elowen stepped closer, drawn as though by invisible threads. Magic resonated against her fingertips, prickling across her skin.

When she reached out, sparks leapt between her hand and the nearest switch, tiny motes that stung like frostbite and soothed like fire all at once. She shivered.

"They're older than the List," a low voice said from the shadows.

She jumped, heart jolting, hand darting back.

Krampus leaned against one rack, half lost in the gloom. Torchlight outlined his towering form, eyes already on her as if he'd been waiting.

"I—" she stammered, clutching her cloak. "I didn't know anyone was—"

"This is not a place for you," he interrupted, stepping forward. His voice was measured, heavy. A warning, not a reprimand.

Elowen lifted her chin. "Then why does it feel like they're calling to me?" She gestured toward the racks. "They...they hum. Like they know I'm here."

His eyes narrowed. Shadow shifted with his breath. At last he said, "Because they know need when it stands before them. Each shows the soul what it must face. Fear. Weakness. Regret."

"So you don't..." She faltered, searching his face. "You don't beat children with them?"

His jaw clenched. "No." The word struck like an axe.

"They are mirrors," he added, softer. "Each person sees what they must. Some tremble at shadows. Some endure pain of their own making. Others...walk free after seeing themselves clearly."

Elowen's hand drifted toward another switch, carved with curling runes that glowed blue. "They don't feel cruel."

"Don't." The word cracked like thunder. But she ignored him.

Her fingers closed around the smooth wood. Energy surged into her palm, thrumming up her arm in a rush that stole her breath. Her magic stirred like tinder taking flame. It was heady, dangerous, alive.

And then another hand closed around hers.

His. Warm, scarred, large. Slowly, deliberately, Krampus drew the switch from her grip. The wood sang between them, its hum changing pitch, sliding down her arm like a whisper.

He dragged the tip down to her wrist, against her sleeve, then lower. The trail it left on her skin seared, intimate as breath on her neck.

Her knees weakened. A shiver ran down the length of her body. She exhaled in a rush.

"It's dangerous," he murmured, voice low as thunderclouds. "You do not understand what you hold."

Her body betrayed her, tensing beneath the lingering trail of magic.

"Don't worry," he said. "I won't use it on you."

The thought struck like lightning, unbidden and impossible to shake. Suddenly, that was all she could think of: what it might feel like if he did.

Her face burned. His eyes darkened, noticing. Of course he noticed.

Krampus bent, his height folding toward her until his breath stirred the hair at her temple. "You wouldn't like it," he said, voice brushing low at her ear.

Her heart stuttered. "I wouldn't?"

The storm in his gaze burned hotter, hungry and restrained in the same breath.

Her hand rose, trembling, pressing lightly to his chest. She meant only to hold distance, to keep space. But her fingers lingered, traitorous, drawn to the steady thrum of his heart beneath scarred muscle. Some treacherous and yearning part of her hoped he would close the space between them.

The switch clattered from his grip onto the stone floor.

Krampus seized her hand, and Elowen looked down at them, his over hers, then up into his eyes. His heartbeat thudded strongly against her skin. His shackles smoldered, branding the air between them.

Her lips parted. No words came.

He bent closer, his mouth grazing her ear. "No," he rasped. "You wouldn't like the nightmares."

She shivered. Not from fear.

Then he moved, pinning her against the table at the room's center. His body caged hers, heat rolling from him in waves that overpowered the chill. His eyes dipped to her lips, then darted away, fighting himself.

Elowen's breath faltered. She closed the distance, brushing her mouth against his.

The kiss was fleeting. A spark, nothing more. But it scorched her down to the bone.

Krampus inhaled sharply, then answered, crushing the spark into flame. His shackles rattled violently, searing white-hot as he kissed her harder, desperate.

Elowen clutched his shirt, rising onto her toes. The table pressed cold against her back. The fire of his mouth seared her front. His hands gripped the wood on either side of her hips, the only barrier left between touch and surrender.

The kiss deepened, ragged and consuming, before he tore himself back with a groan. Flames crawled the shackles, licking red and furious across his arms.

Elowen's eyes widened. "You're—"

He staggered, gritted his teeth. She caught his wrist before he could retreat, sparks flaring at her fingertips. The iron writhed under her touch, runes glowing brighter.

"Let me—" she begged. "Let me take it off. I can help—"

"No!" His roar split the air, pain bending his frame.

Her gray magic leapt, sketching runes she didn't understand across the cuffs. For a heartbeat, they shifted and twisted.

Krampus ripped free with a gasp, stumbling across the room. His shirt clung damp to his chest, scorched raw where the shackles burned. His back struck the rack behind him, and switches rattled against the stone.

"I don't know," he panted, voice hoarse. "I don't know what will happen if you try. Do not touch them again."

Elowen's hand trembled where his arm had been, her magic simmering. Her lips still tingled. Her heart still raced.

Across the room, Krampus bowed his head, chest heaving, shoulders trembling with the effort of smothering fire.

She looked at him and saw not the monster of story, nor the brooding figure on the throne, but a man chained in agony, denied every tenderness.

And it broke something in her chest.

The glow of the shackles was unbearable to watch. Each hiss and flare felt like they seared her own skin. A sob wrenched out of her, raw.

"Follow me," she said, her voice steady though her hands shook.

Krampus lifted his head, eyes glazed with pain. "Elowen—"

"Don't argue." She crossed the room, skirts whispering. She turned, steady, hand extended. "Please. Let me help you."

❄ ❄ ❄

Her hand was outstretched, steady despite its tremor. He hated that steadiness. Hated how it drew him, how it pierced through every warning he had sharpened into armor.

The kiss still scorched his mouth. His breath still bore her name. His shackles still smoked with the truth he had fought to bury: he wanted her.

Not the way he wanted warmth by a fire, or quiet after war. No, this want was rawer, darker, like hunger sharpened to ache. It gnawed through his chest, made his hands twitch with the memory of her tracing his scars as if they were not curses, but maps.

And worse, he had seen her eyes when he dragged the switch down her sleeve. He had seen her shiver. He had *known* what she imagined, and it had pleased him. That memory alone made his pulse thunder now.

Fool. She did not know what she had kissed. She did not know what she begged to follow.

The shackles hissed, branding the thought. *Good,* he told himself. Remember what you are. The monster that rends. The shadow that punishes.

But her face...by the frost, her face when she looked at him. Not with fear, not even pity. With defiance and something softer, something he could not name without breaking.

He groaned, but he followed her. Shadows spilled from him like blood as he matched her pace, the castle shuddering around him, feeling the pain. The corridors stretched endlessly, but all he could sense was her. Her scent of peppermint and parchment, the gray tinge of her magic still clinging to his skin like smoke. Every breath he drew was threaded with her. Every step beside her felt like a trespass.

His body sang with her nearness, the taste of her lips, the heat of her palm pressed to his chest. He wanted to seize her again, crush the distance, devour the sound of her gasp when she yielded. His mouth ached with the memory.

But his chains flared hotter with every thought, branding his arms until his vision blurred. Punishment for daring to want. Punishment for daring to kiss what should be beyond his reach.

He ground his teeth, forcing his pace even, his voice silent. She would not see how close he was to breaking. She would not know that every stride beside her was war.

Her shoulders were set like a banner before him, slim but unshaken. She thought she was leading him. She thought she was saving him.

And perhaps she was.

But in the hollow of his chest, beneath the ache and the fire, a truth struck him, harder than the shackles:

If she asked again, if she reached again, he would not have the strength to stop.

❊ ❊ ❊

Through winding passages they ran, the torches guttering as though afraid of what followed in his wake. She led him to a side door that groaned open into the enclosed atrium.

The ceiling arched high above, but its glass panes were

shattered and rimmed with frost, letting the storm outside bleed straight through. Snow didn't fall so much as surge, drawn in by unseen currents, spiraling down in pale curtains, settling in the corners of stone benches and brittle leaves of frozen ivy. Every flake that hissed into steam against his shackles was replaced by a fresh drift, as though the storm itself conspired to keep him alive.

"Here," Elowen urged. She tugged him down, pressing his arms into the snow.

The hiss was immediate. The snow sizzled and melted away in dark rivulets, steam rising around them. Krampus' jaw slackened as a shudder tore through him. His eyes fluttered closed, breath spilling ragged from his lips.

Relief.

Elowen stayed close, watching the tension leave his frame as he knelt, bent over the snow, chains buried in white frost. The hiss and crackle filled the silence, punctuated by the thunder of his breathing. Steam curled upward, wrapping them in a ghostly shroud. He looked like he was bowing before her, monster, warden, shadow, and something inside her thrilled at the sight.

"This is better, isn't it?" she asked.

His eyes opened, fixing on her. Hunger glowed in them, not only for her touch, but for something deeper, raw, something he had denied himself too long.

He shifted as though to rise, but she pressed firmly on his shoulders, shoving him back down. "No. Wait."

The sound that rumbled from his chest was half growl, half laugh. "My mighty little elf has a monster on his knees. What will you do with him?"

Her pulse skipped, and warmth spread through her core. Steam ghosted across her skin, hot and damp. She shouldn't have liked the power, but she did; she liked the way he stayed, bound by her command. She brushed her fingers through his hair, tentative at first, then firmer, tracing the ridges between his horns. He shivered and leaned into her touch as if it were a balm.

"Maybe I'll keep you here," she teased.

His lips grazed her chest through her dress, a fleeting kiss that seared her. "You have me at a disadvantage."

Heat rushed to her cheeks. He *was* at a disadvantage, kneeling, trembling, undone. But his restraint, how tightly he held himself back, was as intoxicating as his nearness. She wanted to see his control shatter, and she wanted to be the one to break it.

Her hand tightened in his hair. "Good."

She bent, pressing her lips to his forehead, lingering. Steam drifted between them, dampening his dark hair, curling around her mouth.

He lifted his head, eyes burning, beginning to rise again. She shoved him back down, firmer this time. The motion was instinct, but it made her breath catch, because he let her.

He groaned, half from pain, half from something far more dangerous. The shackles flared, snow sizzling louder beneath him. Steam thickened, the atrium turning into a cauldron of heat and shadow.

"Elowen—" His voice cracked.

She leaned down, hands tangled in his dark hair, and kissed him.

It was no fleeting spark this time. It was fire, smoke, and snow all at once. His lips consumed hers desperately, as though he could devour the very breath from her lungs. Her body pressed against him, her weight anchoring him in the snow even as he writhed beneath the twin pulls of agony and need.

The shackles smoldered, runes flaring white hot. Steam boiled up around them, curling like spirits, wrapping them in haze. The frost lights guttered as though they, too, held their breath.

"Stay," she whispered against his mouth.

His groan was guttural, torn from the pit of him. He braced on all fours, horns framing her like a crown, breath hot against her skin. Survival turned into worship; her monster brought low before her.

She liked it, and so did he.

Still she kissed him, steam rising, until the atrium was a sealed world of fire and frost.

When they finally broke apart, both gasping, the room was drenched in haze. Water dripped from the stone walls, melted snow pooling at their knees. Krampus' head bowed, his massive frame trembling.

Elowen stood before him, chest heaving. The snow hissed and steamed beneath his shackles, and still she pressed him down, teasing him with every heartbeat she drew out of him.

For once, he was not a monster, no warden of shadows. Only a man, shackled, undone, brought low by the hands of a woman who refused to let him burn alone.

Krampus lifted his head, steam curling through his horns, his breath wild. His eyes locked onto hers, hungry, desperate, as if she were the only solid thing in a world made of shadow. But his body obeyed. For now.

"You mock me," he rumbled at last, lips curving though his chest heaved.

"Do I?" Her fingers combed slowly through his damp hair, deliberate, cruel. "Because it seems to me you enjoy being here. On your knees in front of me."

The hungry growl that vibrated from him shook her bones and sent heat through her. His hands clenched in the snow, hissing louder with every tremor. "Careful, little elf. You don't know what power you're toying with."

She leaned close, lips grazing his ear. "I thought you were supposed to teach me."

His groan broke against her skin, raw and ragged. The shackles flared brighter, molten runes spilling smoke and steam into the air. His head fell forward, forehead pressing against her stomach. His voice came rough, almost reverent: "Say the word, and I will stay here. I will bow."

Her breath caught. He meant it. Every line of him trembled with the effort to resist. Her hand slid across the curve of his horn, down the strong line of his neck, until her palm rested at his nape. She tilted his face up to hers. "Then stay."

His chest heaved, his jaw clenched, his eyes storm-bright.

"You're cruel, Elowen."

"And you like it."

That broke him.

With a snarl that was half plea, half surrender, Krampus surged upward. His mouth crashed against hers, searing, desperate, every ounce of restraint shattering. His arm wrenched free from the snow with a hiss, shackles blazing white-hot, light flaring across the atrium. He pinned her back against the snow, his massive frame caging her in, horns haloed in steam.

Elowen's gasp turned into a moan as his lips claimed hers again, rough and unrelenting. The cold bit through her dress, the snow seared her skin, but none of it mattered. There was only his heat, the weight, the storm that poured out of him and into her.

Her hands clawed at his shoulders, his hair, anywhere she could anchor herself as the kiss deepened, broke, deepened again. His breath was ragged, his growls spilling into her mouth, swallowed by her own frantic gasps. The shackles pulsed against her sides as his hands slid up her bare thighs, molten brands that threatened to scorch, but she clung to him anyway, refusing to let him go.

"Elowen," he panted against her lips, her name ripped from him like a prayer and a curse all at once. His forehead pressed to hers, their breaths mingling, steam curling around them in suffocating waves. "No more words."

Her answer was another kiss. Reckless, fierce, sealing his vow with her own fire.

The atrium dissolved into haze. The frost lights blinked and guttered, smothered beneath the fog. Snow hissed and boiled away beneath them until water pooled, running dark across the floor. The skeletal tree above chimed and shuddered, shards of ice raining down in delicate music no-one heard.

His shackles blazed once more, a white light so fierce it turned the steam to fire. Chains rattled like a warning bell, but he ignored them, bending lower, his breath breaking against her throat. She held her ground, her fingers threading into his hair, pulling him closer as she arched beneath him.

"You're burning," she gasped, awe and hunger tangled in her voice.

"So are you," he muttered, the words scraping raw from his chest before his mouth found hers again.

Her laugh, breathless and daring, shivered against his lips. His answering groan was broken, guttural, and wholly undone. He slammed a hand into the snow beside her head, steam erupting upward in a violent hiss. She tugged him down harder until the last barrier between restraint and hunger collapsed.

Krampus pressed closer, closer, until there was no space left, no restraint left, only the collision of fire and snow. Each thunder of his body was a testament to how long he had starved himself of this, of her. And she gave back everything, meeting his storm with her own. His growl tore through her as his body fused with hers, raw need claiming what both had already surrendered.

The shackles blazed, searing white, chains rattling like a dirge and a hymn all at once. Steam drowned the frost lights, shadows swallowed the walls, and the world narrowed to the rhythm of their bodies, the wild thunder of two hearts refusing to yield.

"Elowen," he gasped, her name ragged on his lips, a vow and surrender in one.

Her reply was not words, but a cry swallowed into his kiss as the storm broke open inside them, shadow and frost collapsing into one.

When the haze finally stilled, the atrium lay drowned in melted snow and silence, but within it, they burned on.

CHAPTER TWELVE

Silent snow drifted into the atrium, as if the heavens themselves were watching. The storm had pressed inward, bleeding through the fractured ceiling. Flurries spiraled in silver currents, replenishing the snow faster than the hiss of Krampus' shackles could burn them away.

Strange flora clung stubbornly to the stone. Frost-blossoms unfurled with every gust of wind, their petals glimmering like shards of glass. A vine of pale ivy crept along the walls, twitching as if listening. And at the center, the skeletal tree's icy, crystal-tipped branches rang soft, bell-like notes with each strike of snow.

Elowen stirred, her fingers brushing damp curls from Krampus' brow. He lay sprawled across her lap, arms heavy around her waist, his shackled wrists buried deep in the snow. His breath fanned across her stomach, uneven, as if he had fought even in sleep. For once, the great monster looked almost…peaceful.

She feared it wouldn't last.

Her magic prickled, sparks darting across her skin. She had crossed a line, hadn't she? Not by kissing him, but by *choosing* him. Choosing the man beneath the monster when the world demanded she see only his chains. That choice thrummed through her now, intoxicating, terrifying.

Was she still Elowen? Or had she become something else in his arms?

She stroked his hair.

Krampus' eyes snapped open, startled, wild. He surged halfway upright, chest heaving, until he saw her. "What happened?" His voice was rough, jagged.

"You fell asleep," she said. Her hand lingered against his temple until he caught her wrist gently, questioning.

He followed her arm down to her singed gown. The blackened fabric, the thinness against the snow. His jaw tightened. "You're cold."

She shook her head, though her body shivered. "It's alright."

Silence stretched, broken only by the faint crackle of his shackles. Then bells rang above them, faint and chiming, notes carried on the dawn air.

Morning. Another day closer to the end.

Krampus tipped his head back, eyes fixed on the paling sky. "There are only a few days until the end of the year."

Elowen followed his gaze, her chest heavy. The year's end meant reckoning. Kringle would not rest. He saw her power, saw her rebellion. He would come for her. And worse, she shivered; he would come for *him*.

Her heart ached with an impossible question: Could she protect Krampus? Or would staying only doom them both?

"You don't have to go," she whispered, though the words felt like a child's wish.

Sadness flickered across his features, unguarded. His eyes lowered to hers. "I cannot change what I am chained to be. The monster. The punishment. It is written on my shackles."

She reached up, fingertips brushing his jaw. "There should be more gray," she said. She wanted to scream that there should be more choices, more paths than this endless cycle of cruelty.

He gave a hollow laugh, bitter as iron. "Perhaps you've gone too far already, little elf."

Her throat tightened. "Kringle will not stop. He knows what I've done. He'll come for me again."

That cracked something in him. His arms crushed her against him, as if sheer force could shield her. A low groan tore out of him. "I won't let him take you."

Her gaze slid past him, out to the horizon where dawn fractured the snow into shards of pale fire. The light felt merciless, like judgment. She thought of the uniform hiding in her wardrobe, the weight of the machine she had once belonged to. She thought of their kiss, of his hands gripping the snow like chains to keep them from breaking her in two.

Her body longed to stay. Her heart told her she had to go. *I have to try. I have to end this, and it has to start with me.*

She looked down at her own hands. Her fingers flexed, sparks dancing.

Krampus lifted his head. Sharp eyes searched her face as if trying to drag her thoughts from her skull.

She touched his jaw and forced a small smile. "I'm cold, after all. Would you mind if I went back inside?"

Suspicion darkened his eyes, but at last he grunted, "Go."

Elowen rose, skirts damp, her legs trembling. She slipped back into the castle's shadow, the heavy door groaning shut behind her.

Krampus stayed where he was, kneeling in the snow, watching. Frost lights haloed him in a glow that turned him from a monster into a martyr. Smoke curled off his shackles as if the world itself punished him for letting her go.

❄ ❄ ❄

Her chamber was empty; her bed lay untouched. Elowen stood before her wardrobe, her hands quaking against the door. The frost light outside her window spilled long, thin shadows across the floor, tracing bars like a cage.

With a deep breath, she pulled the wardrobe open. The smell of cedar and old wool rose, but her gaze locked on the neatly folded fabric within: the uniform of Kringle Central.

Green. Red. Gold trim gleamed faintly in the dim light.

Her stomach turned. Putting it on again was cutting away everything she had found. Yet she had made her choice.

Elowen tugged the ruined gown from her shoulders. Her breath snagged as the cold air kissed her bare skin, her scars, the faint gray sparks that sometimes crackled when she was most unsettled. She pulled the uniform over her head; it was stiff, scratchy, too bright, too false. Fingers fumbled as if the fabric itself resisted her. Still, she forced it on.

She plaited her hair into two tight braids, the way she once wore it every day as a neat worker in Kringle's machine. Each twist felt like binding herself tighter, erasing the woman who had touched Krampus' brow in the snow. Her slippers, battered, green dye flaking at the seams, slid back onto her feet.

Then she lifted her eyes to the mirror.

The elf staring back at her wasn't Elowen anymore. She was Cubicle C-144: obedient, smiling, hollow. The mask Kringle had molded her into. The mask she would now choose to wear.

Elowen stared until her vision blurred, until the braids and bright colors felt like a stranger's costume. Beneath it, her magic stirred, sparks twitching at the corners of the glass, as if whispering: this is not you.

Her throat tightened. *This is what I must be to win.*

For a moment, she imagined Krampus' hands on her waist, his head bowed against her lap, the raw edge in his voice when he swore not to let Kringle take her. She saw the monster soften, just for her. And now she was leaving him.

She pressed her lips together, steeling her heart. *I have to save him; save us all.*

Elowen slipped from her room into the darkened corridor, her breath shallow as she hurried through the sleeping halls. Her slippers barely rustled against the stone.

The stables loomed large in the courtyard, the air within thick with hay and the musk of beasts. She crept inside, glancing around for Charlie's hulking shape. But the yetlet was nowhere to be found.

Fizz, however, was.

The little frost imp tumbled from a rafter, landing in her path with a gleeful chirp. He spun in circles, icy sparks trailing behind.

"Shhh!" Elowen hissed, crouching to catch him mid-spin. "Quiet, please. You can't give me away."

Fizz cocked his head, eyes glittering like frozen ponds. Then, mercifully, he trilled low and zipped up to perch on a beam, watching silently.

She exhaled relief. "Good boy."

Moving quickly, she found one goat, a sturdy black beast with curling horns. Its golden eyes blinked at her with eerie intelligence. She pulled down a saddle, fumbling with the straps, whispering apologies under her breath.

At last, she led the goat out of the stable, its hooves crunching against the frost. The courtyard stretched wide and empty, frost lights flickering like watchful stars.

She swung herself up into the saddle. Her hands tightened on the reins.

For a moment, she turned, her eyes fixed on the looming black silhouette of the castle. Towers clawed at the sky and frost glinted across the stone. The only home she had left.

Her throat burned.

"Goodbye," she cried.

Then she dug her heels lightly into the goat's side. It bleated, shook its horns, and carried her forward through the gates, out into the wild.

The castle faded behind her, swallowed by snow and shadow.

❄ ❄ ❄

The castle groaned.

Stone trembled as if fearing the wrath contained within its own walls. Shadows boiled up from the flagstones, thick and choking, clinging to the vaulted ceiling like a storm cloud too heavy to hold.

Krampus stood in the middle of the chamber, chest heaving, fists curled. The white-hot shackles filled the air with a metallic tang; every breath from him was thick with smoke. With each snarl, another surge of inky blackness erupted from the floor, writhing upward like serpents and splattering the walls with dripping void.

Fizz screeched and leapt from beam to beam, tiny icicle claws scrabbling for purchase. The imp's chirps were high-pitched, panicked, its frost trailing in chaotic streaks as it tried to escape the shadows that lashed at it.

The chamber doors slammed open.

Charlie barreled inside, snow clinging to his fur, eyes wide as the walls themselves shuddered. He lunged, scooping Fizz into his arms as a tendril of shadow whipped upward, missing the little imp by inches.

"Fizz!" Charlie roared, his voice like an avalanche. "What did you tell him?"

Fizz trembled in the yetlet's arms, chittering frantically, shards of ice bursting from its mouth. Nonsense to most, but Charlie listened. His ears twitched; his frown deepened.

Then Charlie's wide eyes narrowed. "No…"

Across the chamber, Krampus stood rigid, his horns nearly scraping the ceiling, his eyes twin furnaces of black void. His voice was guttural, twisted, rolling from deep in his chest.

"She's gone."

Gloom seeped outward; night slammed against the walls as if the darkness, too, howled at the truth.

He bared his heart to her for one fragile moment. And she had left him. Rage warred with despair, twisting in his chest until it tore free in a roar that rattled the stone and split the frosted glass windows.

❄ ❄ ❄

Elowen clung to the goat's reins so tightly her knuckles blanched white. The beast galloped across the frozen plain, its hooves pounding against the snow-crusted earth, steam rising from its nostrils in ragged bursts.

"Faster!" she urged, her voice cracking. Each breath shredded her lungs, but she didn't dare slow. Behind her, she felt it: Krampus' presence like a storm building, a beast unleashed. He would come; he would drag her back.

I have to save him. I have to end this before he finds me.

Her chest tightened. Not just for him, but for herself, for the elves, for the world Kringle had stolen.

But it wasn't Krampus who found her first.

A sound split the storm; a thin, haunting trill, sharp as a blade dragged across glass. Her stomach plummeted. The Choir.

Shadows streaked across the snow behind her, two figures moving in sync. Their candy cane stripes glimmered faintly in the morning light, twisted song spilling from their throats, tugging at her mind, pulling, urging her to *stop*.

"No!" she hissed, sparks snapping across her knuckles.

The goat faltered, ears flicking at the song. Elowen yanked the reins. "Don't you dare! Run!"

One of the Choir lunged, claws grazing her shoulder, ripping a line of fabric and skin. Pain seared down her arm, blood soaking fabric. Elowen cried out, jerking sideways. Her magic flared; a spark leapt from her fingertips, lightning ripping from her palm. The Choir shrieked, the sound garbling as the spark tore into her chest.

She fell back.

But the second kept coming.

"Please, run a little farther," Elowen begged the goat, pressing low against its back.

The ruins loomed ahead; jagged stone ribs clawed from the earth, half-buried in frost. And within them, the doorway.

The goat stumbled to its knees, collapsing. Elowen pitched forward, rolling into the snow. Pain jarred her bones. She forced herself up, blood dripping down her sleeve.

The Choir's song rose, closer now. The surviving figure stalked through the storm, her mouth splitting into a too-wide grin, voice lilting and sweet as poison.

Elowen staggered to the faint shimmer in the air, her legs shaky as she trudged forward. She slapped her palm to the frostbitten rift, breath ragged, magic sending runes into the air. "Come on! Let me through!"

Nothing. Only the cold, only the storm.

The Choir's steps dragged nearer, crunching through the snow.

Her brow furrowed and her teeth gritted as she shoved harder, magic sparking wildly and unevenly down her arm. She thought of the runes etched into the Black Door, the ones that would send her into Kringle Central, and pushed them into the rift. "Open!"

Elowen gasped as she forced a crack, magic gnawing at her bones.

The Choir's claw stretched toward her face...

...and Elowen hurled herself into the light.

CHAPTER THIRTEEN

Elowen's ears rang as the world reassembled around her. She was curled in a heap against the cold tile, the taste of copper and frost sharp on her tongue. Her nose wrinkled as a smell drifted to her of peppermint, gingerbread, and sugar.

Sweet. Too sweet.

Had it been that long since she had tasted sugar in the air? Her mouth watered at the thought of a cup of warm coffee.

Her eyes adjusted to the gloom, and she discovered she was in a narrow room stacked with rolls of ribbons, crates of wrapping paper, shelves sagging under the weight of plastic smiles. Dolls' heads, porcelain eyes, mechanical toy parts stared blankly at her from their boxes. A supply closet.

What in the frost?

Why hadn't the portal opened at the Black Door on the square? A groan escaped her lips; she must have twisted the runes. At least she hadn't landed miles away like before. A smile danced on her lips. Krampus might even be proud of her for that.

She staggered upright, brushing frost and ash from her cloak. Her fingers trailed across the shelves, and for a wild moment she wondered how many lives had been bent, broken, forced into neat packages tied with bows. A laugh rose in her throat, dry and bitter. *From one prison to another.*

Her hand found a doorknob, and she pushed it open.

Light blazed into her eyes. Not warm light, not the fire of hearth or home, but the white glare of enchanted lanterns and late morning sun flickering through narrow windows. She squinted, raising a hand to shield her eyes from the glare.

When her vision cleared, her heart sank.

She had stepped straight into the toy workshop.

Rows upon rows of elves hunched at long benches, faces gaunt and hollow, fingers working at breakneck speed. Wooden soldiers marched out from hammers and nails, porcelain dolls blinked with mechanical lashes, drums and horns piled high in endless stacks. The air smelled of sugar and sweat, gingerbread icing masking the stench of exhaustion.

And above it all, voices sang. Thin, reedy, weary songs of joy that fell flat, as if someone had wrung every note from their throats. The cheer in it was brittle, forced.

The music died the moment Elowen stumbled into the room.

Hundreds of eyes turned toward her. Tools clattered onto benches. Hushed questions rippled like fire through the rows.

Her cloak hung ragged from her shoulders, smeared with soot and bloody claw marks. Her hair, once carefully plaited, had fallen into a tangle about her face. Compared to their pressed green uniforms, she looked like a wild, battered ghost.

"Elowen?" one elf muttered, voice cracking. "She's supposed to be gone."

Her chest tightened. She had hoped they would have forgotten her since the banishment. It might be harder to go undetected than she thought. Her mind scrambled. If they recognized her, they might listen to her, might help her.

But another thought struck her, colder: *What if they don't? What if no one ever does?*

The words rose in her throat anyway, hot and trembling. She thought of Krampus, how he had shaken the snow itself with his roar, how shadows bent to his command. She had no roar, no shadows. Only a voice. It didn't feel like enough, but it was all she had.

"Listen to me," she said quickly, stepping forward, voice rising above the whispers. "You don't have to do this. You don't have to keep building toys. Kringle has you chained, don't you see? The List is a lie. There's more than this—"

A harsh electric buzz split the air.

"Back. To. Work."

The amplified voice cracked from above. Elowen's eyes snapped upward. On a metal catwalk spanning the room stood a stout elf with slicked hair and a crimson suit, a megaphone clutched in one thick-fingered hand. His round face was flushed, his mouth curled into a snarl.

"You there!" His voice blasted again, rattling down to her. "Trespasser!"

Elves returned to their tasks, fear tightening their movements. Hammers resumed pounding, saws screeched across wood, their song picking up in a shaky murmur.

The overseer descended a ladder, huffing with every step until he landed before her. Another elf scurried up with a stool so he could climb higher; his eyes barely met her chin.

He sniffed, gaze crawling over her soot-streaked cloak, the ruined green uniform beneath, her braids frayed and singed. His lip curled.

"Name. Badge. Papers." His hand shot out, expectant.

Elowen's stomach dropped. Her badge was gone, left somewhere in Krampus' castle.

"I don't have it," she admitted, chin raised.

Gasps flickered through the nearest benches. The overseer's face darkened, a vein pulsing at his temple. "You interrupt my floor, stop my elves, *halt production*—" His voice shrieked through the megaphone, cracking as he swung toward the workers. "Eyes down! Hands moving!"

The elves bent deeper over their tasks, shoulders rigid.

He turned back to her. "You don't belong here." His stubby finger jabbed toward her face, punctuating each word.

Two burly guards appeared from the aisles, taller elves, clad in green uniforms with brass star badges glinting on their chests.

Their heavy boots thudded against the floor as they flanked her.

"Take her," the overseer barked, stepping down from his stool with a grunt.

The guards seized her arms, their grips bruising. Elowen twisted, but their hold only tightened. Her heart hammered as the overseer strutted ahead, leading the way toward the far doors.

Her thoughts spiraled, raw and frantic. *Why won't they hear me? Don't they see the bars, the chains?* She could almost feel her magic pulse beneath her skin, tiny flares at her fingertips, as if it wanted to answer in her place. But it fizzled uselessly, like sparks dying in snow.

The workshop resumed its endless clamor behind her: hammers, saws, the thin drone of a forced carol.

But Elowen's voice cut through it, sharp and desperate.

"You don't have to live like this!" she shouted back to the rows of hunched figures. "You don't have to obey him! There's more than naughty or nice! You deserve freedom!"

For a heartbeat, silence trembled across the floor. Dozens of faces turned toward her, hope flickering like sparks...

...and then the overseer bellowed through his megaphone: "Ignore her! She's nothing but a traitor to the List!"

The elves' gazes dropped, hands moving faster, lips pressing shut.

Elowen's chest ached as the guards dragged her onward, her words swallowed by the pounding of hammers and the relentless, empty cheer. The sting of their silence cut sharper than the overseer's venom. For a moment she wished she could melt into shadow, vanish into smoke, anything but this: the woman with no roar.

❄ ❄ ❄

The guards led her through a set of gilt double doors. Her stomach dropped at the recognition.

The throne hall.

It looked the same as when Kringle first summoned her, and yet not. Then, it had gleamed with gold thread and frosted holly, Kringle seated upon his throne like benevolence made flesh. The glitter was now gaudy, and the holly looked like knives. The air stank of sugar and iron, thick with false warmth.

And there he was.

Kringle rose as the guards dragged her forward. Tall, broad-shouldered, golden hair spilling in immaculate waves beneath that gilded crown. His ivory smile gleamed like a weapon. His eyes twinkled, but the warmth in them was hollow, a light reflected, not born. Bells jingled as he stepped down from the dais.

This is it, Elowen thought, her heart hammering so loud she feared it would echo in the chamber. *This is the moment I wanted. The moment I told myself I'd be brave enough to face him. To stop him. To free them.*

But now, staring up at him, she felt smaller than ever. Her magic fluttered inside her chest, an ember buried in ash, sparking in brief twitches along her fingertips. Not a weapon. Not enough.

"Elowen," he said, his voice a velvet caress that curdled her blood. "The wayward little List Maker."

The guards shoved her to her knees. She gritted her teeth and forced herself not to bow her head.

Kringle circled her, his boots thudding on the marble floor. "Do you know what I admire about you?" he asked. "It takes a certain…audacity…to break the very foundation of our life. And yet you thought yourself cleverer than the system."

Her throat tightened. Her palms itched with heat, a shimmer of frost running up the marble at her knees before vanishing. "The system is wrong," she said, voice cracking but steady. "Children don't fit in boxes. You punish them for being hungry, for being poor. That isn't justice."

Kringle chuckled. "Ah, the bleeding heart. How quaint." He leaned down, his breath sweet as peppermint, sickly. "But do you know what you've done?" His smile sharpened. "Two Choir silenced trying to get you. Do you think I do not feel the tremor when my music falters?"

The words hit her like ice water. He knew. He had *felt* it.

His voice dropped; steel replacing the honey. "And worse, you've tampered with the List. My List."

Elowen's heart pounded, her magic twitching again; static lifted strands of her hair before falling flat. "It was never yours," she shot back. "It was meant for balance, not control. You're twisting it—"

His laughter boomed through the hall, echoing off the vaulted ceiling, sharp and merciless. "Balance? You dare speak to me of balance? Girl, I *am* balance. Without me, everything collapses into ruin. Without me, all is shadow."

"You mean without you, there's freedom," she spat.

His eyes flashed, the twinkle gone, replaced with glacial fury. "Freedom is chaos. And chaos..." he paused, tilting his head, smile curling cruel, "...is my brother's domain."

At the mention of Krampus, Elowen's heart lurched. She felt her magic surge, hot and cold at once, her breath frosting in the air before it faded again.

Kringle's gaze flicked to her, sharp as knives, reading the shift in her face. His smile widened, cold and knowing. "Ah. So that's it." He leaned closer, whispering as if sharing a secret. "The monster's claws are in you, aren't they? Tell me, little elf...do you *love* him?"

Heat flared in her cheeks. "He isn't a monster," she snapped, louder than she meant to. A spark of light flared in her palm. There, and gone.

Kringle's laughter rang like a bell. "Oh, this is rich. My wretched brother, the monster in chains, inspires devotion. You poor, foolish thing." He straightened, voice rising, echoing across the hall. "He has always hungered for what is mine. My lists, my people, my dominion. Now he has taken you as well."

"You're the one who banished me!" Her voice cracked, desperation bleeding through. "He doesn't want any of this. You chained him to it! You forced him to play your monster!"

The words rang through the throne room.

Kringle's smile vanished.

The false warmth drained from his face, leaving only a mask of frost and rage. "Enough." His voice shook the air like thunder. "You know nothing. And you will not live long enough to learn more."

Her blood went cold. *Not like this*, she thought, panic clawing at her chest. Her magic sputtered again, useless sparks at her fingertips. *Please, just once, work. Give me something to fight with.*

He pivoted toward the guards. "Summon the battalions. Prepare the march. It is time my brother remembered his place."

Elowen's breath hitched. "No!" The word tore from her throat. "Leave him alone!"

Kringle pivoted back to her, his fury giving way to a slow, cruel grin. "How precious. You plead for him as though you are his salvation."

He raised a hand. "Take her. Let the record show her crime. Let her punishment be final."

The guards yanked her to her feet. Her chest constricted, terror clawing at her throat. Death. He meant to execute her.

The head guard barked, "To the cells."

As he grabbed her arm, something in her snapped. Fear, fury, desperation; all of it boiled over. Heat surged from her chest into her hands, too much, too fast. Her vision blurred white as the magic burst loose.

A shock wave cracked through the air. Frost spiraled out from her knees, lacing the marble in jagged veins, while fire seared up her palm. The nearest guard shouted, jerking back as his sleeve smoldered, the brass star on his chest glowing red hot. The scent of scorched cloth and singed hair filled the hall.

Elowen stared at him, her own power burning her throat raw.

The guard staggered, cursing, beating at the smoke rising from his arm.

Dozens of eyes turned toward her. *Maybe*, she thought, chest heaving, *maybe this time…*

Kringle laughed.

The sound spread across the throne room, warm and hollow as a cracked bell. He threw back his head, golden strands catching the light, delighted.

"Oh, precious little spark," he crooned, voice dripping mockery. "You think to wound me with tricks? To frighten my soldiers with fire and frost?" He stepped closer, looming above her, his smile sharp enough to cut. "You're kindling. And kindling always burns itself out."

He flicked a hand, dismissive as brushing ash from his sleeve.

The guards, shaken but obedient, tightened their grips, dragging her toward the doors. Her chest burned with magic, her palms stung raw, but it sputtered uselessly now, drained.

Kringle's laughter followed her out, bright and merciless.

❆ ❆ ❆

The cold of the holding cell seeped into Elowen's bones. It was not the bitter, honest cold of Krampus' world; this was sterile, manufactured. A chill designed to keep her small, submissive, and compliant.

Afternoon light sliced through the iron bars, cutting sharp shadows across the floor. Every sound outside echoed too loudly: boots on stone, a jingle of keys, the brittle hum of a song playing somewhere down the corridor. The hollow cheer mocked her.

She sat hunched on the narrow bench, arms wrapped tight around herself, thinking of Cinn's laugh, Charlie's booming voice, Fizz's trills. Of Krampus' hands, heavy and careful, carrying her through storm and shadow. She had left them behind…left *him* behind.

And for what?

She shivered at the finality. The word Kringle had spat rang in her skull: *death.*

Her fingers itched, sparks of magic sputtering before dying.

She clenched her fists. She thought of Krampus' voice, low and gruff, steadying her hands: *You're made for more.*

Tears stung her eyes. "I can't die here," she sobbed into the silence. "I won't."

She dropped to her knees, pressing her palms flat against the seam where stone met stone. The floor was cold, biting into her skin, but something faint and hungry deep below thrummed in answer.

She closed her eyes, drew a shaking breath, and whispered, "Take me out. Take me back."

Gray light bled from her hand, jagged cracks racing outward. They curled into half-formed runes, stuttering but familiar. Her chest pounded. She shoved more magic into the shapes, teeth gritted. "Open!"

The cracks widened. A faint glow swelled upward, like twinkling tree lights caught under glass. Then the floor rippled and split. A slit of darkness yawned open, air rushing out sharp with pine and ash.

Elowen's breath caught. The magic smelled wild, off, untethered.

Boots rang in the corridor. Guards.

She didn't hesitate. She shoved herself through the jagged slit. Magic scraped her raw, tearing across her skin.

She fell, tumbling through blackness that reeked of smoke and winter, before slamming onto frozen ground on the other side of the rift. The impact jolted the breath from her lungs.

The portal snapped shut behind her, leaving only silence broken by her own ragged gasps.

She rolled onto her back, staring up at a bruised-violet sky. Around her stretched snowfields broken by black stone spires, the air thick with the taste of ash.

She was out of Central. She was alive. But she was not safe.

She lay there trembling, clutching her burned palms to her chest. "Please," she pleaded, whether to her magic, or to Krampus, or to herself, she didn't know. "Please let this be close enough."

Elowen pushed herself up from the frozen ground, legs trembling, palms sizzling. The sky above stretched like a torn veil, streaked violet and black, the stars distorted, shivering as though seen through ice.

The air was colder than Krampus' realm. No wind, no birds, no hum of Central's machines. Sound was not biting, but muffled, heavy, like floating in a vast tank of water. The snow crunched under her feet with a brittle, unnatural sound.

She brushed hair from her eyes. "Where am I?"

The land sloped into hollows carved by long-forgotten rivers. Jagged stone teeth jutted from the earth, casting warped shadows. Frost lights glimmered faintly within some hollows, eerie will-o'-wisps pulsing dim and slow. She didn't trust them.

Her chest ached. The magic had gotten her out, yes, but had delivered her into a no-man's-land. *Closer*, she told herself, *I'm closer to him. I have to be.*

A sound cracked the silence.

Not wind. Not snow.

A scrape.

Elowen froze. She swallowed air like glass as her eyes darted over the dark terrain. Nothing moved. She forced herself to keep walking, steps faster now, each crunch of snow too loud.

Then she heard it again. Scraping. Shuffling. Something dragged itself across the stone.

Her heart pounded. Her magic sparked, a faint gray glow in her palm, barely enough to illuminate her trembling fingers as she spun.

From the shadow of a hollow, something pulled itself up.

It was not Choir, or elf, or beast.

It was older.

The figure rose higher than Krampus, gaunt but towering, its limbs too long, its spine bent at sharp angles as though it had been broken and reassembled wrong. Its flesh was pallid ice, translucent in places, showing veins of black frost within. A head tilted toward her, jaw unhinging in a shuddering crack. No eyes, only hollow sockets burning with dim, frost-blue fire.

The scraping sound came from its hands. Claws like splintered icicles dragged across the rock.

Elowen staggered back. *Gingersnaps.*

The thing opened its maw wider. A hollow sound poured out, not a growl, not a scream, but a *whistle*, sharp and cold, like wind forcing itself through a frozen cavern.

The frost lights in the hollows flickered violently at the sound, and the air chilled.

Elowen turned and ran.

The snow crunched beneath her slippers as she stumbled up the ridge, her lungs burning. Her magic sparked as she flung wild bursts of light behind her, striking the creature's chest. It staggered, but continued its pursuit, relentless, its claws biting into the ground as it hauled itself forward.

Her magic wasn't enough. Not like this.

She groaned. This might be the end of her after all.

Her foot tripped, and she rolled down the other side of the ridge, snow and rock cutting her arms. She scrambled up, gasping, and there ahead she saw it.

Another rift, pulsing with runes. Not stable, not open, but *possible*.

The whistle behind her grew louder, closer, piercing her skull. She cried out, clutching her ears, nearly collapsing.

She threw herself against the rift. Her magic flared wild, sparks stinging her skin, runes flickering in half-formed spirals.

The creature's claw slammed into the ground behind her. The impact shook her bones. She felt its frigid breath at her back; the frost burning her neck.

Elowen screamed, shoving everything she had into the seam. All her fear, desperation, her hunger to live. Anything to get back to *him*.

Runes ignited, exploding in gray light. The crack tore wide, unstable, shrieking with energy. The monster reared back, its whistle turning into a scream as the light seared it.

Elowen didn't think. She hurled herself into the light.

Her body tumbled through the doorway, darkness spinning,

her magic sparking as the portal ripped at her. She could hear the monster's scream echoing in the void.

CHAPTER FOURTEEN

Elowen exited the rift to find her hands scraping against a glassy surface. For a long, dizzy moment, she lay there, chest heaving, the echoes of the monster's scream gnawing at her bones.

"Things have got to stop chasing me through doors," she moaned.

When she forced herself to rise, her heart dropped.

This realm was only darkness; vast and crushing, stretching in every direction. A black path glimmered beneath her feet, as though stitched from starlight. Beyond it, there was nothing, only void.

Her throat tightened. Her legs shook. But forward was the only way.

Elowen walked.

The path wound endlessly, her footsteps echoing, as though the void itself listened. Time dissolved. She could not tell whether minutes or hours had passed. Hunger gnawed, thirst burned, but something in this place pulled her onward, an unseen gravity dragging her deeper into its heart.

Finally ahead, she saw it: an exit door.

A towering arch of black stone, its surface crawling with runes. Not red, green, or white. Gray, shifting endlessly across its surface, alive with power.

Her chest seized at the sight. The color, *her* color, smoky, unstable, unclean. People had scolded, hidden, and cursed her for the same sparks.

As she neared, the runes flickered as though rushing into a conversation.

The moment she touched the door, a powerful impact sent her reeling, threatening to knock her down. The runes rearranged, twisting into jagged, crackling lines.

"One more time," she mumbled. Gray magic guttered on her skin as she touched the door again. The runes surged in recognition, answering with the same hue and mimicking the runes she sent.

Her chest heaved. "Please," she cried into the void. "I don't care what I have to give. I have to get back to him. Can you take me to him?"

The runes spun faster. The door trembled. She felt them scraping against her bones, pulling memories from her: the laughter during chores with Cinn, the way Krampus' arms had steadied her when she faltered, the heat of his shackles while he tried to hold her close. They took everything from her life and pressed it against her like a pair of scales.

After a pause, the runes stilled, and then the portal opened.

Elowen crossed into a cathedral-like realm sculpted from darkness, pulsing alive with glowing constellations. As she stepped, the ground beneath her shimmered like the trail of a comet. Great pillars rose into the void, carved with glowing gray runes.

In the center stood a being with vast black wings, each joint dripping with silvery frost. Its body was tall, its skin rippling with gray runes that flared and dimmed like breathing.

Its face...she could not see. Where its features should have been was a blur, a distortion, as though reality refused to render it fully.

When it spoke, it was not in words.

The sound tore through her mind, a chorus of tones too high, too low, too many to belong to a single voice. She staggered, clutching her ears, unable to decipher the message beyond the echoing.

Elowen's heart leapt. "I'm sorry. I don't understand."

The being lifted one long finger, and with a flick, the surrounding space rippled. Images unfolded in the air: Kringle, draped in gold, smiling with hollow eyes as elves bent under their work; Krampus chained, his shackles glowing as he carried his role like a curse; herself, sparks of gray magic flaring at her fingertips, wavering between light and shadow.

Her knees weakened. "That's why I'm here? You want me to fix it?"

The chorus shivered. The runes across its body rearranged themselves, and suddenly, she felt a pressure stab into her chest. A weight settled inside her ribcage. Her vision blurred, her magic surged, gold and shadow sparking together, roaring.

It felt like something *unleashing* inside her. Her magic.

Gasping for breath, she fell to her knees, clutching her chest. "What? What are you doing to me?"

The chorus deepened. The meaning struck her like a bell toll.

Gray is the key. The magic roared through her, breaking open what she already carried. Unsealing it. Unlocking it. *It's always been inside me,* she thought. *I wasn't broken, just bound.*

The world reeled around her. Her magic poured out in violent bursts, but it no longer fizzled and sputtered; it held. It *stabilized*.

Her body trembled, and for a terrifying moment, she thought she might shatter apart. It was too much magic, too much for her to handle. The being reached down and touched her forehead with one burning fingertip.

Everything calmed.

Her magic, her heart, her breath.

When she blinked again, it stepped back, its wings folding slowly, shadows swallowing it whole. The runes across the pillars dimmed. The void hushed.

It had judged her.

And it had unlocked what she already carried.

Whether it was salvation or damnation, she did not yet know.

The void peeled back, bending like smoke under unseen

hands. Where the being stood, a new portal coalesced within black stone and silver fire, gray runes embedded throughout. A gift, or perhaps a dismissal.

Elowen's legs ached as she pushed herself upright, wobbling under the strange new heaviness that thrummed in her chest. The runes inside her veins pulsed, too alive, too loud, as if her own blood were whispering secrets she could not understand.

She staggered toward the portal.

But before she could cross the threshold, the being's hand lowered, vast and rune-carved, settling heavy on her shoulder.

Her heart lurched into her throat. She froze, breath caught in terror, every nerve in her body screaming that she had pushed too far. Slowly, painfully, she turned her head to look up at it.

The face that wasn't a face tilted down toward her. She *felt* its eyes on her, searing, searching. For a moment, she thought it might rip back what it had unlocked for her, unmake and end her existence. Deem her unworthy of the gray and unworthy of what was always hers.

Instead, the runes rippled across its body in a low shudder. The sound that followed was something strange.

A sigh.

Regret.

Something twisted inside her and flickered. She clutched her stomach as a strange protective instinct tightened low inside her. She felt sorrow for what had been taken from her people long ago. For every chain, every lie that had made gray a curse instead of a birthright.

Elowen swallowed hard. "I don't know what you've given me. But I'll do my best to carry it. Thank you."

The being's hand lifted, and the weight vanished.

The portal flared wider, urging her onward.

❄ ❄ ❄

Cold.

Her breath ripped from her chest in a gasp as she left the portal, slippers scraping on the jagged stone of a small cavern.

Frost glittered along the ceiling in jagged spears. The air reeked of old magic, heavy and sharp, thick enough to taste. Torches guttered in sconces, casting long shadows across the walls. And before her rose two doors.

One was carved of bone-black wood, framed in antlers, wildlife, and earth, its runes twisting and flaring as if reacting to her presence. The solemn door thrummed with a familiar dread, its rhythm a song she knew to be his. Krampus.

The other...she flinched.

Bright red and green, gilded with gold filigree, framed in merry loops of holly and candy canes. Its wreath shimmered with bells that jingled softly in an enchanted breeze. The sight of it sent bile to her throat. Kringle Central.

Elowen's breath quivered in her chest. Two paths. Two fates.

Her fingers trembled at her sides. She could almost *hear* their voices. Kringle's booming, hollow laugh, demanding obedience, demanding perfection, but belonging to a place she had called home for most of her life. Krampus' snarl, ragged and rough, chains rattling, yet beneath it something else: the heartbeat she had rested her cheek against, steady even as the storm raged.

She felt the cavern walls closing in. Her breath echoed in the silence. Her eyes burned with tears she hadn't realized were falling.

At last, she turned.

She placed her palm against the door of night.

The runes surged, flaring brilliant white for the briefest instant before bleeding into molten red. They recognized her. Claimed her.

The door swung wide without hesitation.

Elowen exhaled shakily. She had made her choice and would never look back.

The portal yawned before her, dark and vast, leading back into frost and shadow. Her shadow.

And with one last glance at the merry door, its bells jingling faintly behind her, she stepped through.

The cavern dissolved.

The storm-swept air of Krampus' realm filled her lungs again.

"Home," she sighed.

.

CHAPTER FIFTEEN

"I swear," Elowen muttered, "I will scream if I have to step through another portal—"

The words broke off her tongue.

Her heart beat hollow.

In the early light, Krampus' realm burned, its fiery scent filling the air.

Smoke and fire had torn the frost-strewn horizon open. Shattered toy soldiers lay in heaps, their brass gears spilling like entrails across the snow. Splintered candy cane spears jutted from the ground at odd angles, broken rib bones in a corpse. The air reeked of scorched sugar, wood-smoke, and iron.

Elowen staggered forward, her slippers crunching over broken peppermint shards. "No, no, no," she cried.

How long had she been gone? Hours? Days? Her gut told her she had failed, that she hadn't made it back in time to warn him. Kringle's wrath had already spread.

Her lungs burned as she ran, weaving between overturned siege carts painted in cheerful reds and golds, paint peeling, wheels shattered.

Then…voices.

She froze and ducked behind a slab of broken gingerbread barricade. Beyond, in a shallow hollow of snow, a handful of elves huddled around a fire. They wore the red-trimmed uniforms of Kringle's army, their shoulders burdened by strapped packs, their spears tipped with sharpened candy crystal. A battered toy soldier, one leg dragging uselessly behind it, stood sentinel beside them, its jaw clicking faintly as if chewing on the memory of war.

Elowen crept closer, crouching behind a jagged rock.

"Ugly fight," one elf muttered, tossing another stick into the flames. "Didn't think the monster would push back so hard."

Another spat into the snow. "He's desperate. Always is. Won't matter, not this time. His Jolliness wants him back in chains, and that's exactly where he'll end."

Elowen's nails bit into her palms.

Chains. They did not want to defeat him; they wanted to break him.

A third elf shivered, drawing his cloak tighter. "You see the Choir? Sent to soften him up. Gave me chills, hearing her sing."

"She'll finish him if he doesn't break."

The toy soldier's jaw clicked louder, almost like laughter.

Elowen's pulse hammered. She shifted, desperate to run...

A crunch of snow behind her.

Her body locked.

"Oi," a voice said, close, too close. "What's this, then?"

She whirled, face-to-face with a stocky elf, tightening his belt, eyes narrowing. His gaze raked over her bloodied cloak, her dirt-streaked face, and the burns on her arm. Suspicion hardened his features.

"Lost one," he muttered, grabbing her by the elbow. "Come on."

He dragged her out from behind the rock, straight toward the fire.

Five pairs of eyes lifted to meet her, firelight flickering across their faces. One let out a low whistle.

"Jumping jingle bells, you look like burnt gingerbread."

"She's not even got a weapon," another scoffed. "What kind of soldier are ya?"

Panic clawed up Elowen's throat. *Think. Lie.*

"I..." Her mind spun. "Got separated. From my squad."

The elves exchanged a look. Then one barked a laugh, clapping her on the shoulder hard enough to sting.

"Figures. First-timers always lose their nerve."

She forced a weak smile, though her stomach churned.

"Well, lucky for you," their leader, a taller elf with a scar across his brow, cut in, "you're found now. Get her a weapon."

One guard thrust a spear toward her. She took it numbly, the weight of it foreign and wrong in her hands.

The scarred elf kicked snow onto the fire, dousing it with a hiss. "We're moving. Orders for another push by midday. Castle walls before the sun's at its peak."

Elowen's heart stopped.

Castle walls.

Krampus.

Her knuckles whitened on the spear's shaft as the squad marched, their laughter hollow against the surrounding ruin.

She fell in step, dread pounding with every beat of her pulse.

Through the smoke and drifting ash, the jagged silhouette of the fortress loomed.

The march ended on a ridge.

Elowen staggered to a halt with the squad as the scene unfolded before them. The valley below was crawling with soldiers. An entire army. Lines of elves in regimented ranks, candy cane spears gleaming under the pale frost light. Toy soldiers clanked forward in towering formations, gears whirring, bells chiming discordantly with every heavy step. War banners flapped in the storm, golden stars stitched into scarlet cloth. Reindeer in battle armor flanked by snowmen hauling ammunition.

Air stuck sharp in her throat. All of this to capture one monster.

Before her, looming in defiance, was Krampus' fortress.

The castle itself had changed. Where once its black stone had brooded silently against the storm, now its walls were alive. Spiked ramparts bristled with gargoyles and frost-forged defenses. The gates had thickened; iron jaws slammed shut. Frost light pulsed in runes across its surface as though the fortress itself had awakened from slumber. Giant black nutcracker sentinels lined the ramparts.

It was ready.

"Elves above," one soldier muttered, shouldering his spear. "Looks like the monster's fortress wants blood."

The scarred leader barked: "Form ranks! The push begins before noon!"

They moved as one, but Elowen's legs quivered. She shrank back, clutching the spear in clammy hands. She had to find a way inside, warn him, beg him to hold…

"No worries," a soldier said, clapping her back and thrusting her into line. "Stick with us. We'll get that monster."

Horns blared.

The world shattered.

❄ ❄ ❄

The army surged, the valley trembling with boots and gears. War cries split the air, colliding with guttural roars. The sun hung overhead, bright and pitiless, throwing stark shadows across the snow. Krampus' guards, roused from centuries of silence, gathered atop the walls.

Frost arrows rained down, shattering against shields. Screams cut through as toy soldiers marched forward, their gears ticking and blades flashing. Candy-striped lances skewered shadows, peppermint blasts cracked like fireworks. The battlefield was joy turned nightmare beneath the blinding midday light.

Elowen ducked, her breath ragged, the cold biting her lungs like knives. Around her, elves clashed with claw and steel, blood and sugar slicking the snow. She shoved through the tide, deflecting enough to survive, every flicker of gray shielding her.

A roar split the sky.

Her blood froze.

Krampus.

He loomed on the battlements, chains clattering, claws tearing soldiers apart in showers of sparks. Night bled from his body, scattering elves like straw. For one heartbeat, Elowen dared to hope.

She barreled into the courtyard to see Charlie and Cinn. Charlie's fists exploded snowflakes, and Cinn's mace swung wide. They fought side by side until the toy soldiers overwhelmed them. She hauled Charlie behind a barricade of gingerbread corpses and blasted frost to scatter attackers from Cinn. Though her arms quaked with exertion, she was finally defending them.

Then the Choir sang.

Her keening pierced through the din of battle and crawled through bone. Elves faltered, shadows shriveled. Krampus staggered, shackles glowing white-hot. He roared, but the sound broke into a strangled cry.

"No," Elowen whispered, throat raw, vision swimming. The song pressed into her skull and gutted her gray sparks. Every heartbeat felt stolen.

Chains snapped across the battlefield, coiling around Krampus' limbs, his throat.

"Bring him down!"

He roared, a sound that tore the clouds apart, but the Choir dragged him to his knees. Sparks flew as his claws scraped stone.

Elowen shoved through the tide with Charlie and Cinn at her side, but the Choir's song smothered every spell, every strike.

Krampus' roar broke, strangled, and at last he fell face-first into the snow.

Cheers erupted. The elves lifted him high, shackled and broken, the sun glaring down like a witness.

Elowen stumbled forward, lungs burning, tears streaking her frost-bitten face. She wanted to scream his name, but no sound came.

The monster, her monster, was theirs.

* * *

❄ ❄ ❄

The snow crunched beneath Elowen's slippers as she trudged through the valley; the army stretched ahead like a tide of red and green. Soldiers and elves marched side by side, hauling their prize toward Central. His chains glimmered even in the fading light, sparks flickering along the icy links. Every clang and hiss echoed across the plains, a reminder of the power that lay restrained in the fortress's heart.

Elowen wove through the ranks, pretending to march with the others, her heart hammering in her chest. She had to look like another soldier, another elf swept up in the tide, but every glance she stole at him made her stomach twist. He was alive. He was there. Yes, they'd captured him, but he was breathing, and a flicker of defiance remained.

She muttered under her breath, letting her magic hum in her fingertips, a tiny pulse of heat here, a shimmer of frost there. She focused on the chains, the rhythm of the metal, the quiet struggle beneath the white-hot links. Her hands tingled with the effort, and she felt the pull of him like a tether across the distance.

Closer. She had to get closer.

The army's march was long, the snow crunching beneath boots and toy soldier's metal feet. Lantern fires flickered at intervals, their green and red glows bleeding across the snow. The pale afternoon sun dipped lower, shadows lengthening across the valley. Elowen observed the guards as she moved, noting their shifts and patterns, the way their shadows stretched long in the dimming light. Every small gap between them was a chance, a moment she could exploit.

A patrol passed too close, and she ducked behind a cluster of snow-laden trees. From her fingertips, she sent a tiny pulse of frost along the trunk, blending her figure into the shadows. The guard glanced in her direction, frowned, and moved on. Her heart thumped, but she didn't breathe until the danger had passed.

By the time the army slowed, the sun was sliding toward the horizon, painting the snow with low bands of gold and red. They made camp in a frozen glade. Fires crackled in the snow, illuminating rows of elves and toy soldiers exhausted from the march. They led Krampus to a reinforced tent at the center, the chains clinking as they pulled him in. Guards surrounded him, warily glancing at anyone who approached.

Elowen crouched near the edge of the camp, watching, memorizing, heart pounding. Every instinct screamed at her to wait, to plan, but she could not wait. She refused to waste another moment. She crept from shadow to shadow, sliding behind supply carts laden with candy crates, gingerbread barricades, and sacks of peppermint bombs. A toy soldier clanged too close, and she flattened herself in the snow, letting the noise pass over her like water.

She paused by a tent where a pair of guards were exchanging heated whispers. A spark of frost leapt from her fingertips, snaking along the ground and forming a thin icy patch beneath the nearest guard's boot. With a startled cry, he slipped, arms flailing, and Elowen melted into the darkness as the other guard ran to steady him.

Step by step, she edged closer to Krampus' tent. A small circle of enchanted light glimmered from within, illuminating his frame. Her lungs burned. She was careful not to disturb the campfires, every breath held as she crept toward the tent.

The canvas flaps of the tent were heavy, but she found a small gap near the ground. She crawled under it, heart thundering, and froze. There he was, Krampus, massive, coiled in chains, the firelight flickering across his red eyes and the sheen of sweat glistening on his broad shoulders. Even restrained, even bound, he radiated power and danger, and a longing that made her chest ache.

His gaze locked onto hers, and for a heartbeat, the world outside the tent ceased to exist. The chains shivered as his hands twitched, but his eyes were all hers.

"I thought," he muttered, voice hoarse and raw, trembling with relief and something deeper. "I thought you had left me."

Her throat tightened, and she moved closer on unsteady knees, careful not to alarm anyone. "I'm here," she said, tears pricking her eyes. "I won't leave you."

She reached out, her fingers brushing the cool metal of his shackles. Sparks hissed as her magic traced the starlit iron, gentle and probing, testing for a weakness. She wrenched at the links, her magic flaring, but the chains only hissed, unyielding. His hands twitched at her touch, a mirrored longing, his shadows flicking toward her, curling around her hands, her arms, desperate for contact that the chains forbade.

Her eyes fell on the gash along his shoulder, dark with blood. She tore a strip of cloth from her cloak and bound it, pressing soothingly as she worked. "They hurt you," she murmured.

Krampus shivered under her touch, and she felt the tension in his muscles, the raw power coiled beneath his skin. He leaned forward, forehead resting against hers, and a shiver ran down her spine at the heat and scent of him. The smoke of his shadow, the iron tang of his blood, and the dangerous, magnetic pull that made her ache filled her.

She kissed him then, gently at first, fingertips brushing against his jaw, tasting the salt of his pain, the faint tang of fear. The chains hissed white-hot, sparks licking the air, and he groaned, muscles straining, shadow tendrils writhing toward her, desperate to enfold her even as the iron held him back.

"I'll get you out," she murmured against his lips, cheek pressed to his. "I promise."

"Somehow," he rumbled, shadows licking her arms and curling around her shoulders.

She traced the lines of his face, memorizing him as if committing him to memory could ease the chains' cruel weight. He shifted slightly toward her, every movement restrained yet full of longing. He rested his forehead against hers again, letting her steady him.

For a long moment, there was only them. Only the heat of his body, the faint hiss of the shackles, the soft glow of firelight, and their touches. Her hands rested on him, his shadows leaned into her, and the quiet hum of his breathing was all they needed.

Then…a shout ripped through the tent.

Elowen froze, caught between disbelief and desperation, too slow to react. The last rays of the sun struck the canvas from outside, casting long crimson shadows. A heavy blow struck the back of her head, sending her sprawling; stars exploded behind her eyes.

Krampus roared, hands rattling against the iron, shadow lashes slicing through the air in desperate arcs as he tried to reach her. Firelight danced across his strained muscles, illuminating the raw power of his fury.

"Elowen!" he bellowed, voice ragged with rage, fear, and anguish.

But it was too late.

The tent fell into chaotic silence, broken only by the hiss of enchanted chains. She lay for a heartbeat, caught between hope and the darkness, feeling the heat of his magic and the faint echo of his presence, knowing he was fighting, still alive, still hers.

CHAPTER SIXTEEN

Her wrists burned from the bite of iron, heavy links clattering against stone as she stirred. She groaned, her head pounding from the blow that had felled her. When her vision cleared, the world sharpened into the bleakest of prisons: Kringle's throne room, a chamber of pale marble, glowing faintly as though lit from within. Runes crawled across the walls in golden spirals, shimmering like veins of poison through snow.

And across from her...

"Krampus."

He was bound upright between two pillars of white stone, shackles pinning his arms wide. Chains snaked across his chest and throat, glowing white-hot against his skin. His head hung low, horns bent forward, but at the sound of her voice, he shifted.

"You're alive." His voice was raw, shredded with fury.

He surged forward, shadows unspooling as he tried to wrench free. The chains answered with a hiss of fire, searing into his skin. The stench of scorched flesh filled the chamber. He roared through the pain, muscles straining, claws digging into the air as though sheer will could tear through iron.

"Stop!" she cried, yanking at her own chains. The manacles tightened, biting into her skin. "You're burning yourself!"

"I don't care." His eyes glowed, bright as molten coals. "I'll break them. I'll get to you."

Another surge, another hiss. The chains burned deeper into him, his shoulders shaking from the agony, yet he only fought harder, shadows coiling wildly. The chamber trembled with his wrath, dust trickling from the ceiling.

"Please!" Elowen begged, her throat hoarse. "You'll kill yourself!"

Her words cut through, but barely. He sagged against the chains, chest heaving, smoke curling from the scorched flesh around his shackles. His gaze fixed on her, raw and desperate, as though by will alone he could bridge the distance between them.

"Of course," a voice drawled, smooth and sharp as glass. "The two of you."

Kringle stepped through the door with a gleaming smile, every inch the radiant king. His crown glittered with frost. He wore his festive red robe with golden threads shimmering like a net woven from light itself, bells chiming softly at the hem. His blue eyes twinkled with calculated warmth, but his grin was a predator's.

"Well, well. My wayward elf and my disgraced brother." His gaze flicked between them, dripping with mockery as he stood on the dais. "Touching, truly. I should have known you'd find each other. Broken things attract."

Krampus snarled, but the chains yanked him back, sparks hissing.

"Careful," Kringle sang. "You'll blister more than your pride."

Elowen glared at him. "Let him go. He's not your prisoner."

Kringle laughed, head tilting as if she were a fool making a sweet joke. "Not my prisoner? Dear heart, he's been mine since the day mortals first learned to fear him." He walked closer, the faint chime of bells marking each step. His gaze sharpened. "I should have silenced your song when I had the chance."

"You can't kill me," she spat. "You need me. You're losing control of the List and you know it."

For a flicker of a moment, his smile faltered. Then he leaned down, close enough she could smell the cloying sweetness of peppermint and spiced wine on his breath.

"So, you think you're clever? And what, your gray means anything? You're just a useless, burnt-out bulb on a string of lights."

The golden runes on the walls pulsed in rhythm with his words, the chamber humming like a great clock winding tight.

Then...

DONG.

The sound reverberated through the marble like a thunderclap.

As the sun dipped low, a chill filled the chamber, the light fading as torches roared to life.

Elowen's stomach dropped. The first bell of the end of the year.

Kringle's smile spread wider, stretching like ice cracking across a pond. He straightened, arms spread to embrace the sound. "Ah. The hour arrives."

"No," Elowen cried, dread curling in her chest.

Kringle turned to Krampus, his eyes glinting with cruel delight. "Do you feel it? The weight of time? The contract you are bound to?"

Krampus bared his teeth. "You bastard—"

The shackles blazed white.

Krampus convulsed, his roar ripping through the chamber as fire and shadow surged across his body. His muscles swelled, his form twisted, horns lengthened, and skin darkened. His eyes bled into pools of scarlet. Smoke poured from his skin as the shackles branded deeper, forcing him into his monstrous shape.

Elowen screamed, straining against her chains. "Stop it! You're killing him!"

Kringle laughed, throwing back his head as the sound of the bells shook the chamber. "Killing him? Oh no. I am reminding him. Reminding the *world* of who he is."

Krampus' roar deepened, shaking the stones. His claws tore at the air, shadows spilling like a storm, wild and furious. His gaze snapped to Elowen, but there was no recognition now, only the monster the stories had promised.

Elowen's breath came fast, panic clawing her chest. She pressed against her chains, desperate, voice breaking: "Krampus! It's me!"

For a heartbeat, something flickered in his red gaze.

But then the shackles shivered with heat, and he lunged forward, chains straining as the monster inside swallowed him whole.

Kringle's laughter filled the chamber, triumphant and cruel. "Behold! The true face of the Naughty List."

The chamber shook with the force of Kringle's laughter.

"Enough," he declared, voice booming like the bells themselves. He turned, eyes gleaming, to the chained monster thrashing against its bonds. "End this blight so we can proceed with the year's work."

With a wave of Kringle's hand, Elowen's shackles released and clattered to the ground.

Krampus' shackles pulsed and, with a crack like thunder, his chains slithered away, falling in molten links to the floor. Krampus lurched forward, no longer the man Elowen knew, but a beast of shadow and night. His horns scraped the ceiling as he rose to full height. His claws glinted like black steel, his body radiating heat and smoke. The air bent around him, distorted by the weight of his presence.

And his eyes. Red, unrecognizing, empty.

"Krampus!" Elowen cried, but his roar swallowed the sound of his name.

He lunged.

Elowen flung herself away, narrowly avoiding his claws as they tore through the pillar, sending stone fragments flying. She scrambled, heart pounding. Wild magic sparked at her fingertips. Frost hissed across the floor in a desperate barrier.

He smashed through it in a single step.

Krampus swung. Elowen raised her hands, a shield of light flickering into place. The impact shattered it like glass, flinging her across the chamber. Her back hit a column with a thud, pain screaming across her spine. Her lungs burned as the air was torn from her.

Vision blurred, she forced herself up, magic trembling in her palms. She raised a storm of frost and flame and hurled it at him. The blast struck his chest, searing smoke curling up from his skin.

He staggered for a moment before roaring and striding toward her again.

Elowen faltered, fear crawling icy fingers through her. She didn't want to hurt him; she knew deep beneath the monster, the man survived. Every strike that landed on him cut her own heart. Tears stung her eyes as she stumbled backward.

He cornered her against a pillar, his shadow looming over her like the end of the world.

"Krampus, stop. Please!"

He didn't. His claw lashed out, wrapping around her throat.

The stone column bit into her spine. Her feet kicked helplessly against the floor as his grip tightened, sharp claws pricking her skin. She clawed at his hand, choking, sobs shaking her.

"Please...it's me!" she croaked, her voice strangled. Her tears spilled, streaking her face, falling down onto the iron band around his wrist.

The teardrop hissed as it struck the shackle.

Something changed.

For a single heartbeat, his red eyes flickered. His chest heaved as he stared down at her, recognition struggling to surface.

"Elowen," he thundered, her name torn from somewhere deep inside.

Her heart clenched tightly. "Yes! It's me!"

But then the shackles pulsed with ember light, white fire searing his flesh. He roared, jerking back as the monster surged again, his grip tightening reflexively.

"No!" she sobbed, voice breaking. She pressed her trembling hand against the shackle, even as it burned her palm raw. Her flesh sizzled, the pain tearing a mottled scream from her throat. But she did not let go.

Her magic flared, wild and desperate, mingling with her tears. Gray bled into the iron, threads of shadow and light weaving together, biting at the runes carved into the metal.

Kringle's voice thundered in the background, furious, commanding: "End it!"

Elowen shut it out. She felt the runes beneath her hand, the ancient bindings, the cruel starlight iron that had chained him for centuries. And she felt something else, something within her tugging, responding, *fighting*.

Do it.

Her tears fell harder, hissing against the iron. Her magic crackled brighter, pushing, unraveling. The shackles shuddered. Runes flared, their pattern twisting, then cracked, spiderwebbing with light.

"Remember," she hissed through the agony. "Please." The lack of air made her head pound, and her body grew weaker.

And with a sound like shattering glass, the first shackle broke. The iron split, falling in two glowing pieces to the floor.

❄ ❄ ❄

The sound of the shackle splitting was small compared to his roar, but it echoed through him like the breaking of the world.

His claw released her. Elowen collapsed to the ground, clutching her bruised throat, coughing, desperate for air.

With a groan, he collapsed onto his knees. For a breath, there was only silence, his silence. The iron no longer seared his left arm, the weight that had been welded to his flesh for centuries gone. He flexed his claws, trembling, as shadow leapt eagerly to answer him. Not pain nor punishment. Power. His own.

It terrified him.

His gaze snapped to Elowen. She was on the ground, struggling for air, her palm blistered raw where she had touched his fire. And it had been *him*, his claws, his fury, that had nearly snuffed her out. The memory of her neck under his grip, her pulse thrashing against his palm, sickened him. He had wanted to stop, had *fought* to stop, but the shackles drove him, forced his body into the monster.

And yet she had touched him, anyway. Burned herself to free him. Wept and bled for him.

He had roared through countless centuries, endured flame, endured iron, endured Kris' yoke. But nothing had ever undone him like the sight of her broken body still reaching for him.

"Elowen," he rasped, and her name clawed his throat. He wanted to cradle her, shield her, bury her in his shadow until nothing could touch her. But he did not dare. He had almost destroyed her. He was still dangerous, still bound. The other shackle seared brighter, fighting the freedom he'd stolen. The monster inside howled, scenting blood, craving to finish what had begun.

Elowen looked at him, her body shaking. He knew each ragged breath was like a blade, a knife in her lungs.

Fury raged inside him, hot as molten iron. Not at her, never at her. At Kris. At the bells that had chained him, the crown that had twisted him, the centuries of obedience beaten into his bones.

But under the fury was something else. Something unfamiliar. When he flexed his freed arm, when the shadow uncoiled at his command, he felt the faintest crack in the surrounding wall. A breath of air he had never tasted.

Freedom.

It was too much. Too dangerous.

If he let go, he would tear this place down. Tear *everything* down. But if he didn't, his brother would.

Kris' fury split the chamber behind him. "What have you done?" he bellowed, his voice shaking the walls.

His head bowed; smoke curled off his horns as he wrestled against the shackle.

Elowen coughed, clutching her scorched hand against her chest, her battered body trembling. Her defiance reached him, even then, her voice hoarse and unbroken: "I'll break every chain you've ever made."

His shadows flared in answer, and he whispered back, to her, to his brother, to the crown: "And I'll tear down the crown that binds them."

❋ ❋ ❋

The chamber trembled as Kringle descended, fury painted across his once-perfect smile. Golden motes flickered around him like dust turned to fireflies. The bells woven into his robe chimed discordantly, a mockery of cheer.

"Without me, you are nothing but a monster. And you—" His gaze speared Elowen, slumped at Krampus' knees. "You meddlesome elf. I should have snuffed you the day you drew gray."

He raised his hand, and the chamber split with sound. Ranks of toy soldiers marched forth, clockwork gears whirring, eyes glowing an eerie crimson. Their candy cane pikes lowered in unison, the clang of their boots a death march.

Krampus growled low in his throat, his freed arm flexing, shadow coiling around his claws like smoke. He hunched before Elowen, chains binding his other wrist.

Kringle laughed, sharp and hollow.

The toy soldiers marched.

Krampus moved like a storm, his massive claws shredding through rows of iron and candy-striped armor. Each strike echoed like thunder, his shadow lashing out and scattering soldiers like brittle ornaments. Elowen forced herself upright, her knees shaking, and flung her magic outward. A soldier froze mid-step, then shattered into glittering shards.

The floor quaked as Kringle raised his arms, his crown blazing brighter. Streams of golden energy arced from the crown, striking down into his pawns. The toy soldiers grew larger, their candy armor hardening, their pikes burning with flame. They charged again, relentless.

Elowen staggered back, her energy faltering. "There's too many—"

Krampus slammed his free hand into the ground, shadows bursting outward in a wave. The nearest soldiers crumpled into dust, but the effort made him stagger, the shackle on his bound arm flaring with searing light. He roared in pain.

Elowen's eyes locked onto the crown, its form pulsing like a beating heart. Each flare drew energy from *her*, from every elf who had ever bent beneath Kringle's rule.

"It's the crown," she croaked.

Krampus snarled, his eyes flicking from her to Kringle. He ran towards his brother, who met him with a crack of golden lightning, a bolt that split the chamber and hurled Elowen off her feet. She slammed onto the stone floor, pain blazing through her ribs. Gasping, she pushed herself up, vision swimming, in time to see Krampus grapple him.

The two titans clashed, shadows and golden fire colliding in bursts that rattled the walls. Kringle moved with unnatural speed, his crown fueling him, every blow sharp and precise. Krampus was stronger, raw power tearing through the air, but one shackle bound him, holding him back.

"You'll always kneel, brother," Kringle said, his crown blazing brighter.

Elowen staggered closer, clutching her scorched hand. Her eyes locked on the crown, and something inside her tugged. Some instinct, a pull of magic and desperation, tore at her. She reached deep, past pain and fear, into the well of power.

"Hold him!" she said.

Krampus snarled, straining against the golden energy writhing around him. With a roar, he slammed Kringle against a shattered column, pinning him. The shackle seared, smoke rising from his arm, but he held fast.

Elowen raised her hand. She aimed for the crown and with a surge, her magic erupted, a gray light mixed with shadow and frost.

Kringle's eyes widened. "No!"

The crown blazed, runes cracking under the assault. For a heartbeat, pure white light filled the chamber as shadow and flame fought against gold.

The crown screamed.

It cracked; tiny shards of gold and frost rained across the chamber like falling stars. The golden fire fizzled, leaving Kringle gasping, his robes in tatters, his hair wild, his power sputtering.

Krampus staggered, his chest heaving, eyes blazing as the shackle on his arm flickered.

Elowen collapsed to her knees, her body wracked with pain and exhaustion, magic sputtering. She felt the shards of the crown's power fizzle.

Kringle fell to the ground, clutching his crown. His eyes burned with hatred as he rasped, "You'll regret this."

Krampus loomed over him, shadow curling from his claws. His voice was low, trembling with fury barely restrained. "No. No more."

❄ ❄ ❄

Elowen's throat burned with every breath. The taste of ash and copper lingered on her tongue. Her hands, raw and blistered, trembled as she clutched at the torn remnants of her uniform. The stone beneath her shook with every groan of Kringle Central, the great palace-workshop reeling from the cracking of its crown.

And across from her, half-wreathed in smoke, stood Krampus. His muscles strained, shadows twisted violently from him, but the iron burned, shackling not only his body but his soul. His monstrous form haunted him, his eyes flashing between scarlet fire and fleeting glimpses of familiar amber. He staggered forward, half in control, claws flexing as if aching to rend the world apart.

"Elowen," he thundered, voice broken. Her name sounded

more like a growl than a plea. "Go."

She staggered toward him, refusing to heed the command. Her entire body screamed in pain. Her ribs ached from where he had thrown her, and her throat bore the marks of his claw; but, she would not abandon him. "No."

The ruined throne room rang with laughter.

Kringle, though reeling, though bleeding from where the crown had cut against his brow, staggered and leaned against the shattered column, bells tinkling faintly as his breath wheezed in and out. His pristine robe was torn, his face streaked with blood, but his eyes blazed with cold authority.

"Run, little elf," he called, his voice echoing through the fractured chamber. "Run. The List endures. The song endures. And when you've burned yourself out, when the shadows consume you, I will be here."

He lifted one hand, and the ground shuddered. From the wreckage of splintered toy parts and broken candy contraptions, shapes rose. Gears whirred, eyes of painted porcelain glowed red, limbs stitched together from dolls and twisted clockwork. Soldiers of junk and broken joy, their tinny laughter curdling into shrieks as they lurched to life.

One seized mid-motion, its candy cane spine snapping with a hollow crack. Another convulsed, sparks sputtering from its eyes before it collapsed in a twitching heap. The crown's fracture bled through the army; the cheer he commanded faltered, stuttering like a carol sung off-key.

Kringle's smile flickered. His lip curled, fury cutting through the mask. "Defects," he hissed. "False notes in my song."

He raised his hand again, forcing the remaining soldiers to shamble forward in jerks and stutters, like broken marionettes.

Elowen's stomach turned. Even weakened, Kringle commanded creation.

"Go!" Krampus roared. He swung his free arm, and a shadow tore through the nearest abomination, ripping it in half with a screech of grinding gears. But the act cost him; the remaining shackle burned brighter, searing into his wrist. He staggered, choking on the smoke.

Elowen grabbed his arm, her hand small against the monstrous bulk. "The Black Door! Quick!"

His red eyes flickered again, struggling. He snarled, shadows choking in his throat, but nodded.

Together, they left the broken throne room, shadows and steam coiling behind them. Kringle watched with a sneer, making no move to follow, only lifting his hand to summon more monstrosities from the wreckage.

CHAPTER SEVENTEEN

The candy cane halls of Kringle Central twisted into a nightmare. Glittering sugar dust swirled under peppermint pillars; strings of twinkling lights flickered, casting fractured shadows across elves bent to their work. Mechanical rhythms of toy drums and hammering filled the air, but every hollow gaze followed them, eyes flickering with fear and confusion.

Elowen dragged herself forward, bruised and raw, leaning on Krampus' broad shoulder. The shackle on his arm burned, smoke curling. His growls rumbled through the corridor, shadows flaring from his claws, tearing at toy soldiers and marionettes with fractured porcelain faces.

"We can stop," whispered a soft voice. Elowen glanced at an elf hunched over a tiny doll, needle flying through the cloth. Her hands paused, and she stared at Elowen, white hair shifting from her eyes.

"Mirabel," hissed the elf beside her. "You'll get us in trouble."

"Yes!" Elowen cried. "You can fight it!"

Another elf dropped a hammer, staring openly at Krampus' towering form, his chains sizzling. But before he could speak, a supervisor's scowl pressed the hammer back into his hand, and the rhythm of pounding resumed.

Even under Kringle's spell, a spark of defiance lingered in Mirabel's eyes. "But it isn't right—"

A megaphone blared in the air.

Elowen's heart cracked. Even without the crown, they were bound. They were puppets, enslaved not by iron but by belief.

The corridor shook. Marionette dolls dropped from strings, claws snapping. Enchanted toy drums hovered, beating a war rhythm. Elowen raised a trembling hand, forcing frost-laced sparks forward. Several dolls shattered into splinters, glittering like broken candy.

Krampus bent to scoop her up, chest heaving, shackle glowing hotter with every step. His monstrous form staggered, torn between obedience and rebellion. Elowen's vision swam as she clung to him, teeth gritted, breath ragged.

"The door," she gasped. "We have to get to the square."

He roared, barreling through the tide of clockwork horrors, shadows ripping them apart. The shackle flared brighter, trying to drag him under. His free hand quivered mid-swing, eyes dimming, control clawing at him.

"Elowen…" he snarled. "I can't—"

"No," she hissed, tears stinging. Her palm pressed against the burning chain. Flesh blistered, searing agony stabbing her bones, but her magic surged, wrapping around the runes. Sparks hissed, the chain slackened, the glow dimmed. Krampus roared, shadows erupting in a wave that shredded the remaining horde.

She collapsed against him, her body weak and bloody. His chest heaved as he caught her, face twisted with pain and relief. Then, with a bellow that shook the peppermint pillars, he charged forward.

❊ ❊ ❊

The square yawned ahead, vast and alive with frenzy. Elves swarmed like ants around towering reindeer stalls. Sleigh runners were polished, bells fastened to bridles, and gifts stacked in endless pyramids. The air stank of sweat, sugar, and fear.

Krampus' vision swam, red edging his sight. The shackle dragged at him like a leash, each step a battle against submission. The crown screamed in his skull: *Obey. Kneel.* The List demanded fulfillment. He fought them with every shred of will, his shadows snarling against the invisible yoke.

Beside him, Elowen leaned on his arm, fragile and furious, her blistered hand still smoking from where she had dared to touch his fire. She should have been ash. She should have fled. Yet she was here, small body braced against his, leading him through the storm.

He hated himself for wanting her strength. He hated the shackle for reminding him what he was. But most of all, he hated the elves' hollow stares. Bent backs, bloody fingers, lips mouthing Kris' carols like prayers. Their chains weren't metal; they were faith.

When Elowen shouted for them to rise, a spark flickered. He saw *defiance*.

He bared his teeth. If he burned, he would burn for that spark.

❄ ❄ ❄

A supervisor shrieked for the elves to clear the square. One panicked worker bolted, dragging a harnessed reindeer by its bridle. The beast snorted clouds of white into the air.

Elowen's eyes fixed on it.

"That," she rasped.

He didn't understand until she tore herself from him and lunged. The elf yelped as she shoved him aside, seizing the reins with blistered hands. The reindeer reared, hooves striking sparks from the cobblestones.

Krampus roared, shadows lashing back a line of toy soldiers as Elowen swung herself up onto the beast's back. Her silhouette cut against the clock tower, red hair wild, gray sparks curling from her hands into the frosted air. An outlaw saint astride a beast of winter.

The square erupted with elves screaming, soldiers charging, and drums pounding war.

But they were already moving.

The reindeer thundered across the square, Krampus charging beside, his shadows tearing a path while Elowen hurled frost-fire bolts into the ranks. Ice shattered lacquered faces, steam curled from burning gears. Above, the clock tower bell tolled the second hour, a dirge and a promise.

At last, the Black Door. Twisted candy canes, horns spiraling atop, wood charred and cracked.

Krampus held Elowen onto the reindeer. "Hold on."

"Never stopped," she croaked.

The reindeer plunged forward, hooves striking sparks, and with a final shadow-scorched surge, they broke through the last of the horde. Krampus slammed his hand against the door and thrust in the runes for his home. It shrieked open, spiraling with shadow and smoke. Together, battered, scorched, and still burning from battle, they ran through.

❄ ❄ ❄

The throne room lay in ruin, its sugar pillars cracked, its candy cane arches snapped and blackened by smoke. Golden threads of Kringle's robe hung in tatters, his once-pristine gloves seared with ash and blood. His crown lay cracked in his hands, glinting in the dying firelight.

Kringle knelt in the rubble, chest heaving, every breath a wheeze. Then slowly he stood. His body trembled, but his eyes burned with icy fire. He looked at his crown and sneered.

"A single crack does not break the carol. I'll mend it, and it will ring sweeter than before." He brushed the dust off his lapel as if minor soot from a chimney.

The great red robe he wore sagged from his shoulders, threadbare, ash-stained. He tore it off with a snarl, golden embroidery ripping with a harsh sound. An elf rushed into the chamber, wide-eyed and trembling, a new robe clutched in his arms. Kringle snatched it without another word and fastened it across his shoulders. His hands smoothed the velvet as though nothing had happened, as though the surrounding ruin was only a staging ground for his next ascent.

The grand doors groaned as Kringle strode onto the balcony, his boots grinding over shattered glass and broken toys. Below, the square stretched wide, thousands of elves bent to their labor below. Hammers struck, saws shrieked, and wrapping paper snapped under frantic hands. Their half-sung carols stuttered into silence the instant he cleared his throat.

Every head tilted up. Every tool stilled.

Kringle spread his arms, his voice cutting through the frost like a bell: "My children."

The word rippled through the crowd. Some whispered it back, reverent, fearful.

"The crown may falter," he called, his robe flaring in the wind, "the halls may tremble, but the List remains. It *must* remain."

Their voices echoed: *"The List must remain!"*

Kringle's eyes gleamed. He stepped forward, his presence swelling to fill the square. "Without the List, what are we?"

The elves: *"Nothing."*

"Without the List, what is the world?"

"Nothing!"

His smile split wide, cruel and shining. "We are the makers of wonder!"

"Wonder!"

"The guardians of cheer!"

"Cheer!"

"The sugar that scalds the wicked!"

"Burn the wicked!"

The square shook with their brittle chant, voices whipped into a frenzy. Kringle lifted his hands higher, as though conducting the very sound.

"The year will end as it always has," he thundered. "Together we will finish the work. Gifts will be delivered. And when dawn comes—"

The elves erupted, their voices a single, hollow roar: "*All will kneel to the carol!*" Cheers, whistles, clanging of tools against benches. Their song rose, brittle and hollow, but deafening all the same.

Kringle closed his eyes, drinking in the din as though it were music. For a moment, he stood radiant in the ruin, the illusion of adoration crashing over him like a tide. Then, as quickly as it came, his smile withered. He turned from the balcony, his voice dropping low and cold as he addressed the trembling elf at his side.

"Send for my smiths to mend the crown." His fingers curled into a fist. "I will enforce the List until every voice sings in tune...or is silenced."

CHAPTER EIGHTEEN

The reindeer's hooves struck sparks across the frost-bitten stone in Krampus' realm. The beast bellowed, muscles lathered with sweat and steam, antlers tossing as if it too resisted the leash of Kringle's call.

Krampus followed, staggering through behind Elowen, half-monster form crashing down like a storm. His claws raked the ground, shadows streaming behind him. The portal shrieked shut with a crack like bone breaking; the sound echoed until only silence remained.

Snow and ash churned under them. The air reeked of soot and blood. Elowen reined the beast in. Gone were the clawing forests and whispering shadows. The ground was trampled, gouged, littered with broken toy soldiers. Peppermint barricades lay shattered, bleeding their sticky stripes into the snow.

She dropped from the saddle and fell into the drift to clutch a fistful of snow, as if she could mend the ruin with her bare hands.

Krampus staggered beside her. His eyes burned red, shadows writhing. The destruction before him was more than ash; it was his home, desecrated. A guttural groan tore from his throat, grief raw as rage.

He clawed at his shackle, yanking until sparks scorched his flesh. The iron only burned hotter. His roar cracked the night, shadows lashing outward like whips.

"Stop!" Elowen lurched to him, seizing his arm. Her skin blistered, but she refused to release him. "Krampus, look at me!"

His head snapped toward her, eyes wild, chest trembling with restraint. His gaze softened to embers instead of flame.

"You don't have to obey," she pleaded, tears streaking her cheeks, hissing on the iron. "You are not his monster."

The chains pulsed, but she pressed closer, her magic sputtering, wrapping the runes with gray fire. The darkness thrashed, but it recoiled from her touch.

Her words broke on the storm. "You are mine."

Something shifted. The light stuttered. The shackle strained but did not break, its grip weakened by her defiance, her gray. Krampus sagged forward, claws gouging trenches in the snow, until his forehead nearly touched hers.

She held him, trembling, her magic guttering like a candle but refusing to die.

❋ ❋ ❋

The storm came without warning, howling down from the mountains, gnashing with sleet and snow. Elowen tugged the reindeer forward, Krampus staggering at her side, his massive form slowed by exhaustion and shadow. The beast plunged through drifts, antlers glittering with frost, until the jagged mouth of a cavern yawned open in the rock.

"Here," she gasped. Her lungs burned, vision swimming. "Inside!"

He half-fell into the hollow, his bulk crashing against the cavern wall, the shadows bending with him, horns scraping stone. Elowen slid down beside him, cloak drawn tight against the bitter air. The reindeer snorted and shook. Steam rose from its flanks as it settled near the cavern mouth like a sentinel.

Krampus slumped to his knees, breath sawing through his chest, steam rising in ragged bursts. His monstrous form clung to him: horns sharp, claws black as ink, his body thrumming with residual shadow. The lone shackle glowed red, the metal searing against his flesh. He clenched his fist, but it shook as though every nerve rebelled.

Elowen dropped beside him and caught his arm. "Stop."

He gave a humorless huff, head bowing so that his horns grazed the stone floor. "Tear myself apart or let it claim me. That's all there is."

"That's not true," Elowen said, her voice breaking. She reached for his wrist, ignoring the heat. Her palm hovered above the brand seared into his skin. "You lasted longer this time. You fought it."

His jaw clenched, shadows coiling tight around his shoulders. His voice was a rasp, scraped raw by anger and something more fragile beneath. "You don't understand. I never wanted this. Never wanted to rule the Naughty." He slammed his chained fist against the stone, sparks scattering. The cavern shuddered, and the reindeer shook its head. "Kris can still force me." He lifted the shackle, its runes smoldering. "Drag me into his image of a monster."

Elowen's heart twisted. She watched him shake, not from rage, but from terror.

"I don't know how long I have," he admitted, voice dropping. "This…this is the longest I've ever lasted. Next time—" His eyes flashed red for a moment, then dimmed. "Next time, I may not come back."

Elowen pressed closer, ignoring the scorch of the iron. "Then we'll make sure there isn't a next time," she said. "You're not a monster in chains, Krampus. You're more than that."

He gave a dry laugh, bitter, but she caught the way his shoulders eased by a fraction. "More? Look at me."

She tilted her head, lips quirking despite the ache in her chest. "Monsters don't let someone use their lap as a pillow," she said. "I'd say you've already failed in the role."

His shackle burned, but he made no move to resist as Elowen knelt beside him.

"Let me try again," she said. Her hands hovered over the metal, feeling its heat radiate like fire against her skin. Closing her eyes, she felt her magic flicker and let it flow. She searched the runes, probing, coaxing the metal's energy to dull, to cool, to ease his pain without breaking the wards. Sparks flickered but died, leaving a warm hum against the chains.

Krampus exhaled sharply, muscles relaxing as the tension eased. Shadows coiled and twined around her, reaching but hesitant. "You're impossible," he muttered, a rasp of a laugh that trembled with relief.

"You're the one who keeps insisting on fighting everything," she said. Her touch was slow, deliberate, coaxing strength from him in ways words could not.

He flinched, but leaned into her hand. "And yet you touch me, even knowing what I am...what I did to you." His voice was rough, broken.

"You're not just this," she whispered. "I see you. That's enough."

He stared at her, caught between disbelief and something warmer flickering in his eyes. Then, a shadow crossed his gaze. "Why? Why do you keep fighting for them? For mortals who don't know you. Elves who obey him. For a world that hates me?"

She paused, letting the question hang. Her hands smoothed over the curve of his shoulder. "Because even a world that's cruel can change," she said finally. "Because every act of care, every choice we make...it matters, even if they don't see it. I'll fight for them because it matters. And I fight for you because I do."

Krampus let out a slow breath, his darkness coiling closer to her, seeking comfort they couldn't reach.

For a long moment, silence filled the hollow. Then, she asked, "Do you remember life before...this? Before the chains, before the List."

"I do," he said, gaze dropping to the stone beneath them. "With Kris...and my mother. Before mortals' worship, before they demanded gifts and punishment became my burden...the world was simpler. The elves were kind. I remember running through the snow untouched by fear, laughter in the forests that smelled of pine and hearth smoke. I remember...love. Family. And I remember thinking the world was endless and full of promise."

Elowen's hand slid to cup his cheek, careful even as the shadows twitched toward her. "You *can* have that again," she said. "Not the chains, not the List, but you, us. Isn't that worth fighting for?"

He leaned into her touch, the monstrous edge of him softening, his shadows easing in reluctant obedience. The heat of his body, the weight of his power, and the tremor of his words pressed against her.

"I'd like that," he murmured.

Elowen brushed her forehead against his, closing her eyes. Her magic flickered across her hands, soothing the ache in his muscles, and easing the shackle's pull.

"Elowen...I..." His voice was rough, almost lost to exhaustion, but threaded with something fragile. "Thank you."

"For what?" she asked.

"For letting me be more than a monster."

❄ ❄ ❄

Far away, the bells of Kringle Central tolled the hour.

Kringle sat upon his throne, his red robe shimmering in the torchlight, golden embroidery catching the gleam like captured fire. Below him, the clang of hammers echoed as smiths worked feverishly in the night. On their anvil lay the cracked crown, now being repaired with molten gold, frost, and holly. Strands of stolen elf magic twisted into its form.

A cage rattled at the chamber's edge. Inside, the last Choir trembled, bound by silver and shadow. Her voice, raw and radiant, poured unwillingly from her lips, notes plucked and stitched into the crown by Kringle's cruel hand. With a flick of his wrist, the spell of extraction snapped her spirits. Light flared from her chest as the song was ripped from her, each note screaming in agony before she faded forever. The crown drank greedily, golden veins glowing, each ember of magic a stolen life.

The air thickened with iron, peppermint, and sacrifice. A single note, brighter than the rest, hummed along the crown's edge, sparking with new, terrible power. It pulsed, sending tremors across the throne room, the very walls vibrating with the sound of obedience yet unborn.

Kringle leaned forward, elbows on his knees, eyes cold and bright as he watched the forging of the crown. "Easier than a trip to that old Forger," he muttered.

One trembling elf presented a scroll. Kringle snatched it, scanned quickly, then dismissed the attendant with a flick of his hand. "Send word to every battalion," he commanded. "Sweep the valleys, the forests, the caverns. Bring them both to me."

An elf stammered. "They'll resist—"

"Then silence them." His smile curved cruel. "The carol will not falter. The List must endure."

From the tall windows, the chiming of bells spread across Kringle Central. Below, the elves sang brittle cheer, their song stitched into the crown, hollow but deafening. Kringle lifted his chin, as though the false harmony proved his dominion. The circlet pulsed, veins of gold flaring with stolen light, the first spark of new dominion.

"Soon," he whispered. "The world will kneel to the song."

❈ ❈ ❈

The cavern gave them little shelter, only a brief reprieve from the storm's bite. Snow sifted through the cracks overhead, settling in glittering drifts across the black stone. Krampus leaned against the wall, shoulders heaving. Elowen crouched opposite, flexing her fingers against her damp uniform, trying to steady her breath.

Far beyond the wall, bells tolled. One, then another, rolled in hollow waves across the frozen world. She counted them, her stomach knotting with each chime. Seven bells. A warning. A countdown. A chain winding tighter around Krampus' throat.

He heard it too. His head lifted toward the sound, horns glinting faintly in the frost light. Shadows twitched restlessly along his frame.

"We can't stay," she whispered. "Every hour we wait is a risk he'll find us."

Krampus' gaze slid back to her, haunted fire in his eyes. "You don't understand, little snow. He doesn't need to hunt me. The List finds me."

Her brows furrowed. "How?"

His voice dropped, rough as gravel. "The Ledger holds the List within it. I…" He raised his shackled arm. The runes glowed faintly, stirred by the bells. "…bear the Naughty. Every misdeed, every name, delivered through me. That is how he binds me."

Elowen's heart clenched. "So the shackles are the chain…and the List is the lock."

His laugh was bitter, a rasp in the cold air. "And I am the key, whether or not I wish it."

She leaned forward, heart hammering. "Is that why you gave me the archive? So I could do what you can't?"

His eyes flicked to hers. "I cannot change a single name. But you, with your gray, can spare them from punishment. You can unmake the whip before it falls."

Her chest tightened as determination sparked in her chest, despite the ache in her bones. "Then take me to it."

Krampus recoiled, eyes narrowing. "You don't know what you're asking. The Master List realm is dangerous. Even I dare not enter. It was never meant for mortal eyes."

"But I'm not mortal." Her voice came steadier than she felt. "And Kringle doesn't deserve to guard it. If there's a chance…" she swallowed, glancing toward the mouth of the cavern where snow still howled, "…we have to take it."

For a long moment he said nothing, only the storm breathing around them. Then he groaned, a sound weighted with dread. "If the twelfth bell finishes...and I am not...I don't know what will happen."

Elowen's stomach turned to ice. When dawn shone upon the world of mortals, his would end.

Krampus' shadow stirred close, heavy as the storm outside. His last words rumbled like thunder between them: "So be it."

CHAPTER NINETEEN

Elowen and Krampus stumbled into the dark with the first crack of light threatening on the horizon. The storm had broken, but the landscape bore its scars: trees snapped into splinters, ridges carved into jagged peaks, snow churned into pits by marching armies.

She sat astride the stolen reindeer, its flanks still streaked with frost, its antlers rimmed with ice. The beast snorted, tossing its head, but obeyed her hand on the reins. Beside her, Krampus staggered forward, stride uneven, one claw dragging through the snow. She sobbed. The next dawn could be his last. His monstrous form flickered. Horns glinted, shadows caught between man and nightmare. The shackle blazed, whispering obedience into his bones.

Elowen leaned low over the saddle. "Stay with me," she whispered. Her magic sparked at her fingertips, refusing to die.

A horn split the air.

From behind a ridge, a line of toy soldiers marched, steel glinting under candy cane enamel, elves in crimson cloaks flanking them, crossbows ready.

"They've found us," Elowen cried.

Krampus' lips peeled back in a snarl, shadows bristling.

Peppermint arrows hissed through the air. Krampus flung up his chained arm; shadow lashed outward, scattering bolts into snow. Elowen raised her hand, frost sparking, and a soldier froze mid-charge, gears locking before Krampus' claw smashed it to shards. She wheeled her mount, guiding the reindeer into the melee, its hooves striking sparks as it kicked another doll to splinters.

But then the valley shifted.

A deep, impossible song rose, threading through the air, commanding, absolute.

Kringle.

He crested the horizon astride a war-reindeer massive as a stag, its hide sheathed in steel and holly-plate, eyes burning with spell fire. The newly reforged crown glowed on his brow, veins of gold pulsing with stolen light. The melody poured from him, a carol sharpened into a weapon, cutting through the valley with the weight of dominion.

Every elf's eyes glazed. Every soldier's gears locked into perfect rhythm.

Elowen doubled over, clutching her head. Obedience flooded her thoughts: warmth, joy, cheer. A suffocating mirage that smothered her will. She swayed in the saddle, nearly falling.

Krampus snarled, shadows flaring around her shoulders. "Fight it, Elowen!"

She gritted her teeth, forcing frost and fire to spark from her palms. The blast shoved the melody back for a heartbeat, enough to breathe. But Krampus' shackle blazed brighter, pulling him toward the song. His form trembled, torn between chains and rebellion.

"We can't fight them all," he rasped. "We won't make it to the castle. To the Master List door."

He seized her reins, dragging her mount toward the ridge. At its crest, he dropped to one knee, claw etching runes into the stone. Frost and shadow flared, a circle forming beneath his hand.

The crown's song swelled, pressing harder. Soldiers advanced, arrows glinting.

"Open, damn you," Krampus bellowed, shadows straining

against the portal. Sparks danced, runes shuddering but refusing to hold.

Elowen slid from the saddle, dropping to her knees beside him, her hand pressing over his. "Help him," she whispered, willing her magic to blend with his.

"I command you, as a keeper of the List," he snapped.

The circle stuttered, then tore open, a jagged maw of swirling frost and darkness, edges hissing like teeth grinding against bone.

A peppermint arrow sliced toward them.

Krampus froze, the shackle tugging him back, crown-song commanding.

Elowen shoved him forward with every ounce of strength left in her.

"Go!" she screamed.

The arrow struck her shoulder. Hot pain flooded her chest. Crimson spilled across her uniform. Krampus roared, and caught her as they fell together into the portal, shadows snapping shut around them.

Behind them, the reindeer reared and screamed, bolts glancing from its antlers as the portal sealed.

Kringle rode triumphant, crown blazing, his melody rolling across the valley like a hymn of chains.

❄ ❄ ❄

Elowen collapsed hard onto slick black stone, the world spinning. Pain flared in her shoulder, warm and searing where the arrow had pierced. Her lungs fought for breath. The air here wasn't air at all. It was cold, metallic, laced with a bitter tang that scraped down her throat. She coughed, scrambled onto her knees, and pressed her palm to the wound. The floor pulsed beneath her, like a heartbeat buried deep in the rock.

A low growl reverberated beside her. Krampus staggered upright, shadow rippling along his form, eyes blazing. The shackle glowed, runes pulsing in time with the cavern floor, tugging at him, urging obedience.

Elowen's gaze rose, air catching in her throat. The sky wasn't sky at all. Endless parchment stretched overhead, inked with names that writhed and shifted with life. Scrolls unrolled and folded in on themselves, quills of light scratching furiously across them. The sound echoed like endless thunder, relentless, merciless.

Her stomach knotted.

Krampus followed her gaze, jaw tightening, horns glinting in the eerie ink-light. "The Master List realm."

Elowen grimaced and reached a hand toward the arrow.

He gently shoved her hand away. "No," he rasped. He exhaled sharply and grasped the shaft, pulling it free. Her scream shook the cavern. Blood ran down her arm, bright red against pale skin, the stone beneath them vibrating in resonance with her pain.

"Krampus—" she gasped, voice weak.

He waved a hand, staggering slightly, clutching her shoulder to stifle the bleeding. "I guess I didn't realize how dangerous it would be to be around you, little snow," he half chuckled.

After a moment, he moved, supporting her as they began walking. There was no path, only jagged ridges of stone jutting from a sea of black mist. With each step, they marched deeper into the gloom; the ground beneath them hummed with whispered names. Elowen caught fragments. Voices of children, laughter, and screams flitted through her mind in a haunting, endless litany.

After some time, she realized she was trembling. Her magic flickered uncontrollably at her fingertips, sparking frost, then fire, then fading to nothing. Pain flared in her shoulder. Her thoughts tangled. Every memory of her past, her exile, Kringle's mockery, even Krampus' touch, bled together, too bright, too sharp.

"Elowen."

She jerked her head up. Krampus leaned close, his claws

curling around her elbow. His touch grounded her for a moment, though the shackle at his wrist burned bright, shadows writhing hungrily across his arm. His eyes glowed scarlet, but behind them flickered something more fragile.

"You feel it too?" she asked.

He nodded, jaw tight. "This realm devours the longer you stay. Madness first. Then hunger. Then nothing."

She forced her chin up. "Then we have to hurry. We find it. We free you."

They pressed onward.

The deeper they went, the worse it became. Mist clutched at their ankles, whispering in familiar voices. Elowen stumbled more than once, caught between hallucinations. Klaussen handed her stacks of metrics, Kringle's laughter sneered in her ear, and children cried.

Krampus fought his own battle. She saw it in the way his body trembled, his form swelling with every step. The shackle pulsed violently, shadows bursting off him like smoke. He reeled, claws sinking into the stone as his face twisted into a snarl.

Elowen grabbed his wrist, ignoring the burn of the glowing iron. "Stay with me," she begged.

His head snapped toward her, his blood-red eyes blazing, and yet, her voice cut through the heavy fog. His shoulders eased. He exhaled a ragged breath and muttered, "Your voice."

At last, they crested a ridge and saw it: a monolith rose from the mist, taller than any castle, wider than any mountain. Its surface was black stone, carved with endless runes, each glowing faintly with names that shifted and vanished. At its base burned a single brazier, its flame green and cold.

"The Ledger, the heart of the Master List," Krampus said, reverent and hollow.

Elowen's knees nearly buckled. Her body screamed for rest, her magic crackled and sputtered, but her heart pounded with urgency. She could feel her mind bending. She had to hurry. Her feet stumbled beneath her, each step heavier than the last.

By the time they reached the brazier, her vision was blurring. Her breaths came ragged, words slurred in her mind. "It's…it's beautiful."

"No." Krampus' voice was a growl, close at her ear. He caught her by the shoulders, steadying her as her legs gave out. "Don't look too long."

Her eyes lifted anyway. The runes shimmered, rearranging. For one terrifying moment, she saw her own name scrawled across the surface. Then it vanished.

Her head dropped, her body trembling violently. Her mind did not feel like her own. She pressed her forehead into his chest, clinging to him. "Krampus. I can't—"

"You can," he said, arms caging her in, shackle burning against her. His own shadow writhed, threatening to consume them both. "I won't let this place have you."

His words cut through her haze. She blinked up at him, searching his face as it swam before her. He was fighting, his body half lost to the monster, claws twitching as if he longed to tear her apart. Yet his eyes, even blazing red, held her.

They were both being devoured by madness.

"Elowen," he bit out, his voice breaking. "Say something. Anything. I need to hear your voice."

Her breath trembled. She lifted her hand and pressed her palm to his burning shackle. Pain seared her skin, but she held on, her magic struggling to ease his pain. "Stay. Stay with me."

He shuddered, his body jerking, torn between two worlds. His forehead dropped against hers, their breaths mingling. "If I fall…you run."

"I won't," she cried, tears burning her eyes. "You stay. I stay."

The mist howled around them, and the stone monolith pulsed, runes shifting like a thousand watching eyes. The brazier's green fire flared higher, casting their shadows monstrously against the stone.

Elowen's magic tangled with his shadows, gray and dark swirling together. For a heartbeat, the mist recoiled.

They clung to each other, trembling, caught between ruin and salvation.

And the Ledger watched.

Elowen laughed.

The sound rang strangely in the cavern, too loud, too sharp, bubbling from her chest like water from a cracked spring. She pressed her palms to the slick stone floor and cackled until her ribs ached. Thick shadows coiled tighter around her and Krampus, curling and snapping like beasts with a mind of their own.

"Do you see it?" she cried, whirling on him, her braids wild, her cheeks streaked with tears. "All the running, Krampus, all the snowflaking portals, all the chasing! Through teeth and claws, through songs that cut like knives, through fire and frost and arrows. And here I am! Here I am!"

Her voice pitched higher, the laughter bubbling again until it broke into a sob. She slapped her hand against the ground and rose, teetering, her limbs trembling with exhaustion and something fevered.

Krampus growled low, the sound buried deep in his chest. He could hardly make sense of her words, could barely hear her over the roar of shadows in his skull. But he clung to the sound of her voice, latching onto every syllable as though it were a rope in the dark.

"Elowen..." His voice barked raw, his claws dragging furrows into the stone as he strained against the shackle. The iron burned, and smoke rose from his flesh. "Keep talking..."

She spun to face him, eyes bright with something akin to madness. "Do you remember the atrium?"

The shackle flared, runes glowing blindingly as if the word itself burned through him. He convulsed, a guttural roar tearing from his chest.

Her lips curved into a wild smile. She stumbled toward him, dropped to her knees, and caught his face in her trembling hands. She kissed him hard, desperate, full of madness and ache. His lips tasted of salt, of tears, of fire. When she pulled away, she laughed again; the sound shivered down the cavern walls.

"And you should have seen it," she laughed, staggering back toward the towering monolith of the Ledger. Her fingers dragged across the surface, runes sparking and shivering at her touch. "The being. The one who unlocked this—" She flicked her fingers, and gray sparks hissed in the gloom. "Unlocked it all, filled me whole. And now it's waking."

Krampus froze, horror etching through the shadows writhing around him. He dragged himself forward, half crawling, half clawing against the pull of the shackle. "Elowen. What being? What did you *do*?" His voice cracked, torn between desperation and fear.

Her palm flattened against the Ledger, her head thrown back, a mad smile splitting her face. "It judged me, Krampus. Exactly like this." The runes shifted beneath her skin, responding, flaring bright as though tasting her magic. The stone vibrated under her touch, voices whispering, names screaming. Her body jolted. Runes crawled up her arm, her neck, her face. She saw herself reflected in the stone. Not Elowen, not an elf at all, but a shape made of raw script and cinders.

Krampus lunged forward, the shackle burning, tearing smoke from his flesh. "Get away from it! It will consume you!"

She pressed harder, her laughter dissolving into a cry as tears streamed down her face. "And now. Now it judges me again."

Her gray lightning scorched the ground beneath them. Krampus reeled back, his own shadows recoiling as if afraid of hers.

The Ledger blazed, runes shattering into pure white, bright as a supernova.

And then…silence.

Her body vanished, name and form ripped into the stone.

Krampus howled, the sound shaking the parchment sky, as green fire guttered and flared, his shadows twisting higher than the monolith itself.

Elowen was gone. Swallowed whole by the Ledger.

❇ ❇ ❇

* * *

Inside the Ledger, she floated.

Her body dissolved into gray motes as the void carried her. Around her, endless rivers of names cascaded like waterfalls of light, tumbling into infinity. Every name she had ever coded, every name ever whispered into existence, scrolled and spiraled and dissolved into the next.

And then came the voice.

Worthy.

The sound was thought, pressed into her skull until her teeth rattled.

You touched the Ledger. You awakened it. Will you wear the crown?

Elowen clutched her head, hair fanning out into the void. Her laughter came again, but weaker now, cracked. "The crown? You...you mean the parasite's leash. The one that hollowed Kringle, the one that chained Krampus?"

The crown is the instrument. You, the hand. You will bring order. Naughty and Nice. The world bends only when bound. Mortals must be judged. Without judgment, they devour themselves.

Her eyes burned as names whipped past; some she recognized, most she didn't. Her hands trembled as she reached into the river, brushing letters that seared her fingertips. "You feed," she said. "You feed on belief. On obedience. You consume kings, you consume elves. You control."

Mortals are corrupt. Elves are corrupt. Without binary, there is chaos. Without the binary, there is ruin.

Elowen's lips curled into a wild grin. Her voice cracked as she screamed into the void, "And what do you call enslaving a race, then? What do you call chaining them? Mortals may be ruined, but it's you! You've twisted the rules, poisoned the balance, eaten the joy from it all."

The Ledger pulsed violently. The river of names swirled faster, whipping into a storm.

You defy me! You deny the truth. You will submit, or I will consume you.

White fire lashed out, striking her chest; pain tore through her ribs, hot and endless. She screamed, body writhing as her magic sputtered like a candle.

Her thoughts blurred, but she clung to one thing. One thread. "I already changed it," she bit out. "I've been changing the List from the outside. A name here, a name there. I unmade your binary with *gray*."

The Ledger shuddered. Its runes pulsed, frantic, trying to search, to trace her tampering.

And Elowen laughed.

Her gray magic erupted from her chest, a chaotic, uncontrollable surge that felt like a storm within her. It threaded through the rivers of names, streaking like veins of ash through gold. It seeped into the runes, staining them, infecting them, breaking them.

"Who are we to assign fate? To rewrite morality? No more Naughty. No more Nice," she hissed, voice breaking. "Only truth. Our fate is our own."

The Ledger screamed. A thousand names cried out at once, shrieking through her bones. White light cracked, fissures spreading across its endless surface.

With a violent lurch, it spat her out.

❊ ❊ ❊

Elowen slammed back into the Master List realm like a star hurled from the heavens.

Her body crashed against Krampus' chest with a bone-jarring thud, his massive arms locking around her by instinct, claws trembling at the sudden weight. His breath tore ragged from him, thick with shadow.

"You disappeared," he rasped, voice breaking with strain. "For a second...where did you—"

Elowen laughed. A broken, blood-choked laugh, streaks running from her nose down her chin. Her eyes glimmered fever-bright. She raised one shaking arm, smearing blood across her own lips as she pointed past his shoulder.

The Ledger.

Fissures spidered across its surface, glowing like molten veins beneath stone. The runes stuttered, each one sputtering like a dying star.

"Crack it," she croaked, lips curling in a feral grin. She coughed blood and grinned wider. "Crack it like a candy cane."

For a moment, he only stared at her, the madness of her words clawing at his unraveling mind. Then his gaze shifted to the monolith, and understanding blazed crimson in his eyes.

He placed Elowen on the ground and roared.

Shadows howled with him, storming around his body as he slammed his fists into the monolith. Once. Twice. The impact shook the cavern, runes bursting apart with each strike. Each blow tore another vein of light across the monolith's spine. The iron bite of his shackle ate into his flesh, but he struck again, chains rattling like thunder.

Elowen dragged herself forward, every limb trembling, and pressed her palms to the cracks. The stone scorched her skin. She screamed. Gray magic rushed from her veins into the fault lines. Blood poured from her nose, dripping down her chin. Her vision blurred.

"Break!" she shrieked, her voice shredded raw. "Break!"

Runes writhed under her touch, flaring, fighting. Her arms shook. Her magic sputtered. Krampus' fists hammered beside her, blow after blow. Together, their strength forced the fissures wider until, at last...

A thunderous crack ripped through the air.

The sound was like a bell tolling across creation.

The Ledger split, a molten fault carving through its heart. The monolith groaned and toppled.

Krampus seized Elowen, hauling her close as the cavern convulsed. Shadows tore around him like whips as he sprinted, faster than the collapsing tower could chase them. The heat of its destruction seared their backs as the Ledger fell.

It slammed into the ground.

Shockwaves ripped through the cavern and threw them off their feet. They fell as dust choked the air. Shards of searing rock rained from above.

For a heartbeat, silence.

Then, a bell boomed across the realm, its echoes thundering the last hour of the year.

Krampus lay on his side, body wracked with tremors. Shadows surged around him, twisting higher, devouring him. His eyes burned scarlet, his breath a snarl, his free hand clawing at stone as the darkness climbed his limbs. The shackle burned. Pulling. Binding.

Again, the bell rang, a jarring sound that vibrated through her, shaking her to her core.

"Time," he cried, his voice distant, warped. "Dawn—"

Elowen reeled, bile and copper flooding her throat. She vomited blood, gagged, and dragged herself forward on her elbows. *No. Not now. Have I gone through everything just to lose you?*

With another clang of the bell, Krampus let out a guttural yell. Shadows swallowed half his face, teeth lengthening, claws gouging the stone. His body lurched, the shackle searing as it pulled him toward the abyss.

Elowen flung herself against him and pressed her palm to the burning iron. Flesh blistered instantly. The smell of scorched skin filled the air. She sobbed, forehead pressed to his wrist. "No. No, not like this."

She had to do it. Had to try. Another deafening bell toll and her magic sputtered, first as sparks, then as a flood. Gray bled from her veins in a desperate torrent, searing into the iron, searching its runes, twisting them. Her scream tore her throat raw, every ounce of herself pouring out.

"Please," she begged, voice breaking. *Don't let me lose him.*

The twelfth bell toll echoed in the air. And then...

...the shackle cracked with a sharp, metallic sound.

A blinding flare split it, light spilling like molten silver. The iron burst, shards scattering like dying stars across the cavern floor.

Shadows shrieked and recoiled into the darkness.

Krampus collapsed. His monstrous form unraveled. Ragged breaths tore through his chest. His skin smoked, his body scorched, but he was himself. At last.

The bell was silent. The last note was gone.

Elowen sagged into him, limp, her lips stained with blood. Her eyes fluttered, pale as bone.

"You're free," she whispered, voice thready. "Candy canes."

Her body slackened. The last sparks of gray flickered to ash.

The cavern convulsed. The fractured Ledger glowed like a dying sun, fragments raining down as fire and stone split the ground. Fissures bled white light, the air cracking with each second.

Krampus gathered her into his arms, clutching her against him. "Elowen," he thundered, voice breaking. "Stay with me. Stay."

Her lashes trembled. A weak smile touched her lips. Then she stilled.

A boulder crashed beside them, searing debris showering their backs. He surged to his feet, clutching her like the last ember of the world. His shackles were gone, *gone*, but the price was written on her body.

The cavern walls buckled, flames swallowing the runes as the entire realm collapsed. He barreled through the storm, arms wrapped around her limp body.

And as dawn broke in the mortal land, he leapt through the fractured portal, shadows howling in their wake.

CHAPTER TWENTY

The bells in his office had fallen silent.

Kris Kringle stood at the center of the chamber, surrounded by gold and ruin. At the far end, his Master List realm door glowed faintly, pulsing like a dying heartbeat. Its sigils had gone gray.

He touched them.

The portal did not answer.

For the first time in centuries, the realm refused him.

Kringle's breath fogged the air, though the room burned with unnatural heat. His face twisted into a scowl. He felt his brow to assure himself the crown still rested upon his head. It hummed in protest; he felt it like a chain tugging behind his eyes, a tether stretched too far.

He looked at the door and scowled. "Open," he said.

Nothing.

He raised his hand, gathering the residual light that pulsed from the crown. Gold motes swirled around his fingers as he pressed his palm to the runes. The smell of scorched sugar filled the air.

The runes hissed, flickered, and then died. The light drained away.

He staggered back. The crown flared once, searing his temples with white heat. The feedback cracked the air like a whip, and the peppermint marble at his feet fractured into a spiderweb of

158

hairline fissures.

He tasted iron.

For a long moment, Kringle said nothing. His breathing steadied, but his expression did not. Then, as though the moment of failure had been a minor inconvenience, he smoothed his crimson cuffs, straightened the holly in his lapel, and smiled.

"The door forgets itself," he murmured. "But the crown remembers."

Behind him, the office door creaked open. Klaussen entered hesitantly, pointer clutched in both hands like a staff. The faint sound of panic from the Registry bled from the halls below. He heard the scratch of quills, the echo of shouted orders.

"My Jolliness," Klaussen panted, bowing until his bells clinked. "We've stabilized the Sorters' Wing. Production has resumed at sixty percent capacity. The...the clerks—"

"—are afraid," Kringle finished, turning slowly. His voice was smooth, the warmth of a fire that lured one close before the smoke stole their breath. "They believe the List is gone."

"It is, sir." Klaussen's voice quavered. "The orbs stopped transmitting. No reports from the mortal realms are being categorized. The names, the colors, they're gone."

Kringle regarded him with an almost gentle expression. "Do you think good and evil vanish because a few lines of script crumble?"

Klaussen swallowed. "No, sir."

Kringle took a step closer, and the light from his crown bled over the floor, warm and golden, bleeding into the cracks in the marble like syrup. "Then the song continues," he said softly. "It only needs...a new instrument."

He crossed to his desk and dragged a blank tome from his drawer, an enormous book of pale vellum, bound in gold-threaded hide. He placed it at the center of the desk and rested both hands atop it. The crown flashed once, uncertain, then steadied.

"The List," he said, "was never divine. It was merely my reflection. The world calls for order, and I oblige. So..." His smile widened. "We begin again."

Klaussen frowned faintly, unsure if he was meant to speak.

Kringle gestured to the trembling elf. "Ink."

The pointer clattered as Klaussen fumbled for an inkwell. "At once, sir."

Kringle dipped the quill and wrote the first word himself. The nib hissed as it met the page, gold bleeding where ink should have been.

Nice.

The word burned, then sank into the parchment. The crown's hum deepened, the air thick with sugar and heat.

"Everyone," Kringle said quietly. "Every child, every mortal, every elf. All nice. All deserving."

Klaussen blinked. "Everyone?"

Kringle's eyes gleamed. "Oh yes. Imagine it. Endless production. Gifts for all. The mortals will sing of our benevolence until the stars melt. They will *need* us more than ever. Want becomes virtue. Desire becomes worship. And their gratitude..." he pressed a palm over his chest, feeling the crown pulse against his heartbeat, "...their gratitude feeds the crown."

Klaussen hesitated. "But the resources—"

Kringle turned to him, and the smile sharpened. "The work will increase. The joy must multiply. You will all deliver it."

Something in the air shifted. The crown's hum filled the silence, resonating in the elves' bones. Klaussen's protests withered under the sound. He nodded, wide-eyed.

"Of course, sir."

Kringle's tone softened again, honey over steel. "Good. Fear not the chaos. Order must be earned anew."

He moved toward the great glass window overlooking Kringle Central. Below, elves swarmed through snow-choked courtyards, hauling crates of half-finished toys. The air shimmered with residual magic, the afterglow of a fallen god refusing to perish.

Klaussen followed Kringle's gaze toward the courtyard. "They're still confused, sir. Some are frightened. The clerks refuse to continue without authorization. Larkspur says without direction, production violates the old classifications."

Kringle's smile didn't falter. "Then she questions the crown."

"N-no, sir, she's my best List Maker, she meant no disrespect —"

Kringle turned his head slightly. The motion was small, yet it carried the weight of an executioner drawing breath. "Fetch her."

Moments later, Larkspur was ushered in, her curls bouncing with each step. Her notebook was clutched tight against her chest.

"My Jolliness," she said carefully. "We've kept the lines running where possible. But without the Nice and Naughty registers, we can't determine distribution. Production demands will outpace—"

"Outpace *joy*?" Kringle interrupted, his tone almost wounded. "My dear girl, there is no outpacing joy. It is the only current left."

Larkspur hesitated. "Sir, with respect—"

"Respect." He let the word hang, tasting it. "Respect is a kind of faith, isn't it? And faith, I find, needs proof."

He gestured toward the space beside his desk, where the air shimmered faintly. A gilded candy-striped hook unfolded from the wall. It dangled there like a toy made for hanging stockings.

"Step closer," Kringle said gently.

Larkspur blinked. "Sir?"

"Do not tremble," he soothed. "You've done well, truly. You've worked through the noise, the loss, the chaos. You've kept the engines turning. But you *hesitated*. That seed of doubt is a frostbite, and I cannot let it spread."

Her throat worked as she swallowed. "I meant no offense—"

"Of course you didn't. That's why this will be brief."

Before she could step back, Kringle reached forward and laid two fingers against her brow. The crown flared; gold light seared through her eyes. Her scream fractured into a high-pitched laugh, as though joy itself had been weaponized. The sound echoed through the room, bright and hideous.

When he released her, she dropped to her knees. Her eyes were glazed, her mouth parted in a trembling smile. The smell of burnt sugar thickened the air.

"Now," Kringle said softly, brushing ash from his glove, "tell me, Larkspur. Do you still doubt the List's return?"

She shook her head, curls bouncing. "No sir. Never. The List is eternal. You are eternal."

"Good," he murmured. "Rise."

As she stood, the light of the crown shimmered briefly over her. A faint mark, a glowing snowflake, blossomed across her throat, sinking into her skin.

"Do you see, Klaussen?" Kringle asked, turning to him with the patience of a teacher. "The mark of devotion protects them. Faith made visible."

Klaussen nodded quickly, though his knuckles whitened on his pointer.

Kringle placed a hand on his shoulder. "Now send her back to the Registry. Let them *see* what devotion earns. Let them understand the cost of faithlessness."

Larkspur, smiling in dazed reverence, clasped her hands. "They'll understand, sir. They'll sing your name as law."

"Good girl," Kringle whispered.

She left, her steps brisk and sure. The door shut behind her.

For a moment, the only sounds was the low hum of the crown, the faint crackle of power radiating through the floor.

Kringle turned back to the window. Below, Larkspur emerged into the courtyard, the golden mark still glowing faintly on her throat. The elves froze as she passed. One touched her arm; the light leapt from her skin into theirs, faint but visible, spreading like candlelight through the crowd. Murmurs turned to gasps, then to sobs, then to cheers.

Kringle's reflection smiled in the glass. "And thus," he said softly, "faith multiplies."

He looked down at the unfinished book on his desk. The single word, *nice*, still shimmered faintly. More words appeared beneath it, as if responding to the energy below: Larkspur,

Klaussen, Rutherby, Pipp. Names upon names. His kingdom rewrote itself in devotion.

He picked up the quill again, idly sketching a flourish beneath the growing List. "Belief is a simple arithmetic," he mused aloud. "Reward the visible. Punish the invisible. Both will call it love."

He pressed the quill's nib to his tongue, tasting the metallic sweetness of ink before dipping it again. "You see, Klaussen," he went on, "in chaos, one need not command. One only needs to comfort."

He glanced down, watching the List thrum with new life, the pages turning themselves as if feeding on the worship below. "Soon, they'll forget the old Ledger. Forget the cracks, the smoke, the ruin. They'll remember only this: I remained. I gave. I forgave."

Behind him, Klaussen whispered, "You're merciful, sir."

Kringle laughed softly, genuine and terrible. "Oh, I am mercy incarnate."

Outside, a bell began to ring. Then another. Then another.

Kringle's grin widened. The sound was spontaneous, rising from the elves as they struck tools against metal, glass, and stone in rhythm. A chant began to pulse through the air, fragmented but growing:

Nice. Nice. Nice.

Kringle turned from the window and sank into his chair, folding his hands beneath his chin. The crown's light gleamed across his cheeks like reflected flame.

"Do you hear it, Klaussen?" he whispered. "The world hums again."

Klaussen hesitated. "What shall we tell them the word means, sir?"

Kringle's smile lingered. "Whatever I need it to mean."

He looked once more to the dead Master List door, and for a fleeting instant, something raw crossed his face. Fury? Fear? It passed like a shadow under glass.

"The Ledger may be gone," he murmured, voice low and

reverent, "but I am still the List."

The crown pulsed, and golden veins crept outward through the marble floor, threading like roots, spreading down into the depths of Kringle Central, carrying the same faint mark into every wall and hall. The magic rewrote what was broken.

Outside, the chant swelled until it shook the snow itself.

Kringle leaned back, closed his eyes, and smiled. "Merry," he breathed, almost tenderly. "So very merry."

❄ ❄ ❄

The spires of Kringle Central jutted into a sky bruised with the aftermath of the Ledger's destruction, clouds tinted the color of burnt sugar. Inside, the Registry hub had unraveled into noise and panic. Elves scuttled like faulty clockwork, slippers squeaking over peppermint-waxed floors as overseers barked hymns and orders. Scrolls spilled across desks, inkwells tipped, and pneumatic tubes hissed like overworked lungs. The air stank of hot metal and sugared ink.

The *New List* had begun.

Klaussen walked through it all with his peppermint pointer clutched like a scepter, his reflection flashing in panes of gold-tinted glass. Three weeks ago, he was hunched at his desk, lost in numbers no one read. Now he strode past cubicles, rapping wood, slamming the tip against misfiled scrolls. A single rap made one clerk flinch and scramble to correct a mistake. Klaussen's thin smile sharpened. Every slip of another's quill was another rung on the ladder. He used to be another number in the machine; now he was its voice.

"Shift the bins to Queue Four," he snapped at a harried sorter. "And for frost's sake, straighten your margins." His voice cracked like a whip, but behind his eyes the calculations gleamed.

The clerk muttered a blessing and bowed, and Klaussen moved on. Behind his sharp grin flickered calculation. Every name written into the new tome fed the crown's glow above, and every signature written in trembling ink fed *his* assent. Chaos, he'd learned, was the closest thing to opportunity.

The mark of Kringle's new blessing, the golden snowflake that had first appeared on Larkspur's throat, was spreading through the workforce like a contagion of faith. Some bore it proudly; others pretended they did, tracing counterfeit sigils on their collars with trembling quills. None dared ask what would happen if the crown saw through the lie.

From the shadows of a side passage, Larkspur watched him. The faint glow on her neck pulsed like a heartbeat beneath her collar, though she kept it half-hidden. The first *Marked*, the "Blessed Clerk," they whispered. A miracle. A warning. Both.

She let the rumors work for her.

Promoted from clerk in a haste, her station moved to the maintenance halls, for lack of space. The obscurity suited her. She didn't shout like Klaussen; she didn't need to. Her gaze lingered, recorded, tallied. When a shipment buckled wrong on a cart, her quill scratched a quiet note. When the clerk hesitated over a form, her lips curved faintly. Elves felt her attention like a draft at their backs. It was an unsettling reminder they were being watched, weighed. When one muttered the wrong word, had fear, doubted, or was wrong, her lips curved faintly, and the mark on her neck shimmered brighter.

They saw it and straightened, hearts pounding with guilty reverence.

Klaussen caught her watching and turned, pointer tapping twice against his palm before he sauntered closer.

"You glow these days," he said lightly, eyes flicking to the shimmer beneath her collar. "Promotion suits you."

She didn't flinch. "So does obedience. I hear it earns favor faster than flattery." Her tone was mild, but her eyes measured him as if she were taking inventory. "You're loud for someone so new to the upper floors."

He leaned close, voice a whisper meant only for her. "Loud keeps you alive. Fear keeps you noticed. The quiet ones vanish now, haven't you heard?"

Her smile was delicate and dangerous. "I've heard many things." She closed her ledger with a crisp snap. "For instance, His Jolliness asked for you by name this morning."

He stilled. "Did he now?"

Larkspur nodded, lowering her voice. "Your efficiency. Your zeal. He said it was...infectious." Her gaze sharpened. "That word, you know, it means more now."

The mark on her throat glimmered faintly. Klaussen eyed the faint filigree of veins branching outward from it, like frost spreading beneath her skin. It was beautiful. Terrifying. And very much alive.

He forced a grin. "Then I'll try not to disappoint my benefactor."

"Try harder," she murmured, stepping closer until he could smell the faint caramel tang of singed sugar on her hair. "You're not the only one collecting favor."

He arched a brow. "You think you'll climb higher than the crown's mouthpiece?"

"Perhaps I'll become the crown's ear," she said. "Someone must tell him what it wants to hear."

For a moment, their gazes locked. His eager, grasping; hers cool, assessing. Two predators circling the same golden god, not yet snapping at each other, but measuring.

Then Klaussen tilted his head toward the chaos beyond the hall. "Care to share your notes, Larkspur? I suspect you're not just counting names."

Her smile thinned. "You suspect right. But some ledgers are for His Jolliness alone."

She turned, her mark catching the lamplight. For a moment, the shimmer reflected off the polished walls, scattering tiny snowflake patterns that danced across every face in the hall. Elves paused, staring. Awe rippled through the ranks like a prayer.

Larkspur didn't notice, or pretended not to. She simply walked away, her steps slow, deliberate, and commanding.

Klaussen exhaled through his nose. "And here I thought *I* was the ambitious one," he muttered. Then, louder: "Back to work! His Jolliness smiles on the diligent!"

The Registry obeyed.

Rumors rippled faster than the ink could dry.

The Ledger is gone. The Nice has returned. The world reborn in mercy.

And still, the crown's carol hummed faintly through every corridor, steadying trembling hands with the hymn of false cheer. Kringle himself walked the upper galleries at odd hours, robes gleaming, smile fixed. He never raised his voice. He didn't have to. The mere turn of his head silenced entire rows of clerks.

Time lost its edges. Day and night bled together under perpetual torchlight. Benches overflowed with parcels. Departments blurred into one another, scrolls and packages cross-pollinating in the frenzy. A group of elves worked by lamplight in silence, their hands flying too quickly, too neatly, as though guided by something other than will. Lists spread like veins across the walls. No one asked why they wrote or whom the gifts were for. They knew only that they must never stop.

Klaussen carved out new authority one slammed pointer at a time. Larkspur mapped patterns in the chaos no one else could see. And between them, the factory of faith roared to life again, turning dread into devotion, devotion into power.

Above, in his tower, the crowned figure smiled. The carol grew louder.

Order, he promised, would be rebuilt.

No matter how much it cost.

Far below Kringle's tower, the carol carried, past the peppermint walls, through the factory veins into the very marrow of the world. Its golden pulse spread like sickness, rippling across realms once tethered to the Master List.

Wherever the light touched, the snow lost its purity. The white dulled to syrupy gold, and the air trembled with false joy. Mortals dreamed of gifts they did not need. Elves labored until their hands bled sweetness. Even the deep realms felt it. The hum of a god refusing to die.

Beyond the reach of that gilded glow, the light thinned, faltered, and broke against a wall of storm.

There, in the realms where the Nice could not reach, silence swallowed the hymn.

And through that silence, the portal tore open...

...spitting Elowen and Krampus back into a world of frost, ash, and ruin.

❄ ❄ ❄

The snow swallowed Elowen and Krampus as the portal spat them back into Krampus' realm.

She struck the ground first; her soft cry was lost in the frost. He crashed beside her, shadows spilling wild, then lurched forward to catch her before the snow could close over her slight frame. Her lips bled. He brushed the red away with shaking hands as though the gesture alone might hold her together.

"Don't you dare leave me," he whispered, pressing his brow to hers. His breath fogged between them, trembling.

Her lashes fluttered, her hand twitching against his chest. "Not...done yet." Her voice was thin, broken, but her truth rode every syllable.

Not done.

Krampus' teeth clenched as he lifted his head, scanning what remained of his realm. His woods of claw-like trees lay gutted into stumps. Snow ran black with soot, scarred with the churn of foreign boots. Splintered toy soldiers littered the drifts, their faces staring skyward in mockery.

"We could hide," he said hoarsely, stroking her hair with an unsteady hand. "My shackles are gone. I could run, take you where he will never find us."

Her cracked lips quirked faintly. She opened her eyes, fevered but fierce. "Can't just leave them," she croaked. "The elves."

The words bit deeper than any shackle. His scarred hands

flexed helplessly.

"They're in chains," she rasped. "Even without the Ledger, they'll march, they'll sing, they'll *break* themselves for him. If we run…they'll never be free."

He growled low. "Elowen—"

Her bloody finger pressed his chest, right where his heart hammered. "You said you never wanted to punish. That was his lie. If you won't fight for yourself…" Her hand slipped, but he caught it, fingers curling tight around hers. "Fight for them. For Me."

His shadow trembled, torn between recoil and surrender. He looked away, jaw set. "We cannot win. Not as we are. Kris reforged the crown. You saw it. He'll raise another army. I'm spent. And you—" His gaze snapped back to her pallid face. "You're breaking."

Her smile was thin, stubborn. "Then we need help," she moaned. "Somewhere in these sugar-frosted realms, someone, something can help us."

A crunch of hooves cut through the silence. Krampus lifted his head. At the edge of the ruined wood stood the reindeer she had stolen from Kringle's square. Ash streaked its hide; frost clung to its antlers. Against all odds, it waited.

Elowen gave a weak laugh, nearly delirious. "Our accomplice endures."

Krampus' throat worked as he nodded, setting her carefully astride the creature. He steadied her with a hand against her back, though he trembled. "You ride. I'll walk."

They moved across the snow slowly, the reindeer plowing, Krampus trudging at its flank.

Elowen's voice cracked the silence. "The Forger?" She swallowed, forcing the thought past bleeding lips. "The shackles. The crown. If they forged them, they'll know how to break them."

Krampus froze mid-step. The wind howled around him, tugging at the ragged fur along his shoulders. The word fell from him like a curse: "The Forger."

Her head tipped against the reindeer's mane. "Yes. Where do we find them?"

Krampus' jaw tightened. His gaze swept the black horizon. "You do not. They dwell beyond realms where even gods do not tread."

"But someone knows," Elowen pressed, voice fading. "Someone has to know."

His mind stirred with old memories. He thought of the stone ridges marked with runes that hummed beneath his touch; the wards carved with time was young. "The wardens," he murmured. "Older than I. Older than the List. If summoned, they answer."

Her hand curled feebly in the reindeer's reins. "Summon them."

He looked at her pale face, her lips stained with fresh blood, and his gut twisted. The Forger may help. But the cost...he feared what it would demand of her. Of them. Would it be worth it?

They rode until they reached a black ridge split with old runes, half-buried under snow. The marks glowed faintly, responding to him. Krampus spread his hands over the stone. His voice dropped into the tongue of his making; raw syllables scraped the air and made the world flinch.

The ground split. Frost bled away. From the cracks rose a shape vast and terrible, wrought of obsidian and ice, its body carved with the same runes etched into the ridge. Its head tilted, hollow sockets gleaming with icy fire.

His warden.

Its voice ground like avalanches. "Keeper of the Night," it rumbled. "Why do you call me?"

Krampus bowed his head, shadows bending low. "I seek the Forger."

The warden's silence pressed heavy as stone. When it spoke, frost cracked across the ridge. "The Forger dwells where snow cannot cool. Past the wasteland of stone and fire, under the mountain where chains drink starlight and flames feed on oathbreakers."

"We wish to make the journey."

"Travel three days into the black plain, where no tree grows and no bird flies. Through the wasteland of stone and ash, where the sky bleeds. Seek the Veins of Fire. They crack the earth like wounds, and from them rises smoke that chokes the stars. At its heart stands the gate of the Warden of the Forge. He alone may lead you into the fire of the Forger's mountain.

But beware, Keeper. The forge burns truth from falsehood. If your cause is false, you will be ash."

Elowen shifted slightly, and Krampus, seeing her pale face, felt a pang in his chest. "And if our cause is true?" he growled.

The warden's hollow gaze swept over them. Something shifted in its runes, recognition flickering like light through cracks in stone. "Then they may hear you."

Silence thundered after the words. Krampus bowed low, but the weight in his chest grew heavier.

The warden struck its colossal hand into the ridge. Stone screamed open, a fissure glowing ember-red, a portal seething with fire and shadow.

Elowen's gaze flicked to the reindeer. "Can we take him with us?"

Krampus shook his head firmly. "No. The Forger's realm is fire. It would kill the beast."

Her lip trembled. "Then it'll be alone."

He pressed a palm to the reindeer's brow. Shadows rippled into its antlers, curling like brands that faded into nothing. He whispered an older word, one that tasted of ice and oath. The reindeer snorted, pawed the ground, then turned toward the horizon.

"It knows the way," Krampus said, voice low. "Balthazar and Charlie will give it a home."

Elowen leaned forward, whispering into its ear. "Wait for us."

The beast trotted away into the snow, vanishing into the white.

Krampus bent, gathering Elowen into his arms. Her body felt

frail, but her fire still burned beneath the ruin. He pressed his brow to hers once more. "Ready?"

Her answer was a cracked smile. "Never."

CHAPTER TWENTY-ONE

Krampus stood at the wasteland's edge, Elowen trembling in his arms, and felt the weight of his warden's words echo through his chest: *three days into the black plain, where no tree grows and no bird flies.*

Before them stretched a desolation unfit for breath. Black stone lay ahead of them, split like old bone. Ash drifted in thin veils, and the horizon bled with a red twilight that never brightened, never dimmed. No wind stirred. The silence was heavier than chains.

Elowen stirred weakly against him, coughing, blood flecking her lips. Her eyes fluttered open, too wide, pupils unfocused. She whispered something that might have been his name or might have been a curse. Madness from the Master List realm still gnawed at her mind.

He bowed his head until his horns brushed her hair. "Hush, little snow," he murmured, though fear gnawed his belly raw. He could not tell if her madness would fade or if the List had stolen her mind forever. She had freed him from shackles and undone the List with her will. But she was breaking. And the wasteland would not spare her.

He longed for the reindeer, but knew the desolate wasteland would be its demise. Groaning, he shifted her in his arms. He was tired, but this was a weight he was willing to bear. He would carry her to the ends of the world if he had to, and he had a feeling that's exactly what he was doing.

❋ ❋ ❋

The first day bled into itself; time stretched thin beneath a sky that didn't change. Krampus trudged along, every step sinking into cracked stone dusted with ash. The air was thin, scraping the throat raw, and each breath burned Elowen's lungs. She coughed often, the sound like broken glass. Every spasm wracked her body and sent shivers down his spine.

Krampus hated the sound more than her silence.

At nightfall, though no true night fell, only a deepening of the red twilight, he found a hollow beneath a ridge and gathered what shadow he could. The wasteland was poor in shade, its stone stripped of memory, but still his magic shaped a tent of darkness to guard them from the open plain. Inside, the air was close and cold.

He wrapped Elowen in his ragged cloak. Her skin was clammy, fever burning beneath it. He pressed his hand to her brow, helpless to cool her.

"Not done yet," she whispered again, the same words she had spoken in the snow. Her gaze flickered to his. "We find him...the one who made them."

Krampus' throat worked. "Rest," he ordered, though his voice broke. "Do not speak of it. Not now."

But she smiled faintly, as though humoring a child. "You'll see. He'll unmake the crown. He'll free them."

And if he does not? The thought raged within him, but he swallowed it.

She slept fitfully, shuddering with every cough. Krampus sat beside her through the long twilight, shadows curling and uncurling across his hands. He remembered his warden's warning: *If your cause is false, you will be ash.*

He did not fear the fire. He feared the price it would exact from her.

✤ ✤ ✤

The second day was worse.

Ash storms rolled across the plain, veiling the horizon. The sky wept soot that stung the eyes and blackened his cloak. Krampus tore strips from his shirt, binding one around Elowen's mouth to shield her from the worst of the grit. She sagged in his arms, barely able to lift her head. He never let her go.

The plain mocked them with its sameness. Black stone. Red sky. The occasional jagged shard thrusting upward, glowing faintly as if it knew the Ledger's shatter. Krampus avoided those. Elowen's gaze lingered on them too long, her lips moving, whispering words that were not her own.

He snarled and dragged her eyes away. "Do not listen. Do not look."

She blinked up at him, pupils blown wide, and whispered, "They call me."

"They will not have you," he growled, baring his teeth at the dead stone as though it could hear him. Shadow flared, hissing, driving the whispers back into silence.

By the time the storm eased, they were coated in gray, specters trudging through a world without end. Elowen shivered despite the cloak, lips blue. Krampus shifted her in his arms, and she coughed against his chest, blood wetting his shirt.

Every drop was a brand of failure.

That night, he did not sleep again. He hadn't slept since he had lain in her arms in the atrium. It felt so long ago. He crouched beside her, eyes fixed on the horizon, waiting for threats that did not come. The wasteland did not need beasts or soldiers. It was a predator in itself, patient, gnawing them one breath at a time.

✤ ✤ ✤

* * *

On the third day, the sky bled brighter.

The horizon split with a faint glow, ember-red, smeared like wounds across the black. Heat rolled faintly on the wind, dry and acrid.

The Veins of Fire.

Krampus felt it before he saw it: the pulse beneath the ground, like the heartbeat of the world itself. The plain cracked into fissures, red light searing upward. Smoke rose in choking plumes, veiling the stars that dared to peek through the scarlet sky. The air thickened, sulfur stinging the lungs.

He looked down at Elowen. She clung weakly to him; her face was gray, her breath shallow.

Her eyes fluttered open. "The gate," she rasped. "You said there was a gate."

He stroked her hair back, forehead grazing her temple. "Yes," he whispered. "The gate."

Krampus looked at the fissures. Fire pulsed like blood through the cracked stone, the air roaring faint with distant flame. On the horizon, half-shrouded by smoke, a shape loomed: an arch of black rock, vast and jagged, seared with runes that pulsed in time with the earth.

The gate.

Elowen stirred faintly, lips moving. He bent his head to hear.

"Not done yet," she whispered again.

His jaw clenched. "Nor am I."

With the sky bleeding above and the ground burning beneath, Krampus strode into the Veins of Fire, toward the waiting gate and the Warden of the Forge.

❋ ❋ ❋

The Veins of Fire split the earth in glowing wounds, and the gate of black stone loomed before them. Krampus carried Elowen across the cracked ground, each fissure bleeding heat that clawed at his skin. Her coughs felt weak, and her eyes wandered, half-mad, as she clung to his chest as though tethered to him by stubborn will alone.

He crossed the last fissure, boots grinding sparks against stone, and set her down just beyond the arch. The gate pulsed, runes flickering faint with the memory of ancient hands. His hand traced them, muttering words in the tongue of his realm's foundations.

The ground shuddered.

Stone cracked and pulled apart, and from the chasm rose a figure vast and terrible. Its body was molten and skeletal, shifting like iron hammered endlessly into new shapes. Chains dragged behind it, each link carved with runes that writhed like serpents. The heat of it blistered the air; ash spiraled around its vast frame.

Elowen whimpered softly, and Krampus' shadows surged to shield her. His hands flexed, but even he felt the truth coil in his gut: this was no foe he could rend.

The warden's molten eyes fixed on them, and when it spoke, the canyon shook with the sound of anvils striking.

"Who trespasses the veins?"

Krampus' jaws clenched. His shadow bowed low even as his voice rasped defiance. "Krampus. Keeper of the Night." He groaned and added, "And of the Naughty. Freed of his chains. I seek the Forger."

The warden's laugh was a roar, molten fire spilling between its skeletal jaws. "The Forger hears not the unworthy. Return, or be unmade."

Krampus stepped forward, planting himself between the warden and Elowen. His teeth bared. "Then unmake me."

A hand clutched his wrist. He looked down. Elowen had pushed herself half-upright, trembling, eyes fever-bright.

"No," she croaked, forcing sound through cracked lips. "Don't fight. Listen."

Krampus snarled, torn between fury and fear. "You cannot sway this thing. It was wrought to obey. To serve."

But Elowen staggered forward anyway, one hand trailing along the molten stone, her skin blistering at its touch. Madness danced in her eyes, yet her voice, though ragged, rang with defiance.

"You were made for one purpose," she rasped. "To guard the Forger. To keep the world from breaking."

The warden paused. Chains swayed, the runes glowing like fireflies caught in a forge's breath.

"But the world *is* breaking," she pressed, lifting her arm toward the bleeding sky. "The Ledger is shattered. The List is broken. The crown rises again. Can't you feel it? The chains failed. The rules failed. All you've guarded has fallen to lies."

Her knees buckled, and Krampus lunged to catch her. She shoved him weakly aside, staggering forward another step.

The warden lowered its skull-like head, so close its heat curled her hair. A rune flared across its brow: *judgement*.

Krampus' shadow whipped in panic. "Enough! She cannot bear—"

But Elowen laughed, hollow, delirious. "That's all you guardians do, isn't it? Weighing souls against rules written by tyrants. Judge me then. Judge us both. That's all you ever do, isn't it? You want absolutes," she said, her voice cracking, her eyes wet with tears and madness. "Naughty. Nice. Worthy. Damned. But I don't believe in them. Not anymore. I've seen what those chains do. I won't bow to them. Not anymore. If that damns me, so be it."

The canyon rumbled. The runes carved into the stone flared like veins of lightning.

Another rune shimmered across the warden's brow: *unknown*.

Krampus froze. His gut clenched.

Elowen pressed her palm against the burning stone beneath her. Her voice cracked, but it carried. "That's right," she said. "Not one or the other. Both. Neither. Gray."

The chains shuddered violently, rattling sparks into the air. For a moment, the warden's form flickered, no longer molten, but a smith hunched over an anvil, sparks flying from a hammer.

Then it was skeletal again, then molten, then something in-between.

It leaned low. The heat seared her skin raw, but she did not flinch.

With a groan like mountains breaking, the warden raised one chain high, then drove it into the stone. The earth split wide, revealing a stair of molten rock descending into shadow and fire.

A final rune flared over its brow: *forge.*

Krampus caught Elowen as she collapsed, her body shaking, laughter bubbling raggedly from her lips. He lifted her against his chest, shadows curling close around them both.

Like smoke caught in a draft, the warden dissolved, its chains clattering to the ground and fading into ash.

"You could have been destroyed," he growled, voice rough with terror.

Her smile was cracked, delirious. "Maybe. Or maybe… madness was the only thing it understood."

Krampus stared into the molten stair, the path into fire itself. His arms tightened around her, his jaw set. "Then may the Forger accept madness," he muttered, and carried her down the molten path.

❄ ❄ ❄

Walls of liquid fire crawled up either side of the molten path like veins of a living mountain. The heat was suffocating, every breath thick with ash and smoke, yet the path itself held firm beneath Krampus' heavy strides. The glow turned his shadow into a long, rippling specter, dancing across the glowing stone.

Elowen stirred in his arms, her hair damp with sweat. Her cracked lips twitched into something almost like a smile. "If I ever see another door in my life…" she rasped, "…I swear, I'll scream."

Krampus huffed, the sound caught between exhaustion and amusement. "You've already screamed enough to shake realms, little snow."

Her eyes fluttered. "Portals," she muttered, "why is it always portals? Why can't people travel by normal means? I should've worked at the Sleighways Bureau. Chimneys, reindeer..." Her voice slurred, but the petulance of it struck something in him, and his mouth twitched at the corner.

"Reindeer can't cross realms alone. They connect time and space," he stated plainly, shifting his grip on her as the imposing door came into view.

She groaned as she saw the portal. The carved archway rose from the molten ground itself. The frame was forged of blackened iron etched with runes glowing like embers. She swore softly as she caught sight of a few gray runes flickering at the edge of her vision. Those ancient hands bearing gray magic were here long ago. At the door's heart, a slab of dark metal pulsed with fire as though waiting for their touch.

Krampus pressed his palm to the metal. The runes flared, and the slab parted like melting steel, revealing a blaze of light.

Elowen groaned. "Gingersnapping portals."

Krampus chuckled as they walked through.

※ ※ ※

Heat and a blazing sun enveloped them on the other side, searing and dry, but not the wild madness of the Ledger's cavern or the wasteland. This realm felt whole. Ancient. The air shimmered with the weight of fire, and the horizon burned in hues of copper and blood-red. Rivers of lava cut channels through the black stone plains, their molten glow throwing sparks against the haze of ash.

At the center, a mountain rose like a blackened fang, its peak aflame, fire spilling from rents in its surface. The glow crowned it like a forge's heart, alive, furious, eternal.

Krampus paused and took a deep breath. The pull of madness, the clawing shadow of the Ledger's realm, no longer gnawed at him. His wrists were bare, no iron biting, no runes glowing, no leash dragging him toward servitude. He should have rejoiced. Instead, fear twisted through him like a knife.

Free. The word had teeth. He had never known a life without chains. Not truly. The absence of their weight made him feel hollow, unmoored, like a beast without a cage to pace in. The urge to run, to vanish into the fire-lit horizon and never look back, rose sharp and poisonous in his chest.

He wanted her to run with him, but her warmth pressed against him, slight though it was, reminding him of his anchor. Elowen. Fragile. Reckless. And yet, the only one who had looked at him and not seen a monster.

He bent his head, gaze resting on her face as she stirred against his chest. His freedom was hers. She had wrested it from the jaws of madness, and he swore, here and now, he would not squander it. No more running. No more being dragged. He would go only where she asked, do only what she needed. Even if it led him into the fire. *Especially* if it led him into the fire.

Better he face it than she.

Elowen blinked groggily. The fire reflected in her eyes, wild and alive. She drew a slow breath. "It's...different here," she breathed.

"It's still not safe," Krampus said.

He carried her onward, his long strides slow but steady. The heat pressed against him, burning away the last of the madness clinging to his mind.

He didn't know how Elowen bore the madness for so long, even being an elf. He glared ahead; her madness concerned him. Even though he hadn't physically lost her, he didn't know what he would do if her sanity did not return.

They walked for hours across the cracked stone plain, headed for the mountain. As the sun dipped lower, a purple glow blanketed the land. By the time they reached a ridge of jagged rock, Elowen stirred again and pushed weakly against his chest.

"Put me down," she murmured. "I can walk."

"You cannot," Krampus said.

"I can," she insisted, her voice firmer this time. She slid from his arms, her legs trembling as they touched the ground. He scowled but let her stand, hovering close, ready to catch her.

She wavered, swaying like a reed in the wind, but after a few steps her strength returned. She straightened, lifting her chin. "See? Not entirely useless."

He grunted, but there was pride in his eyes as he fell into step beside her. "You're never useless, Elowen."

You're the only reason I'm walking, he thought.

CHAPTER TWENTY-TWO

They found shelter in a cavern carved into the ridge, a cave in the black stone where the heat dimmed enough to breathe without choking. The walls glowed with veins of ember, and the ground was warm beneath their feet.

Elowen collapsed against the stone, sliding down until she sat with her knees tucked up. Her hair clung to her temples; her cheeks flushed from heat and exhaustion. The world blurred at the edges. She could still see names scrawling in the air and hear whispers crawling in the seams of her thoughts. But it wasn't as loud. She felt like she could breathe...almost.

Krampus lingered at the entrance, his silhouette framed by the setting sun. His chest rose and fell with slow, measured breaths, and for the first time in an eternity, he felt the ghost-burn of his shackles...fading. Not gone, but quiet.

Elowen's eyes followed him. Her monster, her shadow, her terror and salvation. The shackles were gone. She had torn the last one from him in the Ledger's madness. Unchained. Free.

She had done it.

A tremor passed through her chest. He was free; truly free. He could leave her here now, in the dust and heat, and no chains would ever drag him back to her side. Yet he hadn't. He had carried her, held her like something precious, not a burden. He was still here.

For her.

Her breath stuttered. How could anyone see him as a monster when he *stayed* with her?

He turned, and his gaze fell on her.

Elowen looked up, eyes half-lidded, a faint smile twitching at her lips. "You're staring."

"You look half-dead," he said, voice like gravel.

Her laugh was soft, fragile but real. "And yet you're staring."

He stepped inside, lowering himself beside her. The cavern's glow played across his face, the harsh edges softened. His hand lifted, hesitated, then brushed a strand of damp hair from her forehead.

She leaned into his touch, eyes slipping shut. "First time you've touched me without burning," she murmured.

His jaw clenched. "Not entirely. I can feel it. Faint. Like ghosts in the skin."

Her eyes opened again, meeting his. "But it doesn't stop you now."

"No." His voice was raw. He cupped her cheek, his thumb brushing the faint bruise. "Nothing stops me now."

She reached up, her hand covering his. Her trembling fingers pressed his hand against her cheek. "Good. Stay."

The heat in the cavern was stifling, and the silence between them felt as heavy as the air. He leaned forward until his forehead touched hers.

Her heart raced, and she leaned into the feeling, breathing deeply.

He kissed her. Softly at first, as if afraid she might vanish beneath him. But she tilted her head, pressing back with a sigh, and his hand slid from her cheek into her hair, pulling her closer.

There was no firestorm this time, no burning chains, no shackles to sear him away. Only the ghost of his pain, and the raw, fragile tenderness that replaced it.

When they pulled apart, her forehead rested against his, both of them breathing hard. She laughed softly, though her eyes glistened. "Hey, the world didn't fall apart."

He grunted, the sound low but warm, and pulled her against his chest. His arms wrapped around her, careful but firm, and she melted into him with a sigh.

For the first time since that night in the atrium, Krampus slept.

Elowen dozed fitfully against him, the steady rise and fall of his chest like a lullaby. There were no shadows writhing at the edge of his body, no rattling chains, no burning metal. Just his warmth, solid and unyielding, and the steady beat of a heart that had survived too much to still be beating at all.

But the peace didn't last.

A harsh caw shattered the stillness. Black wings tore through the cavern's mouth. A raven the size of a wolf dove low. Its feathers gleamed like molten glass at the tips. It circled once before perching on a jagged stone, eyes burning red as coals.

Krampus woke with a snarl, shadows unfurling like blades.

"Wake up," he barked, shifting to shield her.

She blinked awake, groggy at first, then sharp as she followed his gaze. The raven's beak opened, but no sound came; instead, a chorus of low growls answered from outside.

Shapes shifted at the cavern's edge, faintly lit by the soft glow of the early morning.

Figures emerged one by one, clad in dark armor hammered from volcanic rock, their weapons tipped with fire and steel. Their skin glowed, veins of ember pulsing beneath it like living furnaces. A dozen at least, their eyes sharp and merciless.

The leader stepped forward, a towering figure with horns curving back like blades of obsidian. He pointed a spear burning at the tip at Krampus' chest. His voice was deep as rolling stone.

"Who trespasses in the Forger's land?"

Krampus rose to his full height, shadows unspooling, his teeth bared. "Not yours to question."

"Then you die here." The horned warrior's grip tightened.

Elowen staggered between them, fearing the tension would snap, her body dwarfed by both sides. She lifted her chin, voice ringing clear, though exhaustion wracked her body.

"We seek the Forger," she said. "That is all."

The warriors shifted uneasily, but the leader sneered. "The Forger has no time for wanderers."

Elowen's jaw tightened. "We're not wanderers. The warden showed us the path. We are supposed to be here."

The leader studied her for a long moment. Then he waved two fingers in the air. Two of his soldiers stepped forward with blackened chains that smoked with heat.

Krampus' shadows reared like serpents. "No shackles." His voice was a growl, his eyes blazing red. "Never again."

The soldiers froze, his fury holding them back.

Elowen turned to him, her hands gentle on his forearm, her eyes steady. "Please." Her voice was low, but it cut through his rage. "If this is the only way to the Forger, then we bear it. Together."

His hands flexed; his body was rigid. "Elowen—"

"I will never leave your side," she said firmly. "Not again. Not for chains nor crowns. For anything."

A warrior prodded a spear, and the chains rattled. With a guttural growl, Krampus lowered his shadow and offered his wrists, not to the soldiers, but to Elowen. She guided them gently into the heated metal, her hands trembling as the clasps closed.

He held her gaze, silent but burning.

The leader grunted and turned, gesturing to the others. "Bring them."

The warriors marched them from the cavern, weapons at their backs. The raven glided silently overhead. They followed the winding path upward along the mountain's flank, molten rivers cutting gashes through the rock on either side. At last they reached a colossal tunnel, its mouth carved into the stone like the jaws of a beast.

Inside, the air thickened with heat and ash. The walls pulsed with molten veins, casting the space in a deep, hellish glow. Their chains clanked with every step, each sound echoing like a tolling bell.

The tunnel opened into a vast chamber at the heart of the

mountain. The ceiling arched impossibly high, glowing with firelight that streamed from great vents above. Below, rivers of molten metal crisscrossed the floor, their glow illuminating massive anvils and furnaces that lined the chamber like sleeping giants.

And at the far end, raised on a cliff of black stone, stood the Forger.

A figure of immense height, its skin glowing like molten bronze, every movement radiating the weight of creation itself. Sparks fell from their shoulders like stars as they lifted their hammer, resting it across their broad chest. Their eyes, twin furnaces of white-hot flame, fixed on the intruders below.

Anger burned in their gaze, heavy and unrelenting.

The warriors halted, forcing Elowen and Krampus to their knees.

The Forger's voice boomed across the chamber, a sound like anvils colliding.

"You dare trespass in my forge."

CHAPTER TWENTY-THREE

Even bound by the heated shackles, Krampus's chest rumbled with a growl that sent shadows snaking across the cavern wall. His teeth caught the glow of molten rivers as he glared up at the titan on the cliff.

"You," he spat, his wrists jerking as though phantom burns still seared him. "It was you who forged them. The chains that bound me. That branded me as his monster."

The Forger tilted their head, embers scattering from their shoulders. Then, to Krampus' fury, they laughed; a sound like bellows and thunder, rolling deep through the mountain.

Elowen caught the growl in his throat, the ripple of his shadow, the dangerous hunger in him to strike. Her hand, weak but steady, caught his arm before he could lunge.

Her voice came sharply through the heat. "I shattered them."

The laughter died.

The Forger stilled, the hammer lowering an inch. Those furnace eyes snapped toward her, narrowing.

"What did you say?"

Elowen's body trembled, but she forced herself upright. Each breath scraped her ribs raw, but her chin lifted in defiance. She met the glare that would have cowed a battalion of warriors. "I said I shattered them," she repeated. "Your shackles of starlit iron."

The rivers of fire seemed to hush. Even the air quivered, waiting.

The Forger straightened to their full, mountainous height, sparks leaping from their skin in a fiery halo. Heat pressed down like a second sky.

"You claim you broke starlit iron," the Forger said slowly, the weight of disbelief and fury dripping from each word. "Shackles wrought by flame older than empires, tempered by my hand alone. You…" their voice rolled like an avalanche, "…a scrap of elf, tell me *you* undid my craft?"

Krampus' shadows bristled, unease threading through his rage. "Elowen—" he growled, warning, but she cut him off.

"They were cruel and torturous. Made to enforce the rules of tyrants."

Her throat ached. She felt her magic twitch under her skin, wild and gray. She let a spark slip into the hot, suffocating air. It drifted upward, a ribbon of shadow and frost twined with light, impossibly out of place in the blazing cavern.

The Forger froze. The hammer twirled in their hand as though memory stirred in the metal.

Krampus' body was taut as steel, bracing for the hammer-blow of divine wrath.

Then, slowly, impossibly, they laughed again.

"Gray," they rumbled, embers spilling with the sound. "Gray was always my undoing. Neutral, incorruptible. Ancients who held the balance. They saw truth where others saw only shadow or shine. I forged a crown and shackles on the law of two paths. Virtue or vice. But gray was in between. I could not bind it or master it. It unraveled my work then, as it does now." They laughed again. "And now it stands before me again."

They lifted a massive hand and gestured. "Release them."

The warriors hesitated.

"Now."

The command brooked no refusal. Chains fell away, clattering onto stone. Krampus' shadows surged wide, unbound, but he stayed rooted, his gaze locked on the molten titan.

The Forger descended step by step, each footfall shuddering the cavern as though the mountain itself bowed. They loomed before Krampus and Elowen, firelight haloing their furnace eyes.

"So. You bore the shackles," they said, their gaze searing into Krampus. Then to Elowen: "And you broke them."

The heat sharpened, pricking against her skin. But she held her ground, clutching her ribs, her heart hammering.

Their eyes lingered on the gray spark still unraveling in the hot air. "Old magic. I must respect it. To break what I forged, your will must be great indeed."

"We need your help," she said. "The one who wears the crown must be stopped."

The Forger's flames dimmed a fraction. "The crown was forged for the Ledger. And yet you stand before me, crownless."

"The Ledger is destroyed," she said.

The hammer slipped another inch. The soldiers shifted, whispering. Even the chamber's flames guttered.

"You lie," the Forger said, but there was no conviction in it.

"I saw its heart," she replied. "It offered me the crown. I said no. So, it tried to take me, and I broke it." She glanced at Krampus, then back at the molten titan. "We both did."

The Forger's hammer dipped lower. Sparks rained from their shoulders. The molten rivers hissed, guttering. And then, they inclined their head. "Prove it."

Deeper into the mountain they traveled. The heat grew suffocating, the air thick with smoke and molten light. At last they reached a vast cavern where an obsidian pool of water lay sunken in the stone. With a hammer tap, ripples spread, and visions bloomed.

Elowen gasped as the scene replayed: herself and Krampus pressing their hands to the monolith, cracks spreading, the Ledger falling.

Truth undeniable.

Another ripple, and the vision shifted. This time, Elowen's stomach twisted.

The elves. Rows upon rows of them, moving like lifeless dolls through Kringle Central. Their songs, hollow; their smiles, carved and empty. Snowflakes and golden light burned everywhere. Kringle stood above them, resplendent in his crown, his grip on them absolute. Mortals, too, bent knee in droves, their eyes glazed with the false blessing of endless gifts. Kringle's rule was absolute.

Elowen staggered, her hands covering her mouth, nausea clawing at her throat. "No..." Her voice cracked. "It's worse than before. How long have we been gone?"

Krampus' fingers dug into his palms, shadows writhing with rage.

The Forger looked at her. "Time varies in realms, yet it still binds us all." The golden crown filled the vision, its radiance spilling even into the mountain. The Forger's gaze burned hotter as they dismissed the vision. "Someone dared patch what I made," they snarled. "And rather crudely at that, with venomous intent. That crown was for balance. Instead, he's turned judgment into hunger. Balance into corruption. A crown of rulership." Their lips curled. "A perversion of my work. This system is corrupt, bent on power. This is not what the ancients intended."

They stepped closer, looming. Sparks rained from their shoulders. "Chains can be shattered. Shackles reforged. But know this..." their voice dropped, weighty as anvils, "...metal remembers. Even when broken, scars remain. So it is with the crown. And with you."

Elowen's pulse thundered in her ears. She thought of Krampus' wrists, the phantom burns he felt. Of her own mind, splintered from what she had endured. The scars, visible and invisible.

The Forger studied her, then spoke lower, like the glow of coals in the dark. "You have power, elf-child. Enough to shatter even my work. Do you wish to wield it fully? To let me temper you, forge you into something that none could bind? You would never fear chains again."

Krampus' shadows snapped taut, rage seething. "Do not

listen. That is no gift; it's a curse."

The Forger ignored him, its molten gaze never leaving Elowen. "Say yes, and I will forge you into what this broken world needs. A weapon to end crowns, to bend the balance to your will."

Elowen's throat tightened. The temptation was a knife against her ribs. Freedom, power, and safety could be hers. She could end the cycle of chains forever. And yet...

Her eyes lifted to Krampus, still at her side. Scarred. Broken. Free. And choosing her even now.

She shook her head. "No. I won't become what I fight. I don't want to be your weapon. I just want to end his reign."

The Forger was silent for a long, pulsing beat. Then they smiled, a terrible, brilliant crack of light across molten features. "Good," they said at last. Their hammer lowered in salute. "You are not chains. Not shackles. You are the flame that breaks them."

The mountain trembled around them in acknowledgment.

"I will help you. But it will come at a cost."

CHAPTER TWENTY-FOUR

Deep beneath the mountain, the forge raged, its fiery heart casting dancing shadows. It was a furnace vast enough to swallow armies, its doors carved with runes that writhed like living flame. Heat emanated in suffocating waves, and the air shimmered, tasting of iron and old vows.

The Forger loomed beside it, a silhouette of bronze and ember. Their hammer rested across one shoulder, glowing with the embers of every weapon it had ever struck. When they spoke, it was the sound of iron meeting flame, an old, patient tolling.

"Power enough to undo what has been bound cannot be given freely," the Forger said. "It must be forged. And forging requires sacrifice." Their gaze fell heavy and absolute on Elowen. "Judgment, time, and fire. Only you can pay it."

Krampus' hands curled, shadows twitching like beasts in a cage. "No." The single syllable rumbled through the chamber, raw as a breaking chain. "She has given enough."

The Forger's molten eyes narrowed. "You bore shackles, beast. That was your sacrifice. This is hers."

Elowen swayed where she stood. The journey had left her hollow and raw; her legs felt like wet cloth. Her lips parted, dry and cracked, tasting of smoke and salt. Still, there was that stubborn, fevered light in her eyes, the same light that drove her through the Ledger, through corridors of song, and into this furnace room. "If this is the cost," she said, voice fragile and thin as spun sugar, "then I'll pay it."

Krampus moved as if to step before her, but she reached out and took his wrist. The scars on his forearm prickled under her palm; phantom burns itched like old promises.

"I freed you once," she said, her voice filled with stubborn defiance. "I'll do it again."

His breath hitched, something like grief and pride mixing under the surface. He pressed his forehead to hers a moment; no words, only a promise. Then she turned away and walked toward the furnace.

The Forger struck the ground with their hammer, and the runes on the great doors flared to life like waking suns. Metal groaned; the doors parted on a sound like the tearing of the sky. Light spilled out, so fierce it was blinding.

Elowen looked back only once, at Krampus' silhouette in the doorway, at the way his shoulders held her whole life, and then she stepped inside. The doors slammed shut.

Inside, Elowen walked through fire.

The world narrowed to pain and thought. Flames did not scorch and vanish; they spoke. They clawed at memory, laying out her life like a puzzle. Each step a sentence. Every breath, a verdict.

The flames accused first.

The Ledger's mouth opened. Her face distorted, eyes reciting names she'd marked. Children's faces flared, then snuffed. Krampus' shackled hands blistered. The Ledger smiled. The fire hissed: *unworthy, thief, breaker*. For a terrifying beat, she believed it.

She staggered, whispering through cracked lips. "Those are lies. That's not what happened. I decide my worth."

The flames surged, and pain flared low in her belly, sharper than fire: a cramp, a protest that was not only ash and flame. She fell, screaming, hand clutching her core. For a breath, she tasted copper and something like life, quick, fleeting. A glow bloomed beneath her palm, white-hot against her snow-pale skin.

She screamed. "Please, this pain, make it stop," she begged. Something was wrong, horribly wrong, twisting inside her. A sudden, paralyzing fear seized her.

She could lose it all.

The fire drank her fear like a needle drawing blood.

Visions unspooled.

In one: she accepted the Forger's gift. Her body remade, a blade cast from her own heart. Her hair became metal, laughter a clang, the world bending before her. There was a child at her breast, safe, warmed by the iron coat she'd donned. But the cost: faces she loved burned away, kindness sharpened into command. That future gleamed with coldness.

In another: as the crown's hunger grew, the Ledger returned, elves' carols cracked into screams. Krampus' face sagged with worry lines, a child's cry lost in the dark. The safety of one at the expense of many weighed against the risk of every life for a chance at true freedom.

The fire hissed its lies, and then it whispered temptations. It presented a thousand comforts like sugar cubes across the flames. If she accepted now, a child would never know hunger. *Say the word, and Kringle's reign will end. Let the world kneel to you.* The fire's voice threaded through, whispering all around her. *What is a scar if it buys safety? What mattered the cost if it kept the heart beating?*

Her mind frayed, memories she didn't own crawling over her tongue. Children, rebels, blades, or balms. The madness flickered in her mind. Was she choosing, or spinning through choices someone else had written?

Tears welled in her eyes but dried as soon as they dropped, devoured by the flames. "Hold on to the good. Hold on to what's real," she whispered to herself. So she clung to what was hers. How Krampus slept in the cavern, her hand fitting in his. The atrium's coiling snow, and the way he'd knelt with chains hissing about him. How he stayed with her even when he could have run. *He owes me nothing*, she thought.

He owes you everything, the flames hissed.

No. Lies. Madness. She clenched her fists until crescents cut her palms. She refused to become what she hated to save the one she loved.

The furnace roared. Flames licked her legs and then withdrew. Voices crowded, rusted whispers of every failure, every erased name. *You could have spared them,* the fire crooned. *You could have made them obey.*

She forced the words out, each syllable an ember. "No. I will not be your instrument."

Pain lanced through her belly again. She doubled over, ash-streaked tears burning her cheeks. *If I die, let it be on my terms,* she thought.

"I will bear it!" she cried.

She staggered upright. The flames recoiled as if offended, then reared. Gilded runes blazed overhead. The Forger's voice cracked through the heat, vibrating in her teeth.

"You chose. Many would have taken the easy tempering. Become burnished things that are whole but hollow. You remained flawed. Scarred. True. It will not be easy, but it will be real."

The furnace flared. Heat shaped itself into a rhythm of hammer and anvil, strike and breath. Her bones ached, skin sizzled, and through it she heard the ringing clang of something being forged.

❄ ❄ ❄

Outside, Krampus roared. The sound tore from his chest like a wound ripped anew. His hands scraped the stone; nails gouged deep scars as sparks scattered into the air. Shadows spilled from him in violent waves, crashing against the walls like a storm desperate to tear the furnace open and devour the flames within.

But the Forger struck their hammer against the floor, and the mountain itself answered. A shockwave cracked outward, slamming Krampus back against the wall. His ribs shuddered, shadows flickering erratically as though even his darkness staggered.

"Do not touch it," the Forger warned, their voice low and terrible as grinding stone. "Her suffering is the shaping. Her time within is the tempering. The longer she endures, the stronger the shard will be."

And then the hammer fell again, this time against the anvil in the chamber's heart; an anvil wrought of no mortal iron, but of bedrock and flame. Sparks leapt skyward, blazing like newborn stars, and the sound shook Krampus' bones.

He sank to his knees, his chest heaving, his frame trembling with rage and despair. His ears rang with Elowen's screams. They echoed through the furnace walls, muffled yet piercing, tearing through the chamber like claws raking his soul. Each cry seared him deeper than the shackles ever had, haunted him more than the Choir, and was more maddening than the whispers of the Ledger.

Krampus pressed his forehead to the stone. His teeth ground so hard his jaw ached. His hands clenched until his nails cracked and split against the rock. Blood smeared across the ground, dark as the shadows that writhed uselessly around him. They surged at the furnace, but they could not reach her. He could not reach her.

"I should be in there, not you," he said. "The fire should take me. Not you."

Her screams rose again, then faltered. The silence that followed struck him harder than any blow. His head snapped up, terror ripping through his chest. Then her voice returned, ragged, weaker, but alive. Relief slammed into him, sharp as agony.

The furnace roared like a beast devouring her. The Forger hammered in rhythm, sparks raining down like embers of worlds being born. With every blow, the flames inside flared brighter, and Elowen's cries sharpened.

Krampus slammed his fists into the stone, the ground splintering beneath the force. Blood dripped freely now from split knuckles. His entire body shook as he listened, every sound cutting deeper, every silence worse. His shadow writhed like a wounded animal, snapping and curling back on itself in torment.

The Forger lifted the hammer once more, the glow from the furnace spilling across their form. "She endures. You must endure, too."

Krampus snapped his head up, his eyes blazing red, pupils swallowed by fury and fear. With his teeth bared in a snarl, his voice broke into a roar. "She is mine to protect. And I can do nothing but listen!" His cry cracked the chamber walls, dust raining down like ash.

The Forger did not flinch. They struck the anvil again, sparks flaring across Krampus' face. "That is your trial," they said. "To hear her break and not break yourself. To let her walk the fire alone. Trust her strength."

Krampus' shadows slowed at those words, quivering like a beast pulled taut on a chain. His chest heaved as he forced air into his lungs. Rage clawed at him, demanding release. But beneath it was fear. Raw. Desperate. Suffocating. If she fell, he would fall with her. If she endured...

He closed his eyes, trembling, and pressed his bloody hands to the stone. He bowed his head, not in defeat, but in prayer to no-one. Only to her.

❄ ❄ ❄

The Forger's hammer rose and fell, rose and fell. Each strike echoed with Elowen's screams, her gasps, her laughter that curdled into sobs.

Krampus pressed his hands over his ears, but it did nothing. The sound was inside him, gnawing at his soul.

At last, after what felt like centuries, the hammer struck one final time. The furnace flared so brightly the entire mountain shook. And then Elowen's scream tore into the silence.

Flames hissed low.

"Elowen!" Krampus stumbled forward, shadows whipping around him, desperate.

The furnace doors opened.

She collapsed out of it, smoke rising from her skin. Her cloak was nothing but ash, uniform barely intact, slippers gone. Blisters marred her arms, her cheeks streaked with soot, her lips bloodied. And yet, she breathed.

Krampus caught her before she hit the stone. He dropped to his knees, clutching her against him, his hands trembling as he brushed her hair from her face.

Her eyes fluttered open, faintly glowing, and she rasped, "Is it done?"

The Forger stepped forward. In their massive hands gleamed a single shard. Jagged, white, hot, and pulsing with raw power. "The Shard of Undoing," they intoned. "Born of fire. Born of her. It can shatter crown and chain alike."

Krampus cradled Elowen close, his chest heaving. She lay limp in his arms, her skin hot to the touch, her stomach faintly glowing.

He lifted his gaze, his eyes burning red, and hissed, "If she dies…your forge burns with her."

The Forger's molten eyes narrowed, but they inclined their head. "She is stronger than you know."

Krampus bowed over her, his forehead pressing to hers. He whispered her name again and again, as if willing her soul to stay tethered.

The shard glowed between them like a new star, waiting to be used.

❄ ❄ ❄

Krampus held Elowen as though she might dissolve into ash if he loosened his grip. His hands, scarred and burned, cupped her shoulders while his forehead pressed to hers. Her breaths were shallow, ragged, but they came, and for now that was enough.

Between them, balanced across his knee, the shard pulsed with a dim molten glow, like a coal refusing to die.

Elowen's cracked lips parted. "It's…warm," she rasped. "All of that for a blade no longer than my hand."

Krampus snarled low in his throat, darkness flexing around his back like wings folding protectively. "You will not touch it again."

A heavy laugh rolled down from above, echoing in the molten chamber. The Forger descended, hammer in hand, eyes fixed on the shard with reverence. They stopped before Krampus and Elowen, their presence radiating heat that made the stone floor ripple.

"It is not for you, beast," the Forger rumbled.

Krampus bared his teeth, clutching Elowen closer. "She has given enough. Your flames nearly broke her."

The Forger tilted their head, unconcerned. "And yet she did not break. The fire remembers what it consumes. The shard was fed by her, forged by her screams. To you, it is nothing but cold glass and starlight against the crown. Now gray…"

Elowen stirred, her head resting against Krampus' chest. "Then…I'll use it."

"No." The word ripped out of Krampus like a growl of thunder. His hands flexed, carving shallow trenches into the blackened stone. "No more flames, no more pain. Not for you."

The Forger ignored his fury and fixed their gaze on Elowen. "You would wield it, little snow-born? Even knowing the cost?"

Her eyes opened, red-rimmed, fevered, but blazing with that stubborn fire that always undid him. "What cost now?"

The Forger knelt, the ground groaning beneath their immense frame. They tapped the flat of the hammer against the shard. Sparks hissed up. "To break the crown, the shard needs power. It must drink blood. That is how it binds. That is how it bites." Their voice rumbled low, like stone shifting. "Understand this: the shard feeds from the hand that wields it. The greater the act, the deeper it drinks. A mere spark may cost you little. But to wound the crown? To shatter it?" Their eyes blazed. "It will drain more than strength. It will gnaw at your very life, your blood, your magic, until you have nothing left to give."

Krampus surged to his feet, blackness swelling like whips, but Elowen caught his arm before he could move. "I've bled before to break your shackles," she said, her voice shaking. "I'll bleed again."

"Enough!" Krampus roared, the sound rattling the chamber. "I will not let you take her from me."

The Forger stood, towering over them both, and their laugh was deep and merciless. "You mistake me. It is not I who takes. The fire consumes what you give. She endured my furnace, and she lived. She may choose again, or she may not. That is the way of flame."

Krampus trembled with fury, torn between wrath and despair.

Elowen cupped his jaw with her blistered hand. "Listen to me," she begged. "If we can't break the crown, then nothing we've done matters. Elves stay in chains, mortals keep feeding him, and you..." her voice cracked, "...he'll drag you back into his pit."

Her words pierced deeper than any fire. Krampus closed his eyes, pressing his face into her palm, torn apart by her fragility and her strength.

"You wish to reach the crown-bearer again?" the Forger asked.

Krampus' hand dug into the stone, cracking it under his weight. "Open the way."

"The path back is not clean," the Forger rumbled. "The crown will feel the shard. It will call to him. He will know you come."

Elowen coughed, a bitter laugh breaking through her cracked throat. "Then he can wait for us." She pushed against Krampus' chest, forcing him to look down at her. "We can't wait anymore."

He searched her face, shadows flickering wildly as if they might consume the shard and her both. But her eyes held him steady. At last, he bowed his head, a beast yielding not to chains, but to her.

The Forger raised their hammer high. Lava split, a rift of molten gold spilling sparks across the stone. The heat was immense, searing, and an open portal glowed within.

Krampus carried Elowen towards it, his body braced as though he might fight the fire itself.

"Remember this," the Forger called after them, their voice echoing through stone and flame. "The crown can be broken. But not the will that wears it. Do not mistake one for the other."

Krampus stopped at the edge, his jaw clenched, eyes fixed forward. Elowen pressed against his chest, the shard's glow searing between them.

"You stay, I stay," she whispered.

He nodded once, then stepped through the door.

CHAPTER TWENTY-FIVE

For a heartbeat, Krampus thought the Forger's fire had swallowed them whole. Then the heat dropped, replaced by a gnawing cold that cut to the bone.

Beyond the rift, the world was a desolate expanse of bleak silence, with only a faint whistle on the air. Beneath his boots, the ground was frozen and snow veined with black stone, broken by spires that resembled broken teeth. The sky was bruised violet, as though twilight had been strangled mid-breath. Pale frost-lights shimmered in the hollows, flickering like ghostly lanterns. Every exhale hung in the air like clouds of cotton candy.

Krampus' boots dug into the frost as he steadied his footing. His shadow curled against his frame, uneasy, and his throat rumbled with a warning growl.

Elowen stirred, eyes fluttering half-shut, lashes dusted with frost. Her burned hands trembled where they clutched his cloak. The air bit at her lungs, burning worse than fire, but she managed a whisper through pale, cracked lips. "No...not again." She looked at the frozen wasteland. "The in-between."

His gaze snapped to her. "You've walked this place before?"

Her head lolled, breath shallow. "Once." Her words cracked, brittle as icicles breaking. "*It* hunts here. We can't stay here. We have to go."

The whistle's mournful sound echoed louder across the plain, rattling the ground beneath them.

Krampus' grip on her tightened before he lowered into a crouch. "What hunts?"

"What doesn't?" She laughed, the sound dry and fractured, a scrap of her lingering madness.

From between the jagged spires, it came.

The figure loomed taller than Krampus, gaunt limbs jutting at unnatural angles, as if broken and crudely mended. Its spine arched like a bowstring, its pallid flesh stretched thin enough to show black veins of frost running beneath. Dim frost-fire burned in its hollow sockets, and when it opened its maw, the air filled with the sound of winter itself screaming through stone.

Krampus bared his teeth, shadows flaring outward, but the sound stabbed straight into Elowen's chest. She groaned, her stomach knotting with pain sharp as knives. She almost folded, clutching herself, before Krampus hauled her closer against his chest.

The creature's claws scraped the black stone, dragging sparks, its whistle building into a shriek that rattled the spires.

"Portal!" Krampus snarled, scanning the horizon. "There must be another door—"

Elowen's hand clutched his tunic. Her eyes, though fevered, blazed with the strange clarity of someone who had suffered too much to fear. "No door will open for us. Not unless it—" She broke off, laughter bubbling through her cracked lips, madness spilling through her words.

The creature lurched closer, a tower of frost and bone. Its steps cracked the ground, veins of black fire spidering outward. Krampus' shadows surged like a storm tide, ready to strike.

But Elowen saw something he didn't. As its maw gaped wide, she caught the jagged shape jutting from its side: a shard of black ice, buried deep between ribs, frost-fire seeping out like blood.

Her chest squeezed. Pain echoed through her own body. She understood in an instant.

"Wait." Her voice was hoarse but strong enough to cut through his fury. She pressed her blistered palm to Krampus' arm. "It's hurt."

He whipped his head toward her, disbelief burning in his eyes. "That thing is a nightmare, Elowen. It hunts. It kills."

Her cracked lips lifted in something like a smile. "So did you."

His snarl faltered. Shadows paused, caught between fury and the truth of her words.

Elowen staggered out of his grasp, her knees buckling as she stepped onto the frost. Her steps faltered, every movement like glass breaking underfoot, every breath tore fire from her lungs, but she pressed on.

"Elowen!" Krampus' roar cracked the air. "Get back!"

She lifted a hand toward the creature, palm trembling. "Let me help you," she pleaded.

Krampus' hands flexed, torn between snatching her back and letting her gamble with madness.

The creature froze. Its whistle faltered into a low, hollow groan. Frost-fire flared in its sockets as it regarded her, as if no-one had ever dared to speak to it before.

She drew closer, though the cold burned her skin raw. Her gaze fixed on the shard of ice embedded in its ribs. She lifted her hands, blistered and raw from the Forger's flames. "You've carried this pain for so long. I know what that is. Let me take it."

For a moment, Krampus thought the beast would devour her whole. Its head lowered, maw gaping, and frost spilled out in a plume that frosted her red hair. She swayed but didn't flinch.

Her fingers pressed against the ice shard. Pain screamed through her bones as frost-fire seared her skin, but she curled her hand around the jagged piece and pulled, her erratic magic adding to her force.

The shard tore free with a cracking sound.

The creature's howl shook the wasteland. The wound sealed with frost-light, and the shard crumbled into drifts of snow in Elowen's grasp.

She sagged to her knees, chest heaving. "There," she hissed through chattering teeth. "Now you're free."

The creature loomed over her, its breath gusting across her

face like a winter gale. Then, impossibly, it bowed its head. Its whistle softened, like wind sighing through hollow stone.

Krampus rushed to her side and hauled her back into his arms. His jaw worked, his voice thick with restrained awe and fury. "What in the frost, Elowen? You're reckless, and it's going to kill you one day."

She managed a weak grin. "Maybe. I guess in madness there is bravery."

The creature's gaze lingered on them both. Slowly, it drew back, straightening its towering frame. Then it turned; its steps thundering across the plain. With each stride, frost-lights gathered, weaving together into an arch of black stone. Within the arch, silver rippled like a pond struck by starlight.

An open portal.

Krampus narrowed his eyes, shadows bristling. "Too neat. Too close. This reeks of a trap."

"No," Elowen murmured, her head heavy against his shoulder. "I think it's a gift. Or...maybe a promise. We'll be remembered."

He glanced down at her, her hair pale with frost, her eyes fever-bright but unafraid. Then, with a low growl of resignation, he carried her through the door.

CHAPTER TWENTY-SIX

Elowen's bare feet slid over uneven grass on the other side. The twilight world around her was not black wasteland nor a burning forge, but something quieter, stranger. She wiggled her toes and blinked against the stillness. Neat rows of trees rose, their bark so black that it swallowed the last rays of light. From their twisted branches hung silver glowing fruit, each orb pulsing as though a heartbeat thrummed inside it.

Before them sat a house.

Small, hunched, ancient. Various colored shingles patched its roof, and vines crawled like dark veins across its walls. Smoke whispered from the crooked chimney, and through a warped windowpane flickered the orange shimmer of embers. A forgotten hearth glowed within.

Krampus came through after her, his body stiff with pain, his legs shaking. He caught her by the arm as she stumbled. "Stay with me," he rasped. His eyes, clouded and dim, held a weariness that was etched onto his features.

Elowen tried to laugh, but it caught in her throat, half-hysterical. "A house," she croaked. "Of course. After all that... there is a little cottage waiting for us. How...how tidy the universe must be." She pressed a trembling hand to her mouth and laughed harder, choking on the sound until tears spilled down her face. "Portals and monsters and crowns and chains...

and here we are."

Her knees buckled. In her pocket, the shard thrummed, and a silent craving echoed in her mind.

Krampus dropped to catch her, his hands trembling as he pulled her towards him. She shook with laughter and sobs all tangled together, her shoulders heaving against him.

"Enough," he said. His arms wrapped around her, shielding her from the cold air. "Break if you must. But don't do it alone."

She clung to him, shaking, her forehead pressed to the line of his collarbone. "I can't...I can't keep running through doors and realms and death and—" Her voice cracked into a raw sob. "I can't be strong for everyone right now."

His hand cupped the back of her head, horns caging her. He did not tell her to endure, did not snarl at weakness. He simply held her, his form bent around hers, letting her shatter against him until the sobs ebbed.

When at last she fell silent, hollow and trembling, he lifted his gaze toward the little house. Its door creaked slowly, swinging open. Warmth spilled into the twilight.

"...It welcomes us," Elowen croaked.

Krampus' jaw tightened, suspicion in every line of his form. But she looked at him with hollow eyes, pleading silently for rest. He sighed, a sound like stone breaking, and nodded.

He carried her inside the house, eyes searching every corner for some hint of an enemy waiting to attack.

Inside, dust layered the shelves, cobwebs hung in corners, but the hearth burned faintly with red-orange embers as if waiting for their arrival. The air smelled of smoke and ash, yet also of something sweeter: wood long untouched, dried herbs crumbled to powder.

Krampus lowered her to a battered armchair by the fire. She curled against the worn fabric, letting its faded warmth seep into her bones. He sank heavily to the floor before the hearth, his shadows twitching like restless beasts, but his gaze never left her.

Sleep would not come, though her body begged for it. The

whispers clung to her mind like burrs, dredging up names, debts, false reckonings. The Forger's furnace had branded her marrow, the phantom heat clawing through her bones. Even now, she half-expected to look down and see smoke rising from her hands.

Krampus told her she had endured, but the word felt like mockery. Endurance was survival. Survival was not living.

She stared into the low-burning hearth until her vision blurred. The chair swallowed her whole, soft in ways that frightened her. She was afraid that if she let herself rest, truly rest, she would never rise again. And yet, when his shadow curled near her feet, chilly yet tender, she let herself lean sideways, closing her eyes if only for a breath. *Just for a minute.*

❄ ❄ ❄

He waited until her breaths deepened, shallow and uneven though they were, before rising. His joints groaned as if the Forger had hammered iron rods into them. Shadow peeled reluctantly from her chair, following him like wary hounds.

Without a word, he slipped outside.

The orchard stretched in every direction, endless rows of black-barked trees heavy with their silver fruit. The air shimmered with magic, sharp as frost and sweet. Nothing moved, not even the wind. Yet he distrusted the calm. Predators waited in the quiet.

His hands clung to the doorframe as he hesitated. Leaving her alone was torment. She was so fragile, broken, and haunted. What if she woke and the Ledger's madness clung to her? What if she slipped outside, and the orchard swallowed her whole?

But what if something came through the portal after them, drawn by their passage?

He bared his teeth at the dark. Every path left her vulnerable. Every choice was wrong. Yet he forced himself forward, stalking between the rows.

Shadows pooled at his feet, sliding between roots and stones, searching for threats he could not name. He pressed his hand against a tree. The bark was cold and wet as bone, and the fruit pulsed faintly beneath his palm. He recoiled, growling low in his chest.

This realm was no haven; it couldn't be. It was a snare, and they had stepped willingly inside it.

He turned back toward the little house, the orange glow of the hearth barely visible between the rows. His chest ached at the thought of her inside, curled small and shaking. He would guard her here, though he could not guard her from herself.

"Break if you must," he bit out into the orchard, "but not without me."

❄ ❄ ❄

Elowen's scream split the orchard.

Krampus was on his feet in an instant, claws extended, shadows unspooling like spears. The walls shuddered under the sudden flare of her magic, sparks hissing against the ceiling. For one awful heartbeat he thought something had followed them through, some creature or Choir or worse.

But it was her.

She thrashed in the chair, magic crawling over her skin, eyes wide and unseeing. The air rippled with heat as though the furnace had opened again, her hands glowing like half-forged iron.

"Elowen." His voice was a growl, half-command, half-plea. He seized her wrists, pinning them before she burned the cottage down. His own flesh seared beneath her touch, but he refused to release her. "Wake up!"

Her scream guttered into ragged breaths. Slowly, her eyes focused on him. Sweat poured down her face, her hair plastered to her temples. She trembled violently, every bone shuddering as if still under the Forger's hammer.

"I can feel it," she said, choking on the words. "The fire. It's inside me. I can't—" She doubled over, gagging on sobs. "I can't get it out."

He pulled her close, shadows wrapping around her. "It was a dream," he said, though he knew it was a lie. "No flame touches you now."

Her body was drenched, the scraps of her uniform clung damply to her, and the heat rising from her skin was no dream.

"We can't stay here," she said, pushing against him, her eyes frantic. "We have to keep moving. If we linger, they'll find us. And we have to get to—"

He caught her chin in his hand, forcing her to meet his eyes. His gaze burned steadily. "You will not run from this. Not tonight. If you try, you'll break." His grip softened, his thumb brushing damp hair from her temple. "You need rest. Even the hunted must breathe."

She hiccuped and then frowned. Shame burned through her fear, but she could not summon another protest.

He rose, helping her stand, though she nearly collapsed against him. "The waters," he said, glancing toward the orchard's edge. "Perhaps they will cool you."

The lake lay nestled beyond the trees, its surface black as polished glass. It shimmered faintly with the same twilight glow that clung to the fruit, a strange, silver calm amid shadow.

Elowen sank to her knees at the bank, dipping her fingers into the water. The chill shocked her lungs into taking a deep breath. She stripped her sweat-soaked, ruined uniform of Kringle Central and waded in, the cold wrapping her like an embrace.

Relief bled through her skin, pulling the phantom fire from her bones. She sank until only her face broke the surface, floating on her back as the twilight sky spread endlessly above her.

She felt quiet inside; not peace, never peace, but quiet enough to think.

Maybe Krampus was right. Maybe she couldn't run yet. Her body trembled at the thought of another portal, another creature waiting on the other side. But what if rest was surrender? What if she wasted time while Kringle enslaved more elves?

She let herself drift, staring at the endless orchard sky. The water whispered in her ears, murmuring secrets she could almost catch.

When her strength waned, she left the lake, clothes clutched to her chest. Her skin steamed faintly in the cool air, the last of the phantom heat bleeding away. Barefoot, she padded across the orchard to the cottage.

Inside, the chair by the fire was empty. On the other side of the room lay a bed, neatly made, with a folded shift of clean cloth laid across it. She stared at the offering, too hollow to question the magic.

With clumsy fingers, she pulled the shift over her head, dropped the ruined uniform to the floor, and crawled beneath the covers. Her limbs sank heavily into the mattress, exhaustion claiming her whole.

As her eyes fluttered shut, a shadow crept across her face, cool and familiar. She did not fight it. Krampus' presence lingered there, a silent vow in the dark.

❅ ❅ ❅

They woke in the twilight. Without a dawn or sun, a bruised-violet sky was all that spilled through the warped glass panes. A month had passed in Central and the mortal realms while only a full day in the orchard.

Elowen stirred first. She was startled to realize she was lying in a bed, not a chair, with soft linen against her cheek and a blanket over her. For a moment she wondered if she was dreaming, if the cottage had simply invented a comfort to lull her deeper into madness. She tried to remember lying down, but the thought slid from her grasp like water through fingers. A memory of bathing in a lake and the soft feel of a bed flickered at the edge of her mind. Was it yesterday? Or hours ago? Time felt strange in this realm.

Her stomach twisted. A hollow ache clawed up her ribs, gnawing from the inside. She pressed her hand to her middle. Empty. Starved. The thought came with a laugh bubbling at the edge of her throat: after all the fire, the chains, the Ledger, the Forger…was she simply to be undone by hunger?

Something pulled at her. A pulse. A sweetness. It brushed against her mind like a whisper through cracked sugar glass.

Eat.

She rose, bare feet silent on the warped boards. Krampus' shadow stirred from the far side of the room, but she did not notice. Or perhaps she chose not to. Her eyes were fever-bright as she pushed open the cottage door.

The orchard greeted her.

Black trees clawed at the sky, their branches burdened with ripe silver-white fruit. Each orb throbbed with light, a slow, seductive heartbeat. When she blinked, she thought she saw the fruit sway closer to her outstretched hand, as if reaching for her. She twirled beneath them, arms wide, her laugh carrying into the quiet. "So many little stars," she murmured. "All waiting for me."

Her fingers brushed one. It dropped easily into her hand, warm and alive against her palm. She raised it high, staring at it as if it were the moon itself come to earth.

"Elowen."

His voice cut through the air. Krampus; low, sharp, warning.

She turned, hair a wild tangle, her smile too wide, too sharp. "It called to me," she said, and sank her teeth into the fruit.

Juice burst over her tongue, sweet and cold, flooding her veins with light. For a heartbeat, she swore she could feel every fracture in her bones knitting, every scar dissolving. She tried to recall the pain, but it felt distant now, blurred, like a story she'd once read. The hunger roared with delight. The madness hummed, approving. A laugh spilled from her lips. "It's like… life itself."

The whispers in her head clapped and cheered, their voices overlapping: *yes, yes, more, take more.* She plucked another fruit and thrust it into Krampus' hands. "Eat."

His brows furrowed, and he sniffed it, wary as ever. Her laughter, a blend of wildness and relief, cut through his doubts. His own hunger sharpened, as though the fruit's scent was prying open an old ache. He wrinkled his nose and nibbled slowly at first, then devoured with a hunger that matched her own.

Silver juice streaked his chin. His shadow folded closer to his skin, and she watched as his shoulders eased. His wounds pulled tighter, slowly mending. She thought his scars looked shallower already, but maybe she was imagining it. She couldn't quite remember how deep they'd been. The sight made her giddy, dizzy with relief. She laughed again, higher this time, until it dissolved into hiccups.

"See? Not every fruit is a curse. Not every gift is poison," she said.

He wiped the juice from his chin with the back of his hand, eyeing her. "You're drunk on it."

"Maybe." She shrugged, then finished her second piece before swaying towards him, eyes gleaming. "Would it matter as long as I felt better?" Her hand brushed his chest. She could feel his heart pounding beneath her palm. "Have another one. I'm starving."

She sauntered back to the tree, and he followed, his stomach growling. Together they knocked down as many as they could and sat there among the trees, feasting to their hearts' content. She could feel magic flowing, burns healing, her body stitching back together, cell by cell. The orchard hummed softly around them, like a lullaby with no end.

Elowen stretched on the soft grass, reveling in the feeling of her body finally becoming hers again. She looked at Krampus, and a new hunger bloomed inside her, not just for food. It reached further, deeper. For truth, for touch, for him. "Tell me something true," she said.

His jaw tightened. "I really shouldn't."

"You must," she said, grin trembling at her lips. "Don't lie."

She giggled before hiccuping. "Besides, I don't think we can."

He grumbled. She could see his face wrinkling, his mouth twisting as he tried to form words, to say something false, but found them stifled on his tongue. With a frustrated sigh, his shoulders sagged. He leaned close, his breath hot against her ear. "Truth? Then hear it, Elowen. I am afraid."

A startled gasp escaped her, and her heart raced. She hadn't expected a truth so profound. Sweet juice clouded her thoughts. She laughed and shoved him backwards onto the ground.

With a trembling hand, he pulled her beside him, his movements deliberate and careful. His mind swam, and his tongue moved in his mouth before he could stop it. "I need you," he confessed, "more than I should. More than I can bear. If you fall, I—" His voice broke, shadows twitching before he forced them still. "I don't know if I can face Kris without you."

Him. Whispers clawed at her mind. How could she have forgotten for a second about Kringle? Her laughter melted into a sob. She pressed her forehead to his, tears streaking her face. "Then don't."

Their lips met, fierce and desperate, silver juice sweet between them. He kissed her like a man starved, like her mouth was the only thing keeping him as flesh and not shadow. She clutched at him, tasting truth, tasting need.

The orchard glowed brighter, silver light flickering across their skin as if the trees themselves approved. The fruit overhead pulsed, echoing their heartbeat.

Krampus broke the kiss. His breath was ragged, and his hand cradled the back of her head as if she were made of glass. "You don't know what you do to me." His voice was hoarse, strained. "I have dreamed of you, of this—" He shook his head, jaw clenching. "But I will not take more than you can give right now."

Elowen chuckled through her tears and brushed her nose against his. Words felt so simple, so easy to speak, to call out from her heart. "You think I haven't dreamt of this too?" She kissed him again, slow this time, lingering. She could taste the silver fruit and salt on his lips, feel his heart racing beneath her. "Truth," she sighed. "I am yours."

Something in him broke at those words.

With his strength returned, he carried her back to the house, her body light in his arms, the movement swift and effortless. The hearth burst into flame, bright and hot, filling the room with warmth. He laid her down on the mattress and climbed beside her, shadows twitching around him like restless wings.

Elowen reached over and caught his face between her palms, forcing him to meet her gaze. "Look at me. Not at the shadows. Not at what you think you are. Just me."

His throat worked as he obeyed. His eyes burned into hers, wide and raw.

Her fingers traced the lines of his jaw, the scars at his temple, and the trembling curve of his mouth. She could feel the redness clearing from her eyes, her vision returning. She searched his body, his forearms, as if understanding what she had done. "Hey, you aren't bound anymore. No shackles. No punishment." Her voice broke as she added, "There's nothing stopping you from caring now. You don't need snow or bandages."

His eyes flared, and with a low groan he kissed her again with hunger barely leashed. He devoured her, his hands grazed her waist, gently caressing.

She arched beneath him, laughing breathlessly between kisses. "Careful," she teased. "You might convince me you're not a monster after all."

He growled against her lips, nipping before pulling back to rasp, "Don't tempt me. I've spent lifetimes as the monster he chained me to be. You…you make me forget."

"Then forget," she urged, wrapping her arms around his neck and pulling him down. She wriggled to the side and laughed as she flipped to straddle him. Her head felt light, her madness and sorrows ebbing away by sweet, silver juice. Only joy filled her.

Shadow trembled across his shoulders. He took in the glow of her red hair in the firelight, the flush returning to her cheeks. She didn't look like the half-mad, broken creature who had staggered through realms. She looked alive.

Elowen laughed as she looked at Krampus beneath her. Somehow she knew that her laughter could undo him. Her monster. Her fingers slowly trailed down his chest until they rested beneath her. "Such a vulnerable position, yet again, for a powerful monster of the night." She laughed again as he scoffed. "What? No more words?"

His eyes burned red in the firelight, his voice dropping low. "You can say as many words as you want, little snow. And for as long as you want." His hands slid to her waist, grazing over her, and his mouth curved into a smile. "But right now…" he rolled and pinned her beneath him, "…I think we need more."

She cried and laughed at once, half delight, half challenge. Magic flickered unbidden, arcing through the air like gray fireflies caught between them. *Oh, thank the candy canes, it's back,* she thought. "Careful," she said, biting her lip, "I might scorch you."

"Scorch me," he rumbled, his mouth trailing down her throat. "Freeze me. Burn me. I'll take everything you give."

Her laughter broke into a sigh, her hands tangling in his hair, tugging him closer. Her magic surged with her pulse, gray tendrils curling into his shadows until the entire room shimmered with them.

The hearth fire flared high, then bent, as if bowing to them.

Shadows wrapped around them, protective, desperate, while her gray threaded through the dark, soft and stubborn, refusing to be drowned. She arched against him, the orchard's silver glow spilling in through the window to crown her in light.

"Truth?" she asked before tugging at his lip with her mouth.

He growled and then bit her neck, his hands digging into her hips tighter. "Truth? I am yours."

They weren't breaking. They weren't surviving.

They were choosing.

The fire, the shadows, and her magic rose with them, filling every corner of the little house until the walls hummed with their release.

In that blaze, the world beyond their sanctuary ceased to exist.

CHAPTER TWENTY-SEVEN

Five years had worn grooves into Kringle Central. The peppermint-waxed floors no longer gleamed; countless feet trampled the shine dull. The crystal orbs that once sparkled in the cubicles now glowed faintly, their light the color of tired honey. Piles of parchment buried desks, with ink stains everywhere. The carols, piped through brass tubes, sounded thinner, yet bright, with a tautness that made it seem like the building itself was struggling to maintain the rhythm.

The New List ruled everything now.

A tome of gold-leaf parchment filled the center of the Great Registry, so massive it took two elves at once to turn a page. Its script flowed in molten ink, never drying, alive under the quills of Kringle's chosen scribes. Each name that appeared shimmered for a heartbeat before sinking into the paper's veins, absorbed into the crown's hunger. No one questioned why the names wrote themselves faster when the elves worked longer hours. No one dared to.

Klaussen adjusted the emerald sash across his chest, brushing a thumb over the polished insignia pinned above his heart. After five years of loyal service under the New List, he was now Deputy Registrar. He used to carry a peppermint pointer like a weapon of ambition. Now it hung at his belt, ceremonial, its stripes dulled. The uniform fit, the medals gleamed, but the man beneath had frayed. Lines bracketed his mouth, and the cheer in his smile had long since calcified into habit.

The crown had stolen those years. Everyone knew it, though no-one dared say it. The elves worked faster, aged quicker. Magic bled from them like steam, feeding the crown's eternal glow. One clerk's curls had gone white overnight; another's hands shook so badly he could no longer copy names, and he had been quietly reassigned to "Holiday Maintenance." Their stations were filled before their ink dried. This must have been what it was like to be a mortal, aging so fast. He despised it.

Klaussen survived by never slowing. He recorded every mistake and turned every failure into proof of his worth. Ambition had kept him sharp; fear kept him alive.

"Still polishing that pin?"

He turned. Larkspur leaned against the doorframe, ledger tucked beneath her arm, with a cool smile curving her lips. Now, her curls were pulled severely back, and the faint shimmer of the golden snowflake at her throat pulsed softly whenever the carol rose.

On the first day it had appeared, the whole Registry had stared. Faith spread faster than a cold. "A blessing," Kringle had called it. "Proof of the crown's favor."

But he saw the truth: the mark burned when she lied, bright as molten sugar.

He smiled despite himself. "If I don't, someone else will notice first."

"Someone like me." She crossed the room, skirts whispering, and perched on the edge of his desk. Her gaze drifted to the tall windows, where Kringle's silhouette passed in the upper gallery, robes like poured wine, crown blazing like a false sun. The moment his shadow crossed the glass, the carol swelled. Elves below straightened their backs, singing through bleeding lips.

Larkspur's jaw tightened. "He's wasting us away," she murmured. "Every year, more of us burned into nothing so he can glow brighter. And still they call it cheer."

Klaussen set down his quill, studying her. "And yet you bear his mark."

Her fingers brushed the faint glow at her throat. "A gift I didn't refuse quickly enough," she said, tone bitter. "It listens when I lie. Convenient, isn't it? Makes me the perfect auditor. The perfect ear."

"Or the perfect spy," he said softly.

Her eyes flashed. "Maybe both."

A silence hung between them, thick as maple syrup. The quills outside kept scratching. The New List sang faintly through the floorboards, a heartbeat of gold.

"Still," she said after a moment, "we're here. Still standing."

He leaned back with a wry glint in his eyes. "For now."

❄ ❄ ❄

That night, Larkspur stayed after curfew, ledger open beneath the dim glow of a peppermint lamp. The ink shimmered faintly as she wrote columns of numbers, names, and departmental tallies, but her mind was elsewhere.

Quill hovering. The ink pooled into a dark blot, like a hole in the page.

Her parents' letters were dust now, buried under years of state-approved cheer. She had told herself she would climb high enough that they'd be proud. Now she realized pride had no meaning here. Only survival did.

She flexed her hand, watching the mark pulse gold. Once, it had seared her flesh for daring to question a command. She had smiled through the pain and taken notes. Now she used it as a weapon. The mark made her trustworthy, invaluable. She was Kringle's snow-blessed auditor, the one who could never lie.

And no one ever suspected the truth: she had learned to twist her thoughts into half-truths, to speak around the fire. Lies wrapped in niceties. Rebellion written in margins. Because now, the crown consumed even perfection. It didn't matter how sharp her quills were, how straight her ledgers. Kringle would devour her like the rest.

And that, she could not accept.

Her eyes flicked to Klaussen's office. He was ambitious too, tired, but still dangerous in the right ways. He was a risk, but a useful one, and he gave her something the crown could never grant: someone who *saw her* not as a dutiful daughter or a flawless faithful, but as an equal built for clawing upward, plotting survival.

She dipped her quill again, writing neat figures into the ledger. *When the crown falters,* she thought, *I'll be ready. Not used up. Ready.*

❄ ❄ ❄

Later, when the lamps burned low, and the carol dimmed to a distant hum, Klaussen and Larkspur met again. He stood by the window, watching the snow fall gold. It never melted now; it lay over the world like ash.

"He won't last forever," she whispered. "Nothing does."

Klaussen felt a shiver trace down his spine. His reflection met hers in the glass. "And when he falls?"

Her lips curved, but her eyes were hard. "Someone will have to keep the List running."

He hesitated, then reached out, his fingers brushing hers where they rested on the desk. She didn't pull away.

"We bide our time," he murmured. "When the crown falters, it will need hands ready to catch it."

Their eyes locked; his were hungry, and hers burned with cool calculation. It was a pact; he knew it in his bones. An alliance. A promise made in exhaustion and fear.

Outside, the carol swelled again, echoing down the corridors, smooth and unbroken. The elves moved like clockwork. The night shift clocked in, their steps measured, their voices drained of color. Scribes wrote faster, hands trembling.

The golden snowflake on Larkspur's neck flared once, bright

and searing, and then dimmed to a slow, steady glow.

In that moment, both of them smiled.

They were still standing.

And somewhere in the distance, faint as a heartbeat beneath the carol's hymn, the world began to turn against its maker.

❄ ❄ ❄

In the highest chamber of the tower, Kris Kringle sat alone before the New List.

Elves brought the tome from the Registry to live under his hands alone. He did not trust anyone to view it but himself. It spanned half his desk, its parchment gilded and alive, pulsing faintly with every name inscribed. The ink glowed like molten gold, flowing from quills that moved of their own accord, tracing characters faster than any elf could write. Each line seemed to breathe, the letters curling and melting before reforming, as if the book dreamt. This new main List, compiled of every name written by elves in the Registry below, was locked under a golden key held by Kringle himself.

Kringle watched it with something close to tenderness. "So many who believe," he murmured, fingertips brushing the margin.

The crown hummed in response. The vibration thrummed down through his bones, through the marble beneath his boots, down into the endless network of halls below. Somewhere below, the elves stilled for a heartbeat, bowed their heads, then resumed their work, hands quickening in time with the hum.

Every act of obedience was another spark of devotion, and every spark fed the crown. It was a perfect circuit: the List, the crown, the labor, the song. The machine of faith made flesh.

He rose, pacing toward the great window that overlooked the frozen city. Snow flickered gold, catching light that did not exist in the sky. The air shimmered with it, so that even the horizon glowed. "See how it spreads," he whispered. "The mercy of cheer. The warmth of obedience."

He spread his hands, feeling the hum coil up his arms like a heartbeat not his own. The light crawled along the veins of his fingers, tracing his skin in delicate, burning filigree.

Below, an elf collapsed mid-chorus. The others did not stop singing. They simply stepped around the fallen form, never breaking rhythm. The carol rose higher.

Kringle smiled, the expression slow and beatific. "Sacrifice," he said softly. "The finest gift of all."

He turned back to the List. New names appeared now. The endless columns were no longer reserved for children. Adults. Elders. Elves. The world itself, one golden line at a time.

He placed his hand over the page, pressing down until the parchment burned faintly beneath his palm. "All Nice," he said, voice rich and low. "All mine."

The crown flared in answer. Gold light spilled across the floor, crawling up the walls, devouring shadow. The hum deepened into a low, feverish chant.

Outside, the wind shifted. The golden snow drifted higher, climbing like a tide. And somewhere, far beyond its reach, past the glass and gilt, past the horizon of his dominion, the everlasting twilight stirred.

The twilight orchard waited.

CHAPTER TWENTY-EIGHT

The twilight orchard pulsed as day and night blurred for Elowen and Krampus. They kept telling themselves, "just another day" until a full month had passed feasting on the fruit. Five years were gone for mortals.

Elowen woke first most mornings, if morning it could be called in the perpetual silver-lit twilight. She would stir beneath the blankets, listening to the crackle of the hearth that never went out, and revel in the lack of urgency clawing at her ribs. No bells tolling. No footsteps hunting. Only warmth, and the heavy weight of Krampus' arm curled over her waist.

When she rose, he always rumbled awake not long after, shadows twitching faintly before settling again as though reminded they were safe. They would step outside together into the orchard, the black-barked trees shimmering faintly, fruit glowing like silver lanterns against the endless dusk. He fetched the higher ones easily, his hands curling delicately around stems before dropping them into her waiting basket. She would laugh when his height left her little to do but catch, and he would grunt in mock irritation before stealing a fruit for himself.

At the hearth, she stoked the embers until flames licked high again. She pretended she was keeping house, and he pretended to let her, though she noticed the way his shadows helped the fire catch quicker, the way his watchful eyes never strayed far.

They shared food, seated side by side on the rug, knees brushing.

It was domestic. It was absurd. It was perfect.

The lake shimmered at the edge of the orchard, its surface glittering with stars. The water calmed her, washed her of the Forger's flames, and embraced her. She floated on her back, staring up at the endless silver canopy, her hair fanned out like pale fire on the water. Krampus stood nearby, waist-deep, watching her with the wariness of a man who had forgotten what peace looked like.

"Come here," she teased, reaching for his hand.

He grumbled but obeyed, and when she pulled him closer, their laughter echoed across the waters.

The days softened the sharp edges of them both. Elowen's burns and wounds faded, her strength returning with every bite of glowing fruit. Her madness quieted into laughter that no longer broke into sobs. Krampus' shadows no longer writhed with restless violence but coiled loosely around him, like beasts drowsing at their master's feet.

And with the quiet came something deeper. A brushing of fingers across her wrist as he passed her fruit. A kiss pressed to her temple when she stoked the fire. A soft laugh when she teased him. She loved his laughter and the way it made her feel. She was constantly searching for more ways to delight him so she could hear that sound.

They lay before the hearth when they tired, not because they needed its heat, but because the firelight painted them in warmth they had not known for so long.

There was no rush, no need for survival. Their touches grew slower, their confessions quieter. She whispered her fears into his chest, and he murmured truths back to her he would never have spoken before. Their lips met often, sometimes playful, sometimes reverent, until the ache of want melted into something gentler, something celebratory. Gray light and shadow wove together in that realm, in the house, orchard, the lake, everywhere they pleased.

The orchard glowed brighter every day, the fruit always replenishing at will. The realm provided, making sure their wants were filled.

❄ ❄ ❄

Time in that realm was as soft and pliant as the fruit that healed their wounds and loosened their tongues. Another day of bliss for them, another month gone for the elves and mortals.

Krampus lay stretched on the rug before the fire, shadows lazily curling around him like smoke. Elowen sat cross-legged beside him, hair mussed, her cheeks bright from laughter. She had finished telling him the story of a gingerbread man and his icing woes when his rumble of laughter softened into silence.

She turned, and his eyes were on her.

"We could stay here," he murmured. His voice was gravel and storm, but something pleading lay beneath it. His hands brushed her leg tentatively, as though the thought itself might shatter if he held it too tightly. "Forget everything. Just us."

Elowen's breath caught. For a heartbeat, she blinked at him, blank. The words slid past her like a dream. *Forget what?* A strange pressure tightened in her skull. She had to think hard to call up the images: the chains, the List, the elves. They flickered like a fading picture before she could hold them steady.

Then she saw it: herself stoking the hearth while he brought her fruit from the orchard, saw them swimming in the lake, no portals, no chains, no war. Only them.

Her throat tightened. She reached out, her hand grazing the faintest scar where the shackle had once bitten deepest. His shadow rippled under her touch. She leaned down and kissed him, soft and aching.

When she pulled back, her whisper was ragged. "I want nothing more."

His gaze sharpened, desperate, hungry for her agreement.

"But we can't," she finished, and the words cut her as much as

CHRISTINA VEILLETTE

him. Even as she said it, she had to claw the reason back into focus, like a carol she'd almost forgotten. She closed her eyes and swallowed. "The elves are still chained. Mortals are enslaved by his lies. If we don't finish this...even this place could be swallowed."

Krampus' arms tightened around her. His shadow flickered, uncertain. "Who?" he asked, as if the name itself had slipped from his tongue. His eyes flashed, confused, before the answer returned with a painful jolt. "Kris."

A sound of raw pain rumbled through his chest into hers. He wanted to argue. He wanted to snarl that none of it mattered, that only she mattered. But he wrapped his arms around her, pulling her close as though he could anchor himself in her resolve.

After a long silence, his voice rumbled low. "When this is done, I'll bring you back here. I swear it."

She lifted her head, her lips trembling with both sorrow and fierce resolve. She kissed him fiercely, sealing his vow with the heat of her mouth and the promise of her faith.

"I promise," he repeated, his growl low as his kisses traveled down her neck to her navel.

Elowen gasped, her fingers tangling in his dark mane, tugging him closer, urging him on. His teeth grazed the hollow of her hip, hungry, as though he were memorizing her taste, her warmth, every trembling shiver that rippled through her body.

She arched beneath him, laughter and moans tangled, her hands roaming down the ridges of his back, mapping him like she might lose him again at any moment. With a trembling hand, she claimed his scars, his strength, his need, her palms pressing into his skin to anchor him in that moment.

Krampus' shadow curled tighter around them, cocooning them in a dark embrace. Every brush of her fingers over his skin drew a rumble from deep in his chest, vibrating through her bones.

"El," he rasped, his voice breaking as his mouth trailed back up her body. His hands cupped her thighs, her waist, her breasts, reverent and ravenous all at once. "Stay."

She laughed breathlessly, pulling his face back up to hers, her lips swollen and sweet. "Stay," she echoed fiercely, her magic sparking against his shadows. The two forces twined around them, bright and dark, gleaming and humming, spilling out of the little house into the orchard.

Their bodies collided with the hunger for survival, remembering how they chose one another despite every realm that had tried to tear them apart. His hands explored her with aching reverence; hers roved over him with equal hunger until neither knew where one ended and the other began.

The fire in the hearth roared higher. The orchard's glow fought against their magic seeping through the windows, silver light faintly flickering across their tangled limbs. Her laughter broke into cries; his growls melted into whispers of her name.

When they finally fell into stillness, tangled and slick with sweat, he held her as though afraid she might vanish. His chest rose and fell raggedly, his shadows quivering. Her head rested on his heart, listening to its thunder slow into something steady, something safe.

She felt whole. He was her home. How could she ever leave something so good?

❄ ❄ ❄

For a while, they remembered again. For a while, they forgot. Four months had passed since they had first set foot in that orchard, yet ten years had spanned in the mortal realm.

The fruit dulled the edges of memory, sweet silver juice washing over their tongues and into their veins. Time was hazy. Their laughter grew louder, their kisses more reckless. They sprawled beneath the black trees, sticky with juice and tangled together, her hair glowing faint in the orchard light while his shadows spread around them like a great blanket.

They forgot the chiming bells, Kringle's crown, his List, the armies marching. Only the warmth of each other's bodies, the sweetness of fruit on their lips, and the safe hum of a realm that wanted them whole mattered.

For a time, they let themselves believe it could last, and for a time, it did.

Until one day, the prick of her finger ended it all.

Elowen tidied the little house, humming a broken carol, when her hand brushed something sharp hidden beneath the hearthstones. A sliver of memory pulsed there, long-buried and waiting.

The shard.

Its edge cut clean across her finger before she realized what she held. A bead of blood welled, bright against her pale skin, and dripped down the surface. At once the glass pulsed, drinking the drop, flaring with a white light that filled the room. Her veins glowed, her magic and life feeding into the shard for the briefest moment. The shard pleaded, its voice hungry in her mind: *More. Feed me more.*

She frowned and sucked her finger. A wash of gray fell upon the room as the walls trembled. The orchard outside dimmed. The hearth cracked, sparks scattering.

"El?"

Krampus burst through the doorway, shadows flaring, eyes wild. He stopped when he saw the shard glowing in her hand, its light burning against his darkness.

She looked up at him, tears starting as the haze of fruit-laced forgetting tore away. Every battle, every wound, every portal, every scream came rushing back, flooding her veins hotter than the blood that dripped from her cut.

"We forgot," she sobbed, voice trembling, eyes wide with clarity. "Not just days. We lost weeks. Maybe months. I don't know how long we've been here." She gasped. "Or how long it's been out there."

His growl was low and pained. He reached for the shard, fingers closing around it as though it burned. For a heartbeat he held it, staring at her, the glow reflecting in his eyes. Then he exhaled raggedly, realization dawning heavily.

"You know we have to leave," she said.

His jaw tightened, but his eyes flickered with desperation. "It was easier," he muttered. "No chains, no crown, no war. Just you. If I stay, I can forget all of it." She watched as his shadow rippled violently, resisting, fighting. For a moment she thought he might roar, might crush the shard and sentence them to this dream forever. Instead, he looked at her, at her tired eyes, her trembling hands, at the truth that she carried when he could not.

His shoulders sagged. "If it were only me…" His voice broke, rough as stone. Then he shook his head. "No. I will do whatever you want."

Her hand rose to his forearm, brushing over where his shackles used to lay. Her lips trembled, but she forced a smile. "One last night," she said.

A silence fell between them, thick and fragile. Then slowly he nodded.

That night, the orchard glowed one last time, the hearth blazed high, and the silver lake rippled as though reflecting every kiss, every touch, every desperate grasp of two souls who knew the dawn would tear them from their sanctuary. They loved each other as though they could carve eternity into their bodies, as though need and tenderness could hold back time itself.

When sleep finally claimed them, it was tangled and heavy, like drowning in warmth.

But dawn came anyway.

Elowen woke first. The house had changed. At the foot of their bed was a small chest, and when she lifted the lid, the smell of aged wood and lavender wafted out. There were garments neatly folded inside: traveling clothes, sturdy boots, cloaks shimmering with silver thread. Gifts for the road ahead. She touched the fabric, her heart aching with gratitude and grief. For a moment, she thought the house was helping them.

But the timbers groaned, low and resentful, as though every plank wished to hold them longer.

When Krampus stirred, she pressed a kiss to his temple.

"Look," she said. She snapped her dress into the air and then pointed to the rest of the clothes.

He grumbled, as if admitting defeat, and together they dressed in silence.

The orchard had dimmed, its fruit duller, no longer glowing as before. The hollow ache in her chest grew as she realized the fruit had healed them, but at a terrible cost. Each bite had eaten away a memory, a moment, a reason to fight. The realm had stolen time.

The hearth burned low, its flames small and resigned. Even the lake rippled with strange light, watching, mourning.

At the door, Elowen turned back. She placed a hand on the wooden frame, and whispered, "Thank you." The house shivered once more, like a sigh. Something shifted in her core, and she wrinkled her brow. She looked at the hearth and the little bed, remembering all the time they spent there cocooned in their own magic. Lost in time.

Krampus' hand closed around hers. She knew he felt the same as night bled from him, heavy with reluctance.

She checked to make sure she had tucked the shard safely inside a pocket in her dress before they stepped into the twilight. Outside, shimmering like a wound in the air, the portal waited.

She wanted to grumble, make some joke about doors, but didn't have the heart to jest. Not now. No words could console them. Neither spoke as together they walked through, their realm of peace slipping behind them.

CHAPTER TWENTY-NINE

Elowen screamed.

Traveling through this portal felt harsh, unwelcoming, and cruel. It tore through them, vanishing the twilight orchard in a wrench of silver light, and pulled them into a maelstrom of screaming colors. Shadows twisted into flame, flame shattered into frost, and all of it spun into a whirl that stripped Elowen's breath from her lungs. Krampus latched onto her, his hands clutching her as they tumbled through a void that felt alive, clawing at their skin with memories and half-formed shapes.

She thought she heard mad laughter from the wasteland, chasing her through the dark. She thought she heard chains rattling, as though seeking to shackle Krampus, mocking him, waiting.

Krampus' hand squeezed hers, and she returned the pull, feeling the fear and anger welling in him. Madness, darkness, imprisonment.

Then, the ground slammed up to meet them on the other side.

Elowen gasped and fell to her hands and knees in a mound of snow. Her core was on fire, and her stomach churned as she stifled her upheaval, to no avail. Sweet berries forced their way back up, the acid burning her throat. Her hands buried in the snow and she forced back her tears.

A shadow loomed over her. "Are you alright?" Krampus

asked, a hand on her back.

Cold air burned her lungs, the smell of pine and ash mingling on the wind. The shard whispered in her pocket, thrumming with hunger. *It's near. It's near.*

"I'm fine," she groaned as she scrambled upright.

She kicked the snow over her mess and looked at their surroundings. She squinted as her eyes adjusted to the harsh light. A brutal change from life in the unending twilight. The afternoon light cast long shadows over the rolling hills, their pristine snow disrupted by blackened craters. In the distance, the faint glow of fires ringed a city of glimmering towers. Her stomach churned again.

Kringle's realm.

The familiar candy-striped towers and twinkling lights were eerily distorted. The glow was harsher; the faint cheer upon the wind brittle. Snow itself had a golden glow, glistening in the air. *How many years have passed?* Everything looked larger, grander, even from a distance. Elves marched in precise lines along the roads, burdened with sacks, tools, and weapons. Toy soldiers patrolled with hollow eyes, their gears grinding like broken bells.

Elowen's heart clenched. Her absence had cost more than she'd known.

Beside her, Krampus rose to his full height, horns curving dark against the pale sky. Restless shadows licked at his shoulders as he scanned the horizon. He looked every inch the monster mortals had been told to fear.

His gaze slid to her. "So what's your plan?"

She swallowed, the acid burning her mouth, but forced herself to meet his eyes. "We find Kringle. We destroy the crown. Nothing else matters."

As if in reply to her words, the shard hummed again, eager to be used.

He studied her for a long moment before giving the faintest of nods.

But as she looked at him, his horns, his towering form, the

darkness that clung to him like a storm cloud, reality crashed over her. She huffed out a bitter laugh and shook her head. "I'm sorry, but you're not exactly easy to hide in plain sight. This…" she gestured at his body, "…might be a problem."

A growl rumbled from his chest, and he squinted at her. "You are not going in there alone."

Her lips parted, words rising to argue, but the heat in his gaze stopped her. She groaned. He meant it. No matter the cost, no matter the danger, she knew he would not let her face Kringle by herself. She should be mad, but some part of her was relieved.

Elowen tugged her cloak tighter, though the cold wasn't what made her shiver. The world before them thrummed with a false cheer: the ringing of bells, the distant swell of carols, the steady grind of toy soldiers' boots. Kringle's order was everywhere, etched into the core of the land.

Krampus shifted beside her. Even crouched low, he was impossible to mistake for anything but what he was. Elowen pressed a hand against his back and said, "We'll need to move when the bells change."

They waited until the chime rang across the hills, thin and brittle, marking another hour of the endless workday. Elves paused their work only long enough to bow toward the distant towers before resuming their burdens. Toy soldiers rotated in precise unison, their lacquered faces scanning the horizon.

"Now," Elowen breathed.

They slid from their cover, darting between snow-crusted boulders and patches of pines covered in frost. Krampus' shadows rippled across the ground, struggling to remain calm. His jaw clenched tight as he forced them down, but every step left a print in the snow too large to belong to any elf.

Elowen glanced back at him, her pulse hammering. They would be caught soon at this rate. "Softer," she mouthed.

His growl was soft thunder, but he obeyed, placing his boots with deliberate care.

They crept into a ravine, where the snow muffled sound.

Elowen froze as voices drifted above them.

A group of elves trudged along the ridge, sacks slung over their shoulders, muttering wearily.

She held her breath and pressed her hand hard against Krampus' chest. His heartbeat thudded under her palm, steady but fierce, mirroring her fear.

She tugged at her sleeves and willed herself to be smaller, hoping the elves wouldn't see them.

The voices faded. The squad moved on.

Elowen exhaled shakily. "Too close."

Krampus snarled. "Every step will be too close. We are walking into his jaws."

She didn't deny it.

The ravine spilled them out onto a snowfield, barren but for a candy cane watchtower jutting against the horizon. Lanterns burned green at its crown, their light sweeping across the plain in slow arcs.

"Gingersnaps," Elowen swore. She grabbed his wrist and pulled him back into the shadow of a stone. "We'll never make it across open ground. Not with them watching."

Krampus' eyes flared, his shadows bristling in protest. "Then what? We can't hide here until his soldiers find us."

Her mind raced, flicking between every memory of Central's endless machinery and guards. Then, an idea, reckless for sure, but maybe their only chance. She pointed towards the marching elves in the distance. "We blend in."

He stared at her as though she'd lost her mind. "Easy enough for you." His voice was incredulous, darkly amused. "Elowen, I could no more blend with you than the sun could hide in daylight."

"Sure, it's worked for me before, when I marched with the army. But maybe if we make the sun believe the sky is night." Her eyes glimmered with a spark of mad determination. She reached for his hand. "Trust me?"

His hand twitched against her palm. Finally, with a guttural sound halfway between a sigh and a growl, he nodded.

"Now what?" he muttered.

"Now you cloak us."

"I'm not sure if it will hide you."

"Just try."

Krampus exhaled, long and low. Shadows unfurled like wings and crawled over her skin. Elowen sucked in a sharp breath as the cold wrapped her. She was used to the biting of winter, but this cold was deeper, like night pressing close, darkness that made the world forget it had ever seen light. Her body shivered involuntarily as coldness spread through her, leaving her empty inside, lost.

"Breathe," he rumbled, his voice near her ear, low enough that it steadied her pulse.

She did, though the cold lodged deep in her lungs. "Is this how it feels for you? All the time?"

"No," he said simply. "I don't feel it."

Her lips quirked despite herself, the shadows crawling over her like a second skin. "I suppose the best things are done at night."

His chest rumbled with a low chuckle, an unexpected warmth in the dark. "The best things," he murmured, leaning closer, "are done in quiet. Now hush."

She stifled a smile, pressed her lips together, and let the silence consume them.

The light from the watchtower swept over the snowfield, green beams crawling closer. Elowen held her breath as they stepped out into the open, Krampus' shadows folding around them tighter, pulling them deeper into darkness. The beam passed over her boots, so close she swore a toy soldier above would hear her heart hammering, but their gaze drifted on, painted eyes scanning for intruders that weren't there.

Step by careful step, they crossed the snow, the march of elves a steady cover in the distance. Elowen held her hand behind her, her magic casting snow to cover their tracks. The tower's gears whined, turning the light again, but the shadows held. They passed unseen.

Only when the tower was behind them did Krampus ease his

grip, shadows clinging like a cloak. His eyes burned red in the half-dark. "Still think I can't blend?"

Elowen let out the breath she'd been holding and grinned, shaky but fierce. "Guess you make a pretty good night sky after all."

"How else do you think I got about doing my work? But it's easier at night," he grumbled.

"I tried to forget that part."

"So did I," he said with a sigh.

The snow muffled their footsteps, but the silence didn't last. A metallic clank rose ahead, steady, mechanical. Too ordered to be elvish. Elowen's stomach twisted.

A patrol.

The shadows tightened around them as Krampus pressed her back into the cookie of a collapsed gingerbread wall. "Don't move," he growled, barely more than a breath.

The toy soldiers marched into view, their faces expressionless, eyes facing ahead. Their gears groaned with every synchronized step, their hollow voices echoing.

Clank, clank, clank.

They weren't far. Too close. One lagged a little behind the others, its head twisting side to side, lantern light sweeping dangerously across the snow.

Elowen let frost slither across the ground behind them, covering the remaining imprints of their boots. The air shimmered with her effort, but the shadows swallowed the glow, hiding it.

The soldier halted. Its head jerked toward them.

Elowen's heart stopped.

Night wrapped in a cold so deep she felt as though she'd ceased to exist. Krampus' hand pressed against her stomach, steadying her, grounding her to the one thing that was real in the void: his presence.

The soldier's lantern swung across the ruin, green light blazing over where they stood. It paused. Gears ticked. A low whirring noise rose, like a clock trying to decide.

Elowen tensed every muscle, forcing herself to freeze, forcing herself silent. *Please, please don't see us.*

Then, the soldier turned with a harsh *clank*, its lantern beam sliding away. It lumbered back into line, its steps merging in unison with the rest of the patrol as they clattered into the distance.

Krampus exhaled through his teeth, shadows slipping away, allowing Elowen to feel her body again. She sagged against the gingerbread, trembling. "That was too close."

His eyes narrowed after the patrol. "Yes. Too close. If not for —" He broke off, glancing at her, his voice rough. "You covered us well."

She swallowed her nerves and forced a small smile. "I have an excellent teacher."

He gave a short huff, almost a laugh. "I stopped teaching you a long time ago," he said, then nodded toward the horizon. "I can't keep shadowing you forever, though, so let's go."

Together, they slipped past the last stretch of snowfield. The hollow songs of the elves grew louder, rising and falling in unison, their voices robbed of joy.

And then, looming ahead, the gates of Kringle Central rose from the snow. Vast candy cane bars, towers crowned in golden stars, and flags snapping in the wind. Elves hurried in and out beneath the gates, their eyes cast down, their lips moving in brittle carols. Toy soldiers stood like statues at every corner, gears ticking faintly as their heads pivoted side to side, weapons braced in arms.

Elowen grimaced. The gates looked more like the maw of a beast than a cheery entry to a joyous kingdom.

Krampus growled low in his throat, shadows bristling at the sight. "So. After all that, we're finally here."

Elowen squared her shoulders, though her pulse raced. "And now we end this."

❄ ❄ ❄

Krampus' shadows cinched tighter around him as they joined the stream of elves shuffling through the gates. Elowen lowered her head, mimicking their hollow posture, forcing her body into the same weary rhythm to become the shadow of another elf. Krampus loomed close behind her, his shadows stretching, bending, blurring his form into something the eye slid away from, as though he were only another shadow cast by a tower.

No one looked at them. Not really. Elves kept their eyes locked forward, their lips moving in brittle carols. Voices rang in eerie harmony:

"Jolly, jolly, evermore,
Work and sing forevermore."

Elowen's stomach churned. She had always hated cheery work songs, but this wasn't a song. It was indoctrination.

Inside, Kringle Central gleamed, but it was wrong. She remembered bright banners, lanterns that painted the streets with warmth. Now the light was harsh, all crimson and gold, glinting off polished metal. The smell of sugar hung in the air, but it was cloying, sickly sweet, layered over with the sting of oil and smoke.

Elves bent over workbenches that lined the streets, hammering toys with mechanical precision. She wondered what had happened to the bustling city streets filled with joyous elves singing and dancing on their way to work. Where was the coffee, sugar, and sprinkles? Now, everywhere she looked, elves worked out in the open. Had production needs gotten so high as to overflow departments? Toy soldiers stalked between rows of elves, their gears ticking in time with the pounding of hammers. Every mistake was met with a harsh bark from overseers perched above in candy cane towers, megaphones blaring corrections.

Krampus' growl rumbled low beside her. Elowen reached

back, her fingers brushing his. "Not yet," she pleaded.

An elf perked up at her whisper, their needle frozen in hand, doll hair suspended in air. She froze, hunched over, her heart racing. Its eyes glazed over her. A licorice rope cracked in the air, snapping the elf back to their work.

They rushed away, slinking through the shadows, and moved deeper into the city. A parade of sleds rattled past, laden with sacks of toys and ornaments. Elves clung to them, their faces blank, eyes glazed, lips moving in that endless, empty chant.

Tinsel lined the streets, but instead of being cheerful, it glimmered like chains. Banners snapped in the wind, their sweeping golden script proclaiming: "The List is Law."

Elowen's throat tightened. She remembered this place filled with laughter, the smell of gingerbread. Now, it was a prison dressed in ribbons.

A whistle shrieked through the air. The flow of elves stopped instantly. Overseers barked new orders, and soldiers clanged forward.

Krampus leaned close, his breath warm against her ear. "We can't linger here. Where is he?"

Elowen's eyes swept the glowing towers ahead. At its heart, the tallest tower rose, its peak of gold burning like fire against the ashen sky. She nodded. "I bet he moved the throne room higher. That's where he'll be."

Krampus' eyes flared, and he squeezed her hand. "Then that's where we go."

❄ ❄ ❄

Step by step, they wound their way through the narrow streets, Krampus' darkness bending light whenever a patrol passed. Elowen kept her head down, but her eyes darted everywhere, drinking in the horrors.

A child-elf stumbled in the line ahead of them, its small hands dropping a carved toy soldier. The toy snapped in half against the cobblestones. A gasp rose from the workers nearby, but no one moved.

A soldier pivoted, gears shrieking. Without a word, it grabbed the child's wrist and dragged her from the line, the broken toy tossed into the gutter. The child's cries were swallowed by the chant, their small voice vanishing as if they had never been there.

Elowen's nails dug into her palms. She wanted to shout, to fight, but Krampus' shadows coiled around her wrist in warning. *Not yet.*

The closer they drew to the central tower, the thicker the air became. The shard in Elowen's pocket pulsed, its light muffled by cloth, but she knew Kringle's crown should *feel* it, like a signal. She felt it in her bones, and saw it in the way the tower leaned towards her, as though scenting prey.

Krampus noticed, too. She felt his shadow writhing restlessly around him. "It knows," he muttered, low enough for only her.

The whistle shrieked again. Soldiers poured from the tower's gates, their heavy steps rattling the ground in a synchronized march. Overseers cracked licorice whips, redirecting the lines of laborers. The chant grew louder, mechanical.

They turned down a side street, but the pressure grew worse. The shard beat faster, betraying them with every pulse.

And then…

"Elowen!"

Her name split the chant like a blade.

She froze. Slowly, she turned.

A woman was running toward her through the haze of golden snow.

Not the prim, bright Larkspur she remembered, the rival with perfect curls and crisp skirts.

This Larkspur was gaunt, her uniform gray with soot and ink. Her hair hung limp, the color leached by years of artificial light. But even with exhaustion, a mark glimmered faintly at her throat: a golden snowflake, its filigree burned into her skin. It pulsed faintly in time with the tower's heartbeat.

"I knew it was you," Larkspur gasped, slowing to a halt. "The rumor was true. You're here." Awe and disbelief colored her trembling voice as she spoke.

Elowen's heart stuttered. Her mind replayed Larkspur's betrayal, echoing from the dormitories all the way to her banishment. She darted forward, desperate. "Larkspur! Please. Don't—"

Larkspur's gaze flicked past her, catching the shifting shadows bristling behind Elowen. She squinted as if to make out the shape within them. Her face twisted, desperation warring with fear. For a moment, her mouth trembled. Elowen thought she might whisper an apology.

Instead, the golden mark at Larkspur's throat flared, and her lips peeled back. "I've waited a decade for this. Guards!" she shouted. "This way! Here!"

Ten years. Ten years since the betrayal that cost her everything, and now Larkspur was repeating history.

"No!" Elowen lunged, grabbing her shoulders. "You don't understand. He'll never free you! You'll never get what you want!"

Larkspur's hands clamped around Elowen's wrists, nails digging in. "You think I have a choice?" Her voice cracked, wild and raw. "The crown *burns* me when I lie. It *feeds* when I obey. Every day the crown takes a little more. If I give them you, if I deliver the traitor of the List, they'll reward me! They have to."

Her breath came in ragged gasps, and then Elowen saw it: the scar tissue beneath the mark, the rawness of years spent balancing terror with obedience.

"You don't have to do this," Elowen pleaded. "You can come with us—"

Larkspur laughed, a broken, hoarse sound. "Come *where*? There's nowhere left that isn't his. You don't know what it's like to live under him. Every day, another year taken. Another elf vanished. The gold never stops. You can't fight that."

The clang of soldiers rang at the alley's mouth. Krampus' shadow shifted and dropped.

Larkspur's gaze flicked to Krampus, and recognition hit. She stumbled back, horror dawning as the truth took shape. She shrieked. "You brought *him* here—"

Krampus growled low and terrible, the sound vibrating through the stones. Shadows surged from the alley walls like a living tide.

Larkspur screamed. "Guards! Guards—"

"Elowen, *run*!" Krampus barked.

The clang of toy soldiers erupted at the alley's mouth. They spilled in, gears shrieking, boots stomping. Krampus seized Elowen's arm and pulled her behind him as the first soldier charged. Shadows whipped out, slicing wood apart with a sound like thunder.

They bolted through a narrow backstreet, Larkspur's cries and the soldier's march pounding after them. The chant followed, a tidal wave of devotion:

"Jolly, jolly, evermore,
Work and sing forevermore."

Snow and soot blurred past. Krampus' shadows streamed around them like smoke, devouring the light. Elowen stumbled, breath burning, but his hand caught hers again, steady and relentless.

"Left!" she gasped, spotting a narrow passage between two candy cane towers. They ducked through, barely a step ahead of the soldiers.

But the pursuit multiplied. Every turn brought another patrol, drawn by the shard's pulse. The air itself throbbed with the crown's hunger.

Elowen's chest ached. "The crown. It's calling them. He *knows*!"

His shadow writhed, black and furious. "Then we give him what he wants."

They burst onto a broad avenue lit by golden lampposts, every light flickering red like watchful eyes. Ahead loomed the central tower, its gates yawning open, soldiers pouring out in formation. Behind them, more were closing in.

Trapped.

Krampus snarled, his hands flexing. Shadows erupted outward, tearing through wood and gears. Sparks and screams filled the air. Elowen raised her hands, sending frost shattering across the cobbles. Ice climbed the legs of the nearest soldiers, freezing them mid-step.

"Move!" Krampus roared, barreling toward the gates.

Krampus' fury and Elowen's magic slashed a path as they smashed through the front line. Behind them, the iron doors slammed shut with a deafening clang.

Inside, the peppermint scent was caustic, choking. Massive columns of red and gold candy stone stretched toward a vaulted ceiling, every inch carved with runes. A sickly glow spread as the late sun hit the stained-glass sugar windows, the picture of elves kneeling before a gold-crowned figure becoming suddenly vibrant.

Kringle's tower. The belly of the beast.

The doors behind them boomed again, shaking under the weight of fists and gears. Krampus shoved Elowen forward, his voice a growl. "We keep moving."

Above them, bells tolled, reverberating through the tower like thunder.

Her heart sank.

The first bell of the new year.

And with it, the crown's song rose like a storm.

CHAPTER THIRTY

"Pssst."

Both of them froze. The whisper snaked through the shadows like smoke.

Krampus bared his teeth, shadows bristling. Elowen grabbed his forearm and breathed, "Wait."

"Over here."

Against the shadows of the wall, a shape detached itself from the gloom. A crooked figure, limping, one leg dragging stiffly. Elowen's heart stuttered when an icing eye came into focus.

"Cinn?" she breathed.

"Follow me."

They hurried after the crooked figure, Krampus stalking behind like a storm on two legs. Through the pounding of soldiers battering the tower doors, they ducked into a side room stacked with towers of wrapped presents.

The gingerbread man stepped into the light. His form was battered and broken: frosting cracked, limbs chipped, an entire hand snapped clean off. Still, he gave a crooked grin. "By sugarplum, what took you so long?"

Elowen's throat closed, and she threw her arms around him. His jagged edges dug into her, but she didn't care. "Cinn!"

He wheezed out a laugh that sounded half crumble, half cough. "Careful, I might fall apart. Literally. But—" he leaned back, giving her a long, appraising look. "Look at you. Same braids. Same eyes. Glowing bright as winter glass. And…" his gaze tipped toward Krampus, pacing the room like a wolf penned in, "…you've picked up a behemoth of a shadow, haven't you?"

Heat crept across Elowen's cheeks, though she buried it in a tight hug. "I'm so sorry. We…we got lost."

"Lost?" Cinn barked a laugh that crumbled into a cough. "Is that what they call it now?"

Her laugh cracked, relief spilling into her tears.

Cinn spread his jagged arm in mock flourish. "And him. Mr. Tall, Dark, and Don't-Talk-to-My-Elf. You two look disgustingly good together. If I'd known elves aged like fine wine, I'd have kept closer to the vineyards myself."

Elowen's heart stuttered at the words. Aged. The orchard had been timeless, a dream stitched in fruit and twilight. She hadn't thought of years. She hadn't thought at all.

Her voice came out rough. "How long?"

Cinn tilted his head, and something like pity flickered in his frosting eye. "You don't know?" He tapped the air with his stump as if counting fingers. "Ten. Give or take."

The number crashed over her like ice. "Ten?" Her knees nearly gave. "No…we weren't even gone half a year. I swear—" Her gaze shot to Krampus, but his eyes burned quietly, confirming her terror.

Cinn shrugged, the motion brittle. "Crown drinks years like cocoa. Siphons them clean. It's given him power, strength. The rest of us? Not so lucky. Ten years, sugarplum."

The room tilted. Elowen braced a hand against the stack of presents. Ten years of carols turned to chains. Ten years of elves breaking their backs while she and Krampus had lived untouched beneath silver boughs. The orchard's twilight had shielded them, but it had stolen time all the same.

She wanted to laugh, to scream, to apologize until her voice bled. Instead, her whisper cracked the silence: "We left them."

Cinn caught her chin gently with his jagged arm, his smile

weary. "No. You came back. That's more than most do."

Her chest ached, but she nodded. "Then we fix it."

Cinn's grin tilted sharper. "Good. Because Charlie's here too. And he needs you."

❈ ❈ ❈

A side stairwell wound upward through the tower; the muffled sound of bells and cheers bled through the walls.

"Watch out," Cinn muttered. "Keep your eyes open."

They climbed until the stair spilled onto a vast balcony overlooking a grand hall.

Elowen froze.

Below stretched a cavernous chamber lined with golden garlands, evergreen boughs dripping with crimson ribbons. Children's laughter rang from phonographs, echoing too shrill, too perfect, while automatons in painted faces twirled endlessly in a haunted waltz. Tables sagged under feasts no-one touched, sugared geese and candied hams rotting where they sat. Her mouth watered at the perfect pastries gleaming in neat towers of sugar. These were things she had once scoffed at, now dreamed of, but found they were nothing more than poisoned promises.

And the toys.

Piles upon piles of them, stacked high like barricades, gleamed under chandeliers. Scattered about were dolls with grins too wide, soldiers that saluted in unison, and rocking horses that tossed their heads in silent rhythm. At the center, a fountain gushed hot cocoa, its surface coated with a sickly sheen.

High-ranking elves with glittering insignia and pressed uniforms pranced at the edges, singing Kringle's hymns. Starched skirts and polished slippers glided along the pristine floor. Behind their ranks, Elowen swore she heard muffled sobs.

Her stomach churned. It should have been a celebration of their year's hard work. "He's twisted joy into a weapon," she whispered.

Krampus' shadow writhed as he bared his teeth. "It's a carnival of chains."

"This is just the festival floor," Cinn muttered. "You don't want to see what happens when the lights go out."

Before she could ask what could make this worse, another whisper threaded from the gloom. "Cinn?"

A bent elf woman in patched red wool emerged from a hidden passage, her eyes sharp as flint, white hair piled high. Two others followed, lean and wary, their once-bright bells tarnished to rust.

"Elowen?" the woman breathed. "So it's true, you're here."

Elowen's pulse leapt. "Yes?"

The woman's gaze softened, a flicker of recognition in her eyes. "I was there that day when you ran from Kringle. Back then, I was a little younger. You whispered to me I could stop. I remember the doll I was sewing. I remember that moment and the spark you left behind. My name is Mirabel."

Elowen blinked, heart hammering. "Mirabel?"

A shadow of a smile crossed her lined face. "That day, I first dared to hope. Ever since, I've tried to resist in small ways. Sabotaging toys, hiding messages, keeping the smallest sparks alive. Every year, they said I was crazy, that hope was dead, that you weren't alive. But I waited. And now...maybe our chance has come."

One of the younger elves leaned close to Cinn. "They've doubled patrols since Kringle caught wind of their presence," he said, wide eyes flicking nervously to Krampus. "But we'll help. In whatever way we can."

"Can you help us get Charlie?" Cinn asked.

The boy nodded. "His cell is under guard. You won't get near without a trick or two."

Krampus growled.

"Wait," Elowen said quickly, clutching his arm. "We can't waste strength here. We'll need all the help we can get when we face Kringle himself. If Charlie's with us, maybe more will follow."

The elder woman's jaw set. "Then we'll take you to him right now. And we'll handle the guards."

❋ ❋ ❋

The rebels led them through a narrow back stairwell, walls sticky and close. Torchlight flickered across peppermint-iron doorframes, runes glowing faintly. Elowen's stomach twisted with every step. She remembered laughing through the city once, ribbons in her hair, cocoa stains on her fingers. Now the air stank of ash and sweat.

At the landing below Charlie's cell, Mirabel raised a hand. "Wait here." She motioned to the boy and the second rebel, who slipped away. Moments later, a sharp whistle pierced the air. Shouts followed. Boots thundered down a corridor as guards scrambled toward the sound.

Mirabel smirked. "That's your window."

Cinn planted himself at the stairwell mouth, stump raised like a weapon. "Go! I'll keep watch."

Krampus strode to the barred door, shadows seething around the peppermint iron. He strained; the lock hissed but held fast. Runes sparked along its seams. His eyes snapped to Elowen. "Your turn."

Her throat tightened. The seal looked like a sloppy imitation of the Forger's work; it was clumsy, forced, like someone copied without understanding and used the wrong runes.

She laid her palms against the bands, breath shaking. Her magic crawled through her fingers, searching, prodding. Lines of light flared, a lattice of peppermint runes unraveling beneath her touch. She pressed harder, deleting, rearranging runes, and whispering words she wasn't sure she understood.

The lock gave a shudder. The runes blinked, faltered, then bent under her will. With a sharp crack, the seal split open.

Elowen staggered back, her palms sweaty and heart racing. "It's open."

"You'd make a great locksmith," Krampus muttered as he pushed the door wide. "I'm glad you're on my side."

Heat assaulted Elowen's face. Inside, the air was thick with sweat, humid as a steaming oven. A furnace burned in the corner, and chains clinked faintly in the gloom.

"Charlie?" Elowen's voice cracked.

A low growl answered. Then, movement.

From the far wall, a hulking form shifted. Chains scraped, links straining as the broad-shouldered yetlet raised his head. His once bright fur was matted, patches of white streaked with soot. His eyes glimmered, but were hollowed, tired. And yet, when they landed on Elowen, they widened.

"Elowen?" His voice was hoarse, disbelieving.

Her throat closed. "Charlie!" She darted forward, but Krampus' arm shot out, barring her, his gaze sweeping the ceiling, the corners, the locks.

Chains bound Charlie at the wrists, iron biting into his thick fur, pinning him against the wall. And clinging to his broad shoulder was the tiny imp Fizz, covered in soot.

Elowen studied the room and realized it was designed for them. The heat stifled their frost, suppressing them, weakening them. Her stomach twisted into knots. This was more than a prison; it was torture.

The imp hissed at the intruders, spitting out a faint spark that fizzled in the air. Once realization dawned, it let out a high-pitched shriek. It tumbled down Charlie's arm and scampered over to her, bouncing off her legs before clambering up her cloak to perch on her shoulder, trilling wildly.

Elowen laughed through her tears, cupping him gently before looking back at Charlie. "I'm sorry it took so long."

Charlie's chest heaved. His lips curled, something between a growl and a broken smile. "Didn't think you would."

"We're here now," Krampus rumbled, his eyes narrowing at the shackles. "And you won't wear these anymore."

He fought the chains. The rough metal tore into his skin as he wrestled the links, but they would not break. He grumbled and turned to Elowen. "It's not enough. I can't break them."

Charlie groaned. "No, no, please, no." He slunk down, his body quivering as if resigned to his fate.

Elowen ran forward and grabbed the chains. She felt them pulsing in her hands, infused with crude runes. "It's a poor job," she said.

"Can you break these too?" Krampus asked.

"Please, Elowen." Charlie looked at her, his eyes filled with hope.

She hummed to herself as she searched through the runes of the chains, her magic spreading, willing it to break. It was crude, but this smith was not the Forger. Frost spread across the iron, then…snap. One by one, the links cracked and shattered, falling to the floor with a heavy clang.

Charlie staggered forward. His massive frame swayed, but Krampus rushed in, catching him. The yetlet shuddered, catching his breath. Fizz cheered from her shoulder and leapt back onto Charlie, trilling affectionately.

Cinn peeked in the doorway from his guard, his seams glowing faint, his grin sharp. "Looks like we have the band back together."

Elowen hugged Charlie fiercely, her tears soaking into his fur. "I'm sorry, but we're not done yet. We need your help. We're going to end the crown."

Charlie's eyes burned brighter, and he stood taller. "Good. I've been waiting a long time for this."

Krampus loomed beside them, his voice low. "We have to move. Before they sense where we are."

Cinn hobbled into the room. "I think it's too late."

CHAPTER THIRTY-ONE

"Sugarplum sticks," Elowen swore. She'd known it was too easy.

Slow, deliberate clapping echoed down the hall.

"Well, well." The voice was singsong, smug, gratingly familiar. "Isn't this festive? Larkspur was right. Our wayward elf has returned."

Klaussen strolled into the chamber, flanked by a squad of elf soldiers, their candy cane spears gleaming sharp in the furnace light. The peppermint tips glinted like fangs. Their boots struck the stone floor in perfect unison. Cinn was shoved forward, spears leveled at his body, his limp worse with the prodding.

Elowen's heart thudded. Klaussen looked older, though not by much. Gone was the immaculate manager's uniform of his list-making days. Now he wore a pressed uniform, crimson-trimmed, emerald sash across his chest, insignia glittering proudly, and a worn baton at his waist. He stood straighter than she remembered, his once-smug grin sharpened by years of command. He had climbed the ladder as he had always wanted.

"Well done," he drawled, spreading his hands as though welcoming her home. "I knew if I waited long enough, you'd stumble right back here. And look at you, bringing gifts." His gaze flicked to Krampus, and his grin widened, sickly sweet. "He will be *delighted*."

"Klaussen," Elowen hissed, fury knotting her throat. "Still a bootlicker after all these years."

His grin faltered for half a beat, then returned, nastier. "Careful, Elowen. My boots stand a little higher now. And your tongue might get you on the Naughty List...oh, wait." He chuckled, low and cruel. "You're already there."

Krampus' shadows flared, curling up the walls, but the spears angled forward instantly, candy-striped with hard, calculating eyes.

"Do it," her old manager said to the soldiers. "March them up. He's been waiting years for this audience."

Soldiers brandished chains, peppermint links gleaming with runes. Elowen stiffened as they clattered at her feet. Krampus growled, low and dangerous.

"No shackles," he snarled, his eyes burning. "Never again."

The soldiers bristled, spears tightening the circle. Klaussen only smirked. "You'll wear what you're told."

Elowen stepped forward, her chin lifted, fury and dread burning in her veins. "Stop." She turned to Krampus, meeting his eyes. Her voice softened, fierce but pleading. "It'll be fine."

His jaw worked, every muscle trembling with rage. At last, with a guttural growl that shook the walls, he let the shadows recede.

Elowen lifted her wrists. "Only me, shackle only me and we will do no harm. That is the deal, or we end this right now, and none of you will leave this room alive. We will all come willingly."

Krampus nodded and stood there, fists clenched at his sides, his glare boring straight through Klaussen with the fiery storm of a thousand nights.

Klaussen flinched under his gaze, then stared at her, considering her words until he waved his hand into the air. Cold peppermint iron closed around her wrists, stinking of sugar and smoke. She didn't flinch. Krampus watched as the shackles bit into her, his red eyes never leaving hers. The soldiers prodded Charlie forward, Fizz squealing furiously on his shoulder. Cinn stepped in line with them, although his face glared in anger.

Klaussen stepped back, smug satisfaction radiating from every pore. "Up we go, little menace. Time to meet your King."

And with that, they were driven higher into the tower, the spiral stair echoing with the grind of gears and the brittle chant of hollow voices.

At the top, the golden doors loomed. Beyond them waited the throne. And in there, the crown.

❊ ❊ ❊

The golden doors groaned as they opened, slow and ponderous, as if the weight might crush intruders beneath their gilt edges.

The throne room beyond blazed with impossible light. It was vast, cathedral-high, its arched ceiling painted with twinkling stars. Elowen blinked, her eyes squinting. Every surface gleamed gold and red: polished marble veined with peppermint stripes and pillars wound with silver tinsel. At the far end rose the throne itself, carved from candy crystal and set atop a dais of sugared stone, gleaming with sugar frost in the light of a hundred chandeliers.

Elowen snorted. A grand throne room fit for a tyrant holiday king. Either Kringle's ostentatiousness had grown to new heights, or some decorator really aimed to please, on penalty of their head.

Toy soldiers lined the chamber in perfect rows, faces blank, gears ticking faintly, each clutching a pike. Their eyes tracked the intruders with mechanical precision.

And upon the throne sat Kringle.

He looked unchanged. The same golden curls, the same cherubic face, his skin unwrinkled and smooth. Barely a day older than the man who sat upon this seat centuries ago. Only his eyes betrayed him now: bright, feverish, burning with the icy fire of dominion. He wore a crimson velvet robe lined with gleaming white fur and a golden belt that cinched his waist.

The soldiers halted the group in the center of the room.

Elowen frowned. Upon his brow the crown gleamed, humming with power, each jewel pulsing.

Kringle's lips curled into a smile. "Well. Look what the snow dragged in."

Elowen's stomach twisted. The shard in her pocket pulsed hot, thrumming with every beat of her heart. She lifted her chin, hiding her shiver.

Then, a faint whistle.

From shadowed side passages, rebel elves burst in, led by the same rust-belled resistors who helped her with Charlie. They moved like phantoms, brandishing makeshift weapons from various departments. Firecrackers exploded at the soldiers' feet. Guards dispersed, chasing the rebels. One pressed something small and rough into Elowen's hand: a charm of woven bells and bone.

"It'll muffle the crown," the elf hissed.

She clutched the charm tight between shackled hands. Its cool surface hummed, and she felt the edge of the crown's pull ease.

Kringle's eyes widened at the rebels. "Traitors," he spat. "You dare to stand against me? Her fate will also be yours."

"You twisted joy into a weapon," Elowen countered. "And you call us traitors?"

Kringle's smile returned, cruel and sharp. He leaned, elbows on his knees, studying them one by one. His gaze lingered on Elowen's shackles, then slid to Krampus. His smile grew sharp. "Brother."

Krampus stiffened, his muscles tensing.

"You've grown bold," Kringle said, his voice smooth, sweet as spun sugar, laced with venom. "How kind of you to return for the end of the year. And to come crawling back here with…" He flicked his hand at Elowen. "…this elf. Tell me, how does it feel, betraying blood for a plaything?"

Krampus growled, the sound reverberating off the chamber walls. His eyes burned crimson.

Elowen spoke before he could. "He's more man than you'll ever be."

Gasps rippled from the balconies. Klaussen sneered behind them, baring his teeth. Kringle laughed, a hollow, booming laugh that echoed in the hall like bells tolling the end of all things.

"Oh, fiery, isn't she?" Kringle's eyes sparkled with something darker than amusement. "Tell me, brother, is that what seduced you? Her fire? Or perhaps her defiance of me was what made you crawl at her feet?"

"Enough," Krampus snarled, darkness flexing.

The toy soldiers shifted in warning, gears whirring.

Kringle spread his arms wide. "What happened to you, Krampus? You were the punishment, the shadow, the scourge of mortals. You were my balance, my blade. And now..." His eyes dropped to Elowen, shackled but defiant. "Now you've been tamed."

Krampus' roar shook the chandeliers, shadows bursting upward like wings. Soldiers lurched, and the room erupted into battle.

Spears thrust. Krampus seized one and snapped it in two, the peppermint shaft splintering. Shadows wrapped the soldiers and ripped them into clouds of splinters and cogs.

Charlie bellowed, his frost breath stuttering, but enough to glaze the floor, sending two soldiers skidding into pillars. Another spear plunged into his side, and he howled, his fur clotted with thick, dark blood. He grabbed a fallen chain, swinging it like a flail, knocking three soldiers flat.

Fizz shrieked, leaping from his shoulder to spit sparks at an elf, who screamed and toppled from a balcony.

Klaussen tugged at Elowen's chains, pulling her backwards from the fray. She stumbled back a few steps, then planted her boots firmly.

"You're mine," Klaussen hissed.

Elowen's wrists burned. She closed her eyes, willed her magic outward to bend and twist the runes, and with a crack the peppermint iron splintered. Shards of sugar and smoke fell to the marble.

"That was a mistake," she said.

Klaussen stumbled backwards, shock splattered upon his face. A rebel ran by and slashed at him with a pair of large gift-wrapping scissors. He screamed as the blades slashed his arm and ran, the rebel chasing him.

Elowen thrust waves of frost into the toy soldiers, freezing their gears in place.

Kringle's smile faded. His eyes narrowed.

"Clever girl," he said, his voice booming. "But cleverness won't save you. You cracked my crown once. Now you'll break beneath it." He touched his crown. Its jewels flared, and the throne room shuddered.

The elves on the balconies screamed, their voices twisting into carols, their eyes rolling white as the crown's power consumed them. They chanted louder, their voices an eerie hymn. The song thickened the air, pressing against Elowen's lungs like suffocating velvet. She staggered and clutched the charm tighter, her body trembling, but the worst of the crown's song broke against it like waves on stone. In her pocket, the shard pulsed, radiating a heat that threatened to burn her.

"Stay with me!" Krampus barked, his hand clamping onto her shoulder. She looked up, and his eyes bore into hers.

She nodded, breath ragged, and spun on her heels.

Cinn darted forward, surprisingly fast on his cracked legs. He snatched a candy cane spear and drove it through an elf's chest, sugar shards flying. "Did you miss me?" he crowed. But his triumph was short-lived. A toy soldier swung the butt of his pike into his side and hurled him across the room. He struck a pillar with a sickening crack, a leg shattering into crumbs. He slumped, the icing glowing faint and broken.

"No!" Elowen screamed. She hurled frost at the soldier, freezing him before shattering him with another blast.

Charlie staggered but still fought, using chains to pull down two more soldiers. He collapsed to one knee, Fizz clinging to his fur and hissing defiantly.

The toy soldiers kept coming, an endless tide. Kringle leaned back on his throne, smiling, watching the carnage as if it were a show staged for him alone.

Elowen's vision blurred. The shard pulsed hotter. She thrust her hand into her cloak, gripping it through the dress fabric, its edges biting her palm. It hummed with power, aching to be used.

Krampus' chest heaved, and shadows dripped from his horns like molten tar. He bared his teeth, eyes blazing. "We can't hold this forever."

Elowen's gaze darted to the throne, to the crown gleaming above Kringle's smug face. She clenched the shard tighter. "Then we don't. We cut the head off the tree."

"Then let's climb." Krampus growled, shadows writhing.

❄ ❄ ❄

The golden doors slammed shut with a thunderous boom. There was no escape. Elowen's heart thudded. She knew either she would end this now or die fighting.

The throne room was alive with light, song, and death. Rows of toy soldiers shifted with mechanical grace, their spears angling in unison, gears grinding like a thousand ticking clocks. Above, balconies of elves swayed in rhythm, their voices echoing down in a carol that was command.

Kringle leaned on his throne, the crown upon his head blazing with a golden fire. His smile spread like poison. "My little elves," he purred, his voice carrying across the room, "sing louder."

Voices rose into a keening wail. The crown pulsed, drawing their song into itself like molasses.

Elowen's stomach churned. The shard in her pocket beat hotter, hungrier, whispering at the edges of her thoughts. *Take me. Use me. End him now.*

Krampus flexed his bloodied hands. They had to make it to the crown. It was the only way.

Soldiers marched towards them, thrusting spears and axes, tips gleaming sharp with runes. Krampus roared, shadows bursting outward, slamming into them like a wave. Soldiers staggered, gears shrieking, but more pressed in, mechanical bodies relentless.

Charlie bellowed, wrenching an axe from an elf's hands. His frost sputtered, a thin sheen of ice slicking the floor. Two more soldiers crashed into one another, but a third lunged and sliced Charlie's shoulder. He roared, batting it away as blood splattered across the tiles.

Fizz's shriek filled the air as it leapt and tore at its face.

Ice chains lashed out from Elowen, cracking with a sharp, brittle sound as they wrapped around the toy soldiers, shattering them. She staggered, breath tearing at her chest. The shard pulsed harder, urging her to draw more, to take more.

"Not yet," she muttered.

Kringle clapped his hands. "Yes! This is the spirit of the season!"

The elves above wailed louder, their song cracking into hysteria, their hollow faces flushed with unnatural devotion. The crown blazed, light spilling down like chains of fire.

Krampus staggered under its weight, his shadows writhing, his horns blazing red at the tips. He snarled and forced himself upright.

Elowen reached into her cloak, her hand closing around the shard. Pain seared her palm. The shard hissed inside her mind. *Feed me. Strike him. Strike now.*

She held it tight, struggling against the urge to launch herself towards the throne. *Not now, not yet*, she begged. She had to get close enough for it to count. Her eyes blazed as she steadied her breath.

Krampus' shadows ripped soldiers apart in bursts of cogs and candy shards. Elowen froze others solid, shattering them with a wave of her hand. Charlie lumbered beside them, bleeding heavily, swinging a hammer to smash soldier after soldier. Fizz darted between them, spitting sparks at joints to jam gears.

Rebels slashed and fought where they could.

The dais loomed ahead. Kringle watched from his seat, grinning, lounging.

Bells tolled above, the sound shaking the chamber. A reminder of the last hours of the year. Time was ending. She had to end this before another year claimed them all.

They reached the steps. Soldiers pressed from every side, relentless, endless, but they climbed, blood smearing the sugar marble. Krampus shielded her with his body, taking blow after blow, night bleeding in retaliation. She shoved frost and fire outward, trying to carve them a path, but the shard burned hotter, hungrier. Slowly, painfully, they climbed higher.

At the base of the throne, Klaussen marched forward with another squad. His crimson-trimmed uniform gleamed, rank pins glittering, his grin sharp as a blade, blood dripping down his arm. He lifted his spear high, voice ringing with smug venom. "For years I waited for this moment, Elowen. For years! And now I'll be the one to end you."

"Not today," she spat, hurling frost at him.

He ducked, and the soldiers closed around them. Krampus tore through them, roaring, but Klaussen slipped between shadows, climbing the steps with a predator's grin.

Yes, I'm almost there.

Elowen reached into her pocket, ready to drive the shard into the crown's glow.

And then…

Pain.

White-hot searing pain lanced through her midsection. With a sob, she lowered her eyes, her shoulders shaking.

A peppermint spear jutted from her belly, blood running crimson down the candy stripes. Her trembling hands closed around the shaft. Her knees buckled.

Above her, Klaussen sneered, his eyes alight with triumph. "Nice try, menace."

Kringle rose from his throne, the crown blazing, his smile radiant and terrible.

Elowen's vision blurred. She swayed, blood soaking her dress and cloak.

Kringle marched down the steps to lean over her. His voice rang above the chaos, sweet and cruel as a carol: "Happy end-of-year, little elf."

CHAPTER THIRTY-TWO

Elowen swayed on her knees at the base of the throne, her dress dark and wet, each breath rattling sharp through her chest. The peppermint spear jutted out of her, its stripes slick with her blood. She clutched at the wound, but the warmth seeped between her shaking fingers no matter how she held it. Something felt wrong, utterly wrong, fluttering inside her.

Klaussen stood above her, grinning like a wolf dressed in sugar.

Kringle's robe swirled like fire, the crown blazing. "I am the carol everlasting, the feast eternal. You're a single candle in the dark, and I snuff candles with a breath." His voice carried over the wail of the elves' brittle chant. "Sing louder! The end of the year is here! Give us your voices, give us your life!"

The elves shrieked their chorus louder.

The crown pulsed with their obedience, light spilling outward like golden chains, snaring the air itself.

But a deeper sound drowned the carol.

A roar.

Krampus.

His eyes burned blood red, his shadows writhing like a winter storm at midnight. He tore through soldiers, ripping wood and sugar like parchment. Each strike sent shards and bodies flying; each roar shook the floor. His horns glowed. His body was a furnace of rage.

Elowen screamed, and a burst of gray magic knocked Klaussen in the leg. The elf flew down the throne stairs, his scream piercing the air.

Krampus lunged. Shadows erupted, slamming soldiers aside, devouring the light.

Kringle met his brother on the steps, his own hand flaring with golden fire drawn straight from the crown. "Don't tell me you'd throw away eternity for an elf," he yelled, though strain laced his voice.

Krampus bellowed, his claw meeting Kringle's hand. Shadow and light clashed, the impact shaking the tower. The marble split beneath their feet, golden sparks colliding with black smoke.

Elowen hunched, clutching her belly. Her vision swam, and she coughed, lungs burning. She looked through the blur: Krampus and Kringle locked in combat, each strike shattering sugar stone, each roar and cry echoing like thunder.

Her blood dripped freely. She could feel the shard pulsing, hissing inside her skull. *Take me. End him. Shatter everything.*

"I can't," she hissed through gritted teeth.

Her mind flickered, half-mad. And in that madness, she remembered…

The in-between.

Snowfields broken by spires of black stone. The gaunt creature with claws like icicles.

It had listened when she had helped it.

She needed a portal. *Can I do it?* Her hand pressed flat against the bloodstained sugar stone. Frost and runes spread from her fingers laced with pain. She uttered words she did not know, her voice cracking but resolute.

"Creature of the in-between. Please, I need your help."

The air split.

Gray runes flickered, and a portal cracked open, jagged and wrong, black frost leaking out. Wind tore through the throne room. Soldiers froze. Even Kringle faltered, his head snapping toward the sound.

From the wound in the world, the creature slithered forward.

Its body, bent and gaunt, claws splintered in ice, and its maw wide and whistling cold. Its presence smothered the elves' chant, the sound of their song dying on their lips as they stared at the creature in horror.

Kringle's golden glow flickered. "What? What is this?"

Krampus seized the distraction. He slammed into Kringle, claws across his chest, hurling him across the steps.

The creature took one glance at Elowen, hissed, then lunged. Its claws slashed Kringle's leg. Blood sprayed crimson over marble. Kringle screamed, writhing, golden light flaring as he fell. With all her might, Elowen hurled a shimmering ball of gray at Kringle.

The crown tumbled from his head.

It rolled across the steps, spinning once, twice, before clattering in a pool of light before Elowen.

A jolt ran through her.

She crawled towards it, every movement agony, her body screaming. Blood smeared the steps beneath her. The shard burned in her pocket, its voice screaming. *Strike. Shatter.*

She reached into her pocket and pulled it free.

"Yes," she breathed.

The shard pulsed brightly as though newly forged. Its edges drank from her blood. Her veins lit with gray fire, runes racing under her skin, the same runes she had seen carved in the pillars of darkness. Her blood sang with them, too loud, too final, as though her body itself was the last forge. The shard burned her, and in a flash drained her magic, her life, clouding her vision.

"Elowen!" Krampus yelled.

But she knew. She had always known. Neither shadow nor fire could undo the crown. Only sacrifice. Only truth. Only gray, the magic of the ancients, the chains that once bound them, now running in her veins. And she would end it.

The crown flared, rejecting shadow, spitting sparks at fire. But when her gray runes pulsed down her arm, it stilled, trembling, as though it recognized its undoing.

With a scream, she slammed the shard into the crown.

Light exploded.

A blinding flash seared the throne room, white, red, and black colliding. Soldiers yelled, gears burst, bodies collapsed in heaps. Elves shrieked, clutching their ears as the carol froze in their throats. The creature from the in-between reared back, frost fire flaring, shrieking in triumph.

Elowen's vision filled with stars. She smelled burning sugar, copper blood, frost on the wind.

The crown screamed as it cracked, a wail of light shattering against shadow, and then against gray. Gray, the one color it could never chain, the truth it had tried to erase. The Choir's voice shrieked its last song. Once. Twice. Then exploded into glittering fragments, each piece shrieking as it died.

Golden chains burst apart. The song cut off. The elves on the balconies collapsed, their eyes now clearing. Rebels cheered and waved their makeshift weapons in the air.

Kringle writhed on the floor, clutching his leg, his eyes wide, face twisted with fury and fear. "No," he gasped.

Elowen's arms trembled with pain. The shard slipped from her grasp, clattering beside her, its hunger sated, her power spent.

Her body gave out. She collapsed against the throne, blood pooling around her, her veins alight as though the shard had carved its hunger into her flesh.

The world bled away in fragments, crimson streaking the steps, frost creeping over marble, her breath rattling shallow and sharp. Kringle's screams were high and furious, his voice stripped of its velvet sweetness. He threw light after light at the creature, to no avail. The creature's claws carved gouges into the floor as it dragged its prize by the leg toward the flickering, jagged portal. Kringle's screams vanished into the howl of icy wind as the portal swallowed him whole.

Krampus' roar shook the ruined tower as he leapt towards her.

She was too weak to answer. The peppermint spear left her

hollow, the warmth of her blood spilling too fast for her body to replace. She knew this would be one wound she would not heal from. And yet, she felt more than her own life slipping. Something softer, fainter. Something fluttered inside her like a moth's wing. Weakening. Fading.

What is that? What dies with me? Her mind was unraveling.

As her vision dimmed, she heard it again, that low, ancient sigh, heavy with regret and release. Not the crown's, not Kringle's, but the ancients'. And she understood: this was why she had been unlocked. Not to live, but to give.

Darkness swelled.

Shadows engulfed her. His shadows, cold and vast, wrapped her as though he could hold her together with will alone. She felt herself lifted, pressed against the furnace of his chest. He smelled of frost and iron and smoke, and his voice broke in her ear, a growl strangled into a plea.

"Stay. Don't you dare leave me. Elowen, *please.*"

Her lips parted, a tremor of breath, but no words came. She coughed, wet with blood, and his shadows recoiled as if burned.

The throne room shattered, sugar stone cracking, toy soldiers clattering lifelessly to the floor. The elves, freed but terrified, scattered into the streets. No-one dared look back. Charlie carried Cinn and Fizz.

Only Krampus stayed with Elowen, his horns casting jagged shadows across the fallen banners, his arms tightening around her limp body.

CHAPTER THIRTY-THREE

He looked at the open, howling portal of black frost, the echo of Kringle's screams faint upon the wind. His red eyes blazed with one terrible thought: *there is no other way.*

He ran.

Shadows carried him faster than mortal legs could move, sweeping up the steps, leaping through the portal. The black frost devoured him, the door snapping shut behind with a sound like shattering bone.

The in-between realm greeted them with silence.

Black spires broke the endless snowfields. The horizon glowed bruised violet; the air was bitter with ash. The whistle of the creature wound through the air like a dirge, always close, never visible. Somewhere distant, Kringle's screams echoed, ragged and fading, like a curse dragged into shadow.

But Krampus had no time for his brother's fate. His every step was for her.

"Elowen," he rasped, running, his arms locked around her. His hands trembled against her back, terrified to feel how cold she had grown. Her hair, once radiant as fire, clung damp and dark to her cheeks. Her eyes fluttered half-shut.

A hand twitched against his chest. "Cold…"

"Stay. You're not leaving me," he growled, louder now, as if his fury alone could anchor her. Shadows billowed around them, lashing the spires, shattering ice. "Do you hear me? Not now. Not ever. You can't."

Her breath rattled. Her lips moved, but only blood bubbled between them.

Krampus' shadows, for all their vastness, could not shield her weakening heartbeat.

He staggered. For a moment, the monster in him wanted to roar, to rend the world until someone, something, *answered*. And in his fury, a memory returned: her voice, hoarse, but alive, telling him of the being she met in the realms between. The one who judged her, the one who gave her more power in her veins.

"That being," he said, his eyes burning. "That one that gave you the power. Show me. Where is it?"

She didn't stir.

But in the distance, as if answered by his call, against the endless snow, a door waited. Black towering arch of black stone, gray runes burning across its surface. The same door that had once judged her in the dark realm, here now, and alive with gray fire.

Krampus' throat closed. His feet carried him faster, shadow whipping around him, until at last he stood before it. He pressed one clawed hand flat against it.

"Let me through," he snarled. His voice cracked, dropping into a whisper. "Judge me if you must. But let me through. She will not die. Not her."

The door groaned, runes flaring to life. A deep vibration shuddered across the plains. His shadow writhed and snapped, clawing at the ground as the door weighed him, his chains, his wrath, his countless nights of fear and punishment.

He pressed harder, baring his teeth. "Take me. Take all of me. Just…save her."

The runes flared gray. And then, the door opened.

❄ ❄ ❄
★ ★ ★

The vast realm stretched beyond, carved from darkness itself, studded with pulsing constellations. At its center, the being stood, its vast night wings stretching all around, skin rippling with breathing gray runes.

Krampus stared, and his heart thudded with fear. He had not known Elowen had found an ancient older than his own mother. Older than the Forger. She found *gray*. He swallowed. He could not let his fear bind him.

The being looked at Elowen in his arms, and the air itself trembled.

"You came carrying ruin," it said. Its voice echoed in the realm, speaking in an ancient tongue, a chorus of tones that Krampus had to strain to comprehend. "A choice weighs upon you, Krampus of the night."

Krampus fell to his knees, clutching her tighter. "Help her. You gave her your gift once. Please heal her. I will pay any cost."

The being's head tilted, fire deepening. "Any cost?"

"Yes," Krampus growled, desperation raw. "Name it. Take it. Only…save her."

The being's runes burned hotter as its distorted face scanned Elowen's, her wound, the blood that stained her body. And then, lower. It lingered over her stomach, faint light glowing beneath her skin.

"You must choose. Which life to save."

Krampus looked at them, his face twisted in confusion. "Hers. Save hers."

"And the child?"

Krampus froze. His chest constricted.

"The elf bears more than her own life," it said. "The one made of gray and night."

His hands shook. "No," he breathed. Then, a strangled whisper: "I did not know."

"Your child's heartbeat falters," the being said. "Blood sacrifice and shard's fire have touched it. Magic has touched it. Changed it. It might not be as it was meant."

Krampus bowed his head, his horns scraping the floor. His

chest burned, his shadows coiling around them both like desperate hands. "Then save them both. Please. If you can."

The being's voice thundered, filling the void. "You cannot have both. One or the other. Choose."

Krampus' throat tore with a roar. "NO!" His magic lashed at pillars, clawing, tearing. "You cannot ask this of me. She is all I have. But—" He broke, choking on his words. "The child...her... our child..."

The being's face twisted, runes flaring brighter. "Which life, Krampus? Which shadow do you cast aside?"

Krampus bowed low, his forehead pressing to Elowen's hair. She was cold, so cold, but he felt the faint tremor of her breath against his chest.

His voice broke as he rumbled, "Do whatever you must. But if you must take a life...let it be mine. Take me instead. Leave her. Leave them both."

The realm shook. Frost cracked around them. The being's form shifted, runes whistling with icy fire. For a long, terrible silence, it stared at him, a monster, begging, pleading not for his own life, but for hers.

Finally, the echoes died. The being's voice fell soft as snow.

"You would give yourself. Even after chains. Even after ruin. You would yield your eternity for hers."

"Yes," Krampus said. "Always."

The being lowered, vast wings curling around them like a cloak. It touched Elowen's wound, and Krampus felt warmth.

"Krampus of shadows, know such bargains leave scars. A gift then. Years for the years taken from you. She will live, but the child's fate is uncertain. It is beyond what we know."

Frost fire spread. The spear disappeared into a flurry of peppermint stars. Elowen stirred, a flicker of breath easing into her chest. The second heartbeat trembled, faint, uncertain, but there.

Krampus clutched them tighter, trembling with the fury of hope.

And above him, the being's runes flared brighter.

CHAPTER THIRTY-FOUR

The orchard smelled of silver fruit and sweetness. Elowen blinked awake to soft twilight and a roof of swaying branches above her. All she remembered was bleeding, falling, the shard's song burning her alive. Now she lay on moss, her body whole, no pain in her limbs, no iron biting her wrists. Her breath trembled as she tested her fingers, her ribs, her belly. All of her was there. Alive.

A figure with vast night wings knelt beside her. Not Krampus.

The being from the darkness brushed a hand against her belly, over the place where the spear had torn through. Its touch was cool. "You are not finished." Its whisper echoed through bone and marrow. "Your unborn is safe. The gray thread pulls you forward. But your choice remains yours."

Her lips parted. Questions tangled in her throat. *Why save me? Why now? Why at all?* But the word it left behind crashed harder than all of them.

Unborn.

She clutched her belly, horror and awe twisting together. A child? After everything? Her mind reeled. If she had known, would she have hurled herself at the crown, broken chains, spilled blood, screamed until her throat was ash? Or would she have faltered? The orchard spun with panic.

But the ancient was already gone, its wings dissolving into

dusk, a shimmer of gray runes falling like rain in its wake.

"Elowen."

Her head jerked. Krampus was beside her, crouched low, his frame trembling. His eyes burned with a relief so raw it hurt to look at. He pressed a cup of silver fruit juice to her lips. "Breathe. Drink. It'll take the edge away."

The juice burst cool and sharp across her tongue, sweetness filling her chest and her shaking limbs. The orchard hummed through her, easing the madness that still clung to her bones. Her fear throbbed quieter.

But her mind blazed. She saw Kringle's crown, the elves bent in chains, the blood they spilled to break it. She saw herself screaming, shadows and light shredding the soldiers apart. And Krampus, shackled, burning, always turned toward her. Chose her.

Tears stung her eyes. "We really did it," she whispered. "The elves. They're free?"

Krampus brushed her cheek with one scarred hand, his voice breaking. "We did. They're free."

Her chest loosened, collapsing into a sob that was almost laughter. She sagged against him, weary beyond words. "Then please...please, let me rest here. Just a little while."

He tilted the cup again until she drank. She let it spill sweetness down her throat, dulling the terror, softening the ache in her ribs. She curled against him, so tired she could hardly breathe.

Before sleep pulled her under, she pressed her palm to her belly, her words a rasp against his chest. "There is a child."

His shadow shivered. He stroked her cheek.

"If it meant the child was safe," she whispered, her voice breaking like glass, "I would give up all my magic."

Krampus bent low, his voice hoarse, a vow threaded in each word. "Then you'll never have to. I'll do anything to keep you both safe."

Her eyes closed. Relief unspooled through her like silver thread, light as breath. For the first time since the snow, the song, the crown, she let go. The orchard rocked her in its hush, washing the ruin away. She found comfort in Krampus' heartbeat thudding steadily beneath her ear.

Her last thought was not of chains or crowns or shadows. It was of life. Warm, fragile, unbroken.

And then, Elowen rested. At last.

❆ ❆ ❆

Snow blanketed Kringle Central, but the songs had stopped.

The grand square was a ruin of toppled toy soldiers half-buried in slush, broken presents spilling ribbons like entrails, and smoke curling from the jagged stump of the shattered tower where the crown had once blazed. The peppermint-polished cobblestones were cracked, stained with soot and blood.

No carols. No rhythm of production lines. Only the ragged shuffle of frantic elves with no orders left to follow. Fear crept in first, then hunger, then desperate eyes searching for anyone, *anyone*, who might lead.

And Klaussen was ready.

He climbed the fountain's rim, steadying himself with a candy cane crutch, the other arm bound in a torn strip of cloth where the rebel's scissors had cut deep. His once-pristine uniform hung in tatters, the brass buttons blackened with ash. The emerald sash was gone, and the insignia was dull. Despite everything, his eyes, sharp and unyielding, blazed with purpose and ambition.

"Brothers and sisters!" His voice cracked the silence like a whip. "The crown is broken. The tyrant is gone. But we are *not lost*."

He lifted the crutch high until its hook caught the gray light. "We are elves. We *endure*."

A murmur rippled through the crowd, hesitant and uncertain, but the sound grew, one voice catching another, until a trembling cheer broke out. Relief, confusion, and awe mixed into one raw sound. They wanted order. They wanted *anything*.

Klaussen smiled, thin and sharp. He had always known what the desperate needed most: direction.

Beside him, Larkspur moved through the throng with quiet, efficient grace. Her curls were streaked with soot, her uniform ink-stained and torn at the sleeves. Yet even now, the faint shimmer of the golden snowflake pulsed faintly against her throat. The brand had once burned with every lie, but now, in the crown's absence, it glowed softly, uncertain of its purpose.

"Elves to the square!" she called, voice firm but calm. "No pushing. There's room for all. You'll be fed. You'll be safe."

Her tone carried none of the fever it once had under Kringle's reign. She didn't need to shout anymore; she had learned that true authority whispered. Wherever she passed, trembling elves straightened their backs, soothed by the order she brought.

Klaussen watched her work, admiration and calculation flickering behind his eyes. She had been the most loyal, the most terrified, and yet, she was still standing. Perhaps they *both* were, because they had learned to bend without breaking.

She glanced back at him through the smoke. For a moment, the air seemed to still, the unspoken recognition that they had outlasted everyone else. The golden mark at her throat dimmed to a steady glow, like an ember that refused to die.

"We'll rebuild," Klaussen said, more to himself than to her. "We'll do it better."

Larkspur's gaze lingered on the ruins of the tower, where molten gold still seeped between the cracks like blood. "Better," she echoed.

He turned back to the crowd, raising his voice once more, shaping the next chant, the next rhythm.

"The season endures!" he called. "Together, we make it anew!"

The elves cheered again, louder this time.

Lines took shape. Broken ranks became marching rows. The chaos bent toward order; not the old order of carols and chains, but something new, sharper.

Whispers spread. *He will keep us safe. He knows what to do.*

Larkspur stepped beside him at the fountain's edge, her breath misting in the cold. "You've always known how to make them listen," she said quietly.

"And you've always known how to make them obey," he replied, half smiling.

He offered her his uninjured hand. "Survive with me. Lead with me."

She hesitated...then took it.

The wind swept through the square, scattering the ash and ribbons. Above, the sky glowed pale gold from dawn breaking through the smoke.

The carols were gone, and in their place, the sound of hammers rose.

He smiled. They had stepped into the vacuum together, and the elves were already falling into place.

But safety under Klaussen had a sharp edge.

❄ ❄ ❄

Far from the square, a gingerbread man dragged himself through a half-collapsed alley, crumbs trailing with each dragging step.

Cinn leaned against a wall, pressing his stump to his chest, wincing at the cracks running deep in his dough. His frosting eyes flickered in the shadows. "Still standing," he muttered, half to himself, half to the icy night. "Barely."

He tipped his head back, staring at the sky where smoke dimmed the stars. Once, he would have heard the endless drone of carols. Now, silence. Only silence.

"Guess that makes two of us," he said. His eye twitched, catching faint sparks.

He shifted his jaw, frosting eye glittering. Somewhere behind the walls, he could hear the faint clanking of chains being broken, the chaos of elves scattering.

He chuckled bitterly. "Well, Elowen. You did it. I hope you're okay wherever that shadow took you."

A low growl rumbled from the snow.

Charlie crouched in the drift, white fur streaked with ash and blood, his once-bright coat now matted and gray. His eyes were tired, but burned steadily. Not hollow. Not enslaved.

Fizz trilled from Charlie's shoulder, sparks lighting the air.

"About time," Cinn croaked. He straightened as much as his cracked spine would allow. "You look like a dirty snowball."

Charlie sighed. "Better than I did."

Cinn barked a laugh. "Fair. But we can't stay here. Let's get out of here before they decide to chain you up again."

"Good idea," he replied. He offered one hand, palm open. Cinn grunted and scrambled into it, crumbs scattering from his broken side. Fizz spat frozen sparks into the air.

The yetlet tilted his head toward the horizon, snow stretching endlessly and black. Together, the three turned from the ruined square and trudged into the night.

❅ ❅ ❅

Between realms, where no sun shone, and no fruit grew, ice cracked.

Kringle dragged himself across the jagged stone, blood smearing the frost. His crimson velvet robe trailed behind him in tatters, white fur lining blackened and stiff with soot. One leg hung useless, bound from the creature's slash that had cast him down. He gritted his teeth, each movement grinding shards of ice beneath his palms.

The air here was hungry, humming faintly, the same note the crown had once sung, though off-key, broken, searching for its master.

He shouted, though no one could hear him, his voice swallowed by the gray between. He pressed a trembling hand to his chest and felt the phantom ache where the crown's light had lived.

"Gone," he whispered, almost in disbelief.

His reflection glimmered faintly in the ice beneath him. He wiped a bloody hand across his face, clearing his golden curls matted with frost and sweat.

The crown was gone, shattered. Only the echo of its song lingered in him, a gnawing hunger where its power had once burned.

But as he crawled forward, his breath steaming in the void, the disbelief curdled into something darker.

"I made them," he hissed. "Their joy. Their faith. Their order." His fingers clawed at the ice until it split. "You think a little frost will stop me?"

Silence answered him. Then, slowly, the gray shifted.

Memory stirred. The aftertaste of every carol ever sung, every prayer whispered to his false benevolence, echoed in the emptiness. The pitying, familiar sound twined around him, taunted him.

He laughed, a ragged, bitter sound that bled into the stillness. A smile, twisted and ravenous, flickered on his lips. Even lost, even forsaken, he whispered promises into the dark.

"They will sing again," he rasped. "They always do."

The gray void stirred. The in-between listened.

And somewhere, faintly, something answered. One note, sweet and hollow, rose like the beginning of a song.

❄ ❄ ❄

The orchard was twilight forever.

Black trees swayed with their silver fruit, glowing softly in the dusk that never broke into dawn. The lake shimmered with its mirror of the violet sky, rippling when the breeze brushed the shore. The little house, with its hearth that never died, waited for them each night with warmth enough to hold shadows at bay.

And there, on the porch of that house, Elowen sat.

Her hands rested on her lap, fingers splayed gently over the curve of her belly. The swell was small, but undeniable. Life grew within her, fragile and stubborn, casting a glow on her face even when the embers of madness sparked in her laughter. She sat there humming under her breath, and her belly glimmered in response.

"What are you singing?" Krampus asked as he sat beside her.

She leaned against him. "I'm not sure, something that feels like from long ago."

Krampus' eyes flickered. He knew what she was humming, some softer, sweeter version of a carol from Kringle Central. His hand trembled before he willed it to still and brushed over her belly. He would not tell her what it was she sang. She was content, and he would not take that from her.

Each morning she plucked the silver fruit herself, slicing it open, drinking deep of the glowing juice. She always smiled afterward, as if the orchard lifted a burden from her chest, smoothing the edges of thought until nothing sharp remained. Krampus never urged her, but he helped keep the fruit within reach, his hands always steady when she passed him the empty cup. *Her choice, always hers.* And he was happy for it, even more so to see her laugh, even if the orchard's haze made her forget what they had survived.

He had buried the shard far away, where the orchard ended and the broken plain began. Deep beneath the black soil, far from her hands, far from her eyes. It pulsed sometimes, as if alive, but he made certain she would never hear it. He dug with his own hands until they bled, stomped the earth down hard, and swore his vow, his curse, into the dirt: *you will never touch her again.* A faint glimmer of shadow, and he was sure he had hidden it from ordinary sight.

Still, some nights when the wind slid cold through the orchard, he swore he heard his brother's scream; it was distant, echoing, clawing its way through the trees. On other nights, the shard thrummed louder beneath the soil, like a muffled heartbeat. He told no one, not even her, especially not her. That weight was his alone.

The fruit's silver juice worked on her. He could see it in her cheeks, hear it in her laughter, the way she sighed with relief as though at last she had nothing to fear. For her, the orchard was healing, forgetting, home.

For him...it never could be.

He let the fruit touch his lips but never enough to drown him fully. The memories stayed: years of fiery shackles, Elowen bleeding for him, for the world, the choice he had made in the realm of darkness. He wore those memories, burned them into his heart, and he embraced them. If someone had to remember the snow and soot, the blood and ruin, it would be him. He would bear it so that she would never have to. That was his price, his alone to pay. And he was happy to do it.

At night, when she slept curled against him, her breath soft, he would drift asleep for a bit, then startle awake, the shadows coiling restless at the edges of the bed. He listened to her heartbeat, and deeper beneath, to the fragile flutter of another within her. Anchored by those sounds, he calmed and remembered eternity wasn't his own anymore.

He chose this.

They were his, and he was theirs.

The orchard whispered around them, the trees sighing as though to calm him themselves, the lake rippling with its strange silver light.

Elowen turned on the porch light and caught him watching her from the shadows. Her red hair spilled about her, tumbling in waves, and she stood there barefoot, a smile spreading across her weary face.

"You're brooding again," she teased.

"Always," he rumbled.

"Stay," she said as she patted the step beside her. He sighed to himself, knowing she didn't fully remember their meaning of the word, and joined her for her nightly habit. His shadow spilled until it wrapped them both like a cloak. She shivered and then leaned against him, her head on his chest. He brushed his lips against her hair and breathed her in.

For now, they were at peace.

For now, he would keep her here, safe in the orchard's embrace, as long as the twilight held.

And if the day ever came when the fruit's spell dimmed or the shard's call returned, when the world outside dared to rise again, he would be ready.

Because he remembered.

And he would do anything to keep her.

Anything.

ALSO BY CHRISTINA VEILLETTE

Song Beneath the Black Sky, short story
The Witch They Wanted, short story
Crown of Thorns and Starlight
Snow & Soot

www.ingramcontent.com/pod-product-compliance
Lightning Source LLC
Chambersburg PA
CBHW050033120726
47903CB00006B/2019